Lady Stanhope's Manuscript
and Other Stories

Also by Dale Nelson

J.R.R. Tolkien: Studies in Reception (forthcoming)

Lady Stanhope's Manuscript
and Other Stories

Dale Nelson

Nodens Books

2017

Lady Stanhope's Manuscript and Other Stories

First published by Nodens Books, 2017
This edition copyright © Nodens Books, L.L.C.
ISBN 978-0615677347
Printed in the United States of America
First edition: October 2017

Nodens Books   www.nodensbooks.com
PO Box 493
Marcellus, MI 49067

Table of Contents

To Dorothea

Preface

This book includes several ghost stories; how many, depends on how *ghost story* is defined. M.R. James, to whose tradition I have desired to contribute, used the term so as to include, for example, the haunter in "Canon Alberic's Scrap-Book." Used thus capaciously, *ghost story* accommodates most of the stories gathered here.

A given Monty James story evokes a particular place—a lonely stretch of Suffolk seacoast, a Copenhagen hotel room, a cathedral city in the Pyrenees. Settings in the present volume include the Upper Midwest in the Dust Bowl era, rural Sweden in the early nineteenth century, the wine country of northern California, and the Russian Far East, towards the end of the Tsarist era.

Here are eleven stories. My thanks to Margit Eastman, Mary Chilvers, and Shannon Hofer of the Mayville State University interlibrary loan department, and to Barbara and Christopher Roden, R.B. Russell, Rosalie Parker, Pierre Comtois, Colin Langeveld, and M.L. Logsdon who escorted them into print. The texts offered here may be revised as compared to the published versions. Occasionally I have restored passages formerly omitted.

Notes on the stories appear at the end of the book along with an Afterword in which, for those who are interested, I've set out some thoughts on ghosts, formulated recently and thus some years after the stories were written.

D. N.

Lady Stanhope's Manuscript
and Other Stories

Lady Stanhope's Manuscript

There had been one of those controversies which occur in the most cheerful of households. Mr. Fletcher did not think it necessary that the children have a hot meal between breakfast and tea everyday. His wife held otherwise, while also maintaining, inconveniently, that the preparation of this repast added a considerable burden to the number of those already borne by one who had abundant daily tasks. The good woman referred to herself, for the Fletchers did not enjoy the services of "help" seven days of the week.

"Well, why don't you ask the children what they think?" Mr. Fletcher had pacifically inquired; but this gave Mrs. Fletcher opportunity to remonstrate with him about his absorption in his employment, which, she averred, was so great, that he was ignorant of the fact that the children would undoubtedly demand cakes and lemonade, should she be so imprudent as to request *their* advice. The question of the young Fletchers' *dejeuner* was unfinished business when Mr. and Mrs. Fletcher parted that morning, she to wait upon two spirited children and their pets mammalian, avian, and (alarmingly and in defiance of household order) reptilian, he to walk into the town, to resume the duties, set down only for the Sabbath, of proprietor of a general goods store. He took the morning post with him.

Over a cup of strong tea at midmorning, Mr. Fletcher opened his letters, having first carefully wiped the flour from his hands. (He had found that if he did not examine each barrel carefully, Stephenson, the miller in Fettys, was apt to pass off beetle-invaded goods on him.) The return address was unfamiliar, but he sensed that the penman should be known to him. So he turned to the signature: *Geoffrey Cleeve*; and through Mr. Fletcher there passed a sensation of the present life of things that had been long forgotten. Geoffrey had been his first friend. They had been two small boys in a rainy seaside town hiding in the Fletchers' untidy rose garden or playing, with clumping feet, at Red Indians in the Cleeves' attic. Geoffrey had an untrainable terrier named Clapper, because an aged lady had once said that the dog's penetrating barks compelled attention just as forcibly as the rapping of a heavy brass clapper on a door. And there had been the games, word-games, candle-games, secret and compelling. "Now wouldn't it be something if I could remember what *those* were about?" he said to himself. The games were presumably Geoffrey's invention; not his own, certainly. There had been nonsense rhymes and mysterious, prohibited syllables and imperative syllables, those that were prohibited and those that were imperative sometimes changing places, and it had all been very complicated and absorbing, more so than any of the word-games his own Arthur and Rosamond played; so far as he knew, of course! But what did the letter say?

My dear Wilfred,

I heard you were a clerk in Bigglesfield from Mitchell. [Mr. Fletcher did not remember who Mitchell was. Someone at the Grammar, presumably, for Fletcher and Geoffrey Cleeve had seen each other there, although they had ceased being friends even before Geoffrey's family left the seaside town. The letter continued:] Are you well? please write to me immediately; O, my friend, my friend from happier days—I am not. If you are still well, I would, selfishly, ask you to come to see me if you possibly can. If you are not well, it is too late, and I may only say that I have not been spared. Perhaps we shall be forgiven; we were only *children*. Please write to me. But better yet, come to see me, even without writing to me. When you arrive, if you do come, someone from the Red Lion can bear a message to me, or give you directions to the house. I am cared for by the *dearest woman* and the *wisest old man* in England. But they cannot take me out from under the hand that is so heavy upon me.— Perhaps when you come, if you are so good, you will find my mind more orderly than now.

I am
      your friend,
           Geoffrey Cleeve.

Mr. Fletcher was not forty years of age. He was not yet accustomed to the expectation that around him many of his friends would be declining in health of body and mind, he himself also bearing ever more wounds from the battle of life against time. Therefore, he was shocked by the evidence of a contemporary's deteriorated health of the flesh, or of the intellect, that was before his eyes in the form of this unlooked-for letter. Was Geoffrey deranged? It seemed probable. Was the woman a longsuffering wife and the old man a doctor; or the woman an attendant of some sort, and the old man Cleeve's father, perhaps?—What was Geoffrey's malady? And why should Geoffrey fear that he, Fletcher, suffered from it?

Like many another of his rank and station in life, Mr. Fletcher could not help it—he must needs take stock of his health when challenged. Surely he was just what he should be, a stout, manly figure; he'd put on a little flesh, perhaps more than a little, as a beef-eating Englishman ought. He was in a moderately prosperous way of business, though far from wealthy, and he slept like the dead. Between himself and his wife subsisted the lively affections of their first year of marriage.

Now, as he reflected, recognizing his agreeable lot for what it was—a boon not granted to all of Adam's children, so many of whom, indeed, he felt, could scarcely be blamed if they looked upon life as a struggle for survival, in the manner of Darwin's apes—he recognized a duty owed to those whose lives were marked by misfortune.

His wife, through twelve years' association with him, knew the business well enough to manage it for a week or a fortnight; although the store was no sweets-and-thread shop such as was more suited to the tender sex, untroubled by unscrupulous suppliers, customers who must be dunned again and yet again, and a rival who seemed determined to drive Mr. Fletcher's smallish store out of business. That evening, when he read the letter to his wife, she was quickly sympathetic; indeed, something bright shone in her eyes for a moment. Sophia Fletcher blinked, and said she would do her best until he returned.

II

As the train crept from unremarkable small town to town, and cold rain spattered the compartment window, Mr. Fletcher tried to remember so much as he could of Geoffrey Cleeve. A pale, fair-haired lad without much of a chin; later, a thin youth who, unexpectedly, proved, so he had heard, to be a notable oarsman at University. What had he studied?—

Archaeology, perhaps? Or some Eastern language or other? Had he taken a degree? They had long since ceased to be friends by that time. Why not friends? As little boys they had been true blood brothers. (A bit of broken glass found at the bottom of the Cleeves' garden had been the instrument by means of which their loyalty had been sealed.) Fletcher had not had such a friend since then, although he had never lacked good company.

But—the boy Geoffrey had had a nervous collapse. Or something like that; Geoffrey had been twelve or so when his parents left the town, and the boys were no longer friends by that time. The young Fletcher had heard, vaguely, about the Cleeves' departure from someone else. Fletcher's own parents had withdrawn him from the other boy's society. He thought, now, that there might have been some incident that had estranged the boys' fathers; yes; Walter Fletcher had returned from the Cleeve house looking angry and frightened; his son, some twenty-five years later, remembered. He remembered, too, that he himself had urged—had begged—the fathers' consultation, but it seemed it had gone askew somehow.

Outside his compartment, late afternoon sunlight, slipping under the rags of rainclouds, slanted across a level landscape. The bright flat sheet of a pond raced by. Mr. Fletcher had visited this region once or twice years ago, but it meant little to him and pleased him less than the hills of his own environs. He knew that the sea lay somewhere out in the deepening gloom that would be visible to passengers on the other side of the corridor, but that would not, he thought, be a very lovely stretch of British coastline; rather, poor, sandy patches of land imperceptibly surrendering to salt marshes and lonely shingle, dreary clumps of grass, and, at last, grey water flowing over the shoals, and crying birds.

An hour later Mr. Fletcher roused himself from his nap, which had carried him through the one metropolis on his journey (for when he slept, he slept soundly). The face of a very old man had risen before his mind's eye, perhaps while he was yet truly asleep, perhaps as awareness was returning; he could not have said which. That face smiled; but the effect was unpleasant, as if the ancient creature were merely assuming a demeanour that might beguile an innocent child, but could never deceive a man or woman of mature years, who would detect its corruption immediately. But could even a small child fail to mark the so evident signs of deathly *illness?* The cheeks were colorless hollows; veins twisted across the temples; the skin across the nose was coarse and tight, while the grey lips contracted and loosened constantly. The eyes were horribly quick and hot; and compelled one's stare. He could attach no name, no place, to that face. One glimpses so many faces, year by year, Mr. Fletcher thought, uncharacteristically bemused. As he pondered, his anxiety receded. Perhaps his eyes had fallen upon this face, just once, as he scanned some street thronged with London's teeming multitudes, or looked up at a curtain drawn aside for a moment; he had visited the great city more than once.

III

Arrived in Croatley, given as his friend's village of residence, Mr. Fletcher had no trouble finding the Red Lion, a clean-looking place of accommodation for the traveller, established on the main street. Therein he was able to secure directions to Geoffrey Cleeve's dwelling place: a private house, not, then, an hospital or asylum, as Mr. Fletcher had feared. However, Mr. Fletcher's informant had no evident personal knowledge of the house or its inmates. A walk of half an hour should bring him there, but Mr. Fletcher was in no hurry to proceed. His friend did not know that he was coming and would not be expecting him; moreover, Geoffrey's appearance and manner, given how ill he must be presumed to be, seemed likely to be distressing, and Mr. Fletcher had already had a day of tiring travel crowded with the uncertainties of fragmentary memory. For the moment, he approved of the fact that none of the presumable habitués of the house appeared to contemplate rising and approaching him, or calling out to him, but were deep in their own counsels. A cutlet and a bit of pudding that had been passed over during the supper hour imparted some small cheer to Mr. Fletcher's table; and here it may be confessed that Mr. Fletcher attempted to revive himself with something stronger than beer, although he was a temperate man.

A tall, stooped man, his overcoat damp from the night air, approached the traveller.

"Do I have the honour of speaking to Mr. Wilfred Fletcher?" he asked, in quiet, agreeably-modulated tones.

"Why, yes—"

"I'm Elias Trefillan. A parson, though unencumbered by the cares of a parish. I am staying with Mr. Cleeve; may I conduct you to the residence of your friend?"

As they strode through the chilly autumnal shadows, Mr. Fletcher wondered what connection his companion might have with the Cleeve household. He appeared to be of late-middle years, vigorous, his face dark and of strong features.

"Perhaps your friend has spoken of me?" the cleric asked.

"Well, he mentioned a woman and an elderly man as his attendants in his—illness. There was no mention of a clergyman, I'm afraid."

"Oh, but there was; for I am his 'elderly man,' without doubt. For myself—I confess that I feel there are many years left to me! But it is a whimsy of your friend—and a charming one—to pretend that I am a greybeard. As perhaps I should be, if I were hirsute! As it is, I became accustomed to smooth cheeks during one of my sojourns abroad on behalf of the Established Church's mission to one or other of the swarthy breeds, during which I found facial hair rather too hot for comfort. The warmth that would be afforded by a full beard, however, would be welcome on a night such as this!"

Mr. Fletcher felt that the clergyman was exerting himself more than was necessary to impart an impression of affability, but reflected that, living in foreign lands, his companion might have had few opportunities for the enjoyment of the society of white men. He himself had never taken much interest in the ways of foreigners, and had never been across the Channel, although he didn't mind wandering the Lakes with a guidebook in hand, provided Sophia didn't come off with any nonsense about climbing some Peak or Fell for the view. He hoped that Trefillan would not indulge himself in a discourse upon the costume and manners of natives, winding up with an invitation to contribute to some Mission Society.

"Geoffrey's letter said that he was unwell," Mr. Fletcher said.

"It is very true, Mr. Fletcher. Your friend has some odd habits and certain quirks of the mind, which you may as well know. He did not even tell me that he had written to you, at first. What part his present illness has had to play in producing these caprices, I do not know. Nor have the doctors been able to ascertain the agency that has effected your friend's decline, whether it be organic illness or some debility of the mind, or even of the soul. Yes, I am afraid that you will find him an invalid. I take it, however, that he was never of a robust constitution? Miss Fieldfare—who in so many ways, I may say, has been a blessing to us—Miss Fieldfare holds that he works too much; but I cannot agree; I believe his work gives Mr. Cleeve a reason to live, and a rallying-point for his energies, without which he should have succumbed many months ago. As it is, I cannot believe that he will live much longer, unless he invests his work with a greater determination than he has done so far."

"You do not approve of Miss Fieldfare as his attendant?"

"Miss Fieldfare is quite devoted to Mr. Cleeve, but—" The clergyman paused. "I suspect her affection for him, which perhaps exceeds what is strictly proper for an unmarried woman employed by an unmarried man, sometimes colors her judgment, while leaving her convinced that she knows better than anyone what is in your friend's best interests. I may just mention that on occasion she has, I believe, overtaxed his strength by persuading him to join her in extended sessions of prayer." Elias Trefillan smiled. "Perhaps it is unbecoming in a clergyman to object to excessive praying. Still, one might have thought that a much briefer session would have been sufficient. Also, surely it is right that the Christian should bow his head before the inscrutable decrees of Omnipotence, and let It find him properly resigned when his day of reckoning comes."

Perhaps Mr. Trefillan sensed that the visitor was not much interested in his account of Miss Fieldfare's actions.

"Mr. Cleeve is engaged upon the translation of a document which has never been rendered in our language—indeed, it is not in print in any tongue—but Miss Fieldfare disapproves of its subject. The schoolmistress and the clergyman's daughter, of course. I may say that she can be tiresome in her objections. She has little use for reading matter less *improving* than that which is read on Sunday afternoons in *rectories*—there, I fear that I have spoken amiss again! Although she has been observed to inspect the works of Sir Walter on occasion, and has been sufficiently yielding to Mr. Cleeve's importunities as to read from Mrs. Ward or Mr. Wilkie Collins of an evening. But I hope that you may encourage your friend to persevere in his labours. It is, I am convinced, very likely that *Oxford* would publish his edition."

Their way led them past ranks of commonplace dwellings. The Reverend Mr. Trefillan turned in at the gate of one of these and preceded Mr. Fletcher along a short path to the door of a two-storey house erected perhaps sixty years before. Mr. Fletcher was not sure that he liked his conductor, but acknowledged, inwardly, that he had brought him to Geoffrey's house more speedily than he should have managed on his own, and that this was welcome, given the dampness of the night.

Elias Trefillan twisted his key in the door and they stepped into a dark house.

Mr. Fletcher's immediate sensation was that several persons—if "persons" was the word he wanted—were close by, but when an instant later Mr. Trefillan turned up the gas, the visitor saw that no one but themselves was in the room. It was furnished with shabby chairs and tables, all burdened with books and papers. A few lively, if cheap, hunting prints, which might have been in place when Geoffrey took the lease of the house, hung from the walls. Mr. Fletcher was pleasantly reminded of *Handley Cross* and *Jorrocks' Jollities*.

"Miss Fieldfare has returned to her aunt's residence until tomorrow morning, Mr. Fletcher. It is she who prepares our humble meals. She takes only a couple of pupils now, so that she has time to play Sister of Charity, albeit without Puseyite habit .... Geoffrey retired three hours ago. As it is, I can offer you bread and cheese?—Then it but remains to show you your room." This was done; the room, tidy enough, did not appear to be much used. "I cannot speak for the provenance of the mattress or bedding, Mr. Fletcher; you took us unawares; I have been looking for you at the Red Lion for just the past two evenings, on the chance that you were coming. Had we known certainly that you were to be favored with your company we should have done better credit to ourselves.

These were on the premises when Mr. Cleeve took the house, I believe. The sheets have been aired, at least; Miss Fieldfare will have seen to that. We breakfast at eight."

IV

Fletcher slept well. Morning came.

"Hello, Wilfred. I'm grateful to you," the small, worn man in the bed said, very quietly. The room was dim, the only light coming through a window to the invalid's left. In a chair at the bedside, her back to the light, sat a still woman who said nothing, though Mr. Fletcher felt that she watched him keenly.

"Geoffrey. Are you—at ease?" he asked.

"Never better.—No, I shouldn't quiz you. Not so well. But let's not talk of that just now. This is Miss Fieldfare. She looks after us and sees to it that I don't simply fold up and—hibernate. I had hoped that we might be married, but I must make sure of not turning this young lady into a widow too quickly!"

Mr. Fletcher noticed that they were holding hands, and must have been doing so when he entered the room. He expected the woman to say something sympathetic, but what she said, not altogether forbearingly, was, "Geoffrey, when you say such things, I'm not sure that I want to marry you. You must hold to your resolve to get well." Mr. Fletcher thought that she looked young enough to be his friend's daughter, but then Geoffrey was so marked by his malady that he seemed many years older than he was. In truth, Mr. Fletcher supposed, she must be no more than ten years younger than Geoffrey.

"Yes, listen to Miss Fieldfare," Elias Trefillan said. "You must not think of the candle of life guttering out!"

The woman rose to her feet. "Geoffrey, perhaps Mr. Trefillan and I should permit you to talk with Mr. Fletcher privately. Mr. Trefillan, shall we—?"

The clergyman hesitated, then followed the young woman from the bedchamber.

From the silent room, Mr. Fletcher heard a dog barking, and, at the edge of audibility, an intermittent sound that might have been that of children playing in the street. Geoffrey began to speak, quietly, of how he had come to live in this small town. His mother's family, long since dead, had lived here, and she had sometimes spoken of it; so it was a place he knew about, a little, and it was a cheap place for living.

Within a moment or two, the two men were quite at ease in one another's company again, despite the passage of years. Mr. Fletcher thought it had been a long time since anyone had listened with such interest to his account of his children and his wife. Soon he was relating one after another of his favorite anecdotes. The invalid listened almost hungrily, as if drawing renewed life from the pictures that were formed, by imaginative sympathy, in his brain, as he listened.

"You love them very much, Wilfred."

"Well, well—I suppose I do. Of course I do. Boy's a fine little chap. Clever as can be. Heaven help you if he gets into your tool chest in a room by himself. Rosamond is growing into just the little lady her mother was when I first met her. Sings a hymn like a bird, she does. But now look, Geoffrey, what about your life here?"

"Oh, Wilfred, it passes day by day like something in a dream. I work at my translation, I eat my meals, I take a little exercise sometimes . . . Diana reads to me . . . We'll never marry, old friend. I'll be dead in a year."

"Is that why you wrote to me? Not that I believe it for a minute."

"It wasn't just the thought of dying, Wilfred. Most of the time I feel that I am ready. My will's made, and I don't fear too much what—what will become of me, you know. Having a man of God under one's own roof most of the day is comforting . . . I suppose he's probably let his tongue run away with him, hasn't he?—It's his way. He's a good man. Done the world of a lot for me. You must hear about the manuscript. I'll be famous if I can get it all into English. Well, not famous, but I'll be known by scholars of—such things. Trefillan has shown me a fragment of the manuscript. You must get him to let you see it sometime. I think such things are fascinating. Here in my house, my rented house, that is—there's something you wouldn't expect to see outside a museum, or the home of a scholar who has travelled the world."

"Geoffrey, I'll have to take your word for it. You know I went to work in the shop at thirteen. Sometimes it's more than I can do, to puzzle out my Testament. That's my English Testament, not Greek! But it must be a fine thing, translating, like you are."

"Only sometimes I feel that I'm wasting my life—don't tell Trefillan, he hates me to talk that way—and I want to shout, 'Devil take the manuscript and all its cycles, conjurations, and superstitions! Life's too short for such trash, however antique.' But I sink back into it, like some insect that has blundered into a cobweb. And after all, it is actually rather fascinating. Sometimes I think it's all true, that one might be able to compel invisible brutes to do one's bidding, and so on. But it's the only way *I* can earn enough money to have something to leave Diana. I said I had had my will made, but I have little enough to leave her. My income is enough to keep us comfortably in an out-of-the-way place, such as this, but that isn't good enough. That's my view. Diana never sighs for fashionable clothes or a county dance! Anyway, a work of scholarship, done the right way, can earn royalties for a man for many years. Or his heirs. Such things continue to sell copies for years, not many copies in a given year, true—I should perhaps drop the manuscript and write a story about the New Woman or a bigamous clergyman!"

"You could ask Mr. Trefillan for details about the life of the clergy, you know!" said Mr. Fletcher, and they both laughed.

Then Geoffrey Cleeve came round again to the occasion of his writing to his friend. "I still haven't explained to you. Diana and I had been talking things over, you know—about my illness and all. I'm afraid I was in a pretty glum state of mind. I couldn't help feeling that maybe God was punishing me. You know, Wilfred, I don't think those word-games we played when we were children were good for us—I see you remember. I used to nearly have fits sometimes in the dark, in my little upstairs bedroom, after we had been playing during the day. Once or twice, I am sure, I saw myself sitting on the edge of the bed, just ready to walk away from my body and never come back. The old man—you remember him, too?—the one who taught us?—he could come through walls. He would just walk through the wall into my bedroom and . . . it's horrible, I'm sorry—he would stretch himself out across me and cover my mouth with his mouth—I would just about swoon—I was breathing in through him somehow—"

"Geoffrey—dear God!"

13

"All some kind of juvenile madness, Wilfred, of course. I can hardly bear to think of it sometimes. Diana knows about it all—I told her once I was sure we should never marry, I couldn't bear that I should pass my madness to our children. But she shook me by the shoulders (she's rather strong for a woman, Wilfred, I had bruises the next day from her thumbs!) and said that was all very long ago. Perhaps it was some kind of fever that passed off and left me just somewhat weak, but not in the head, you know . . ."

"But what's this about being punished?"

"Oh, Diana said it was wicked to think of God like that. She had some Bible verses to prove it. But at the time I couldn't get it out of my head that that was just what it was. That it would be wicked to wish for something different from life. But I wrote you.—When we were boys, I'm afraid many times I told you things the old man told me, or—that I dreamed he told me—wicked things—but you don't remember, do you?"

"I remember that I could never keep up with you. We'd be chanting things back and forth, faster and faster, I never could give you the words back fast enough without running them all together. It was all mostly gibberish to me. Sometimes I felt light-headed, I remember that. I came over queer-like. Sometimes the rest of the day I couldn't eat.—When my dad found out, he didn't like any of that one bit. I'm sorry I didn't find a way to get around him and see you, once he stopped me coming to your house."

"I'm sure your father was right, Wilfred."

"What happened to the old man?"

"After you stopped playing the games and knowing me, he stopped visiting. That was about the time my father's fortunes fell off and we had to move house. My father was a strange man. He would sit with his paper for hours at a time, growling at my mother or me if we approached him. He died of cancer many years ago, but not before I went up to university. My mother is dead, too. She seems to me to have been bewildered, as I look back . . . bewildered, all the time. She used to get into rows with Father. About me and the old man and things. . . . She wanted him to send him away. Father would say horrible things to her, horrible. For many years I hated him for that, speaking to Mother that way. Diana has heard all about these things, Wilfred, and I'm afraid I'm getting too tired to go over them again—would you excuse me?"

14

And when Mr. Fletcher had asked his friend if he bring him anything, Mr. Cleeve thanked him, declined, and closed his eyes. The room was quiet again; from outside still came the sound of a barking dog, but the children were no longer playing. Mr. Fletcher closed the door carefully.

V

That afternoon, over tea, Geoffrey Cleeve explained that he was translating an ancient magical text, which Elias Trefillan had discovered and brought back to England from the Holy Land.

"Geoffrey is omitting to mention some piquant details regarding the origins of his treatise. I suppose, Mr. Fletcher, you will find them to be of more interest than the contents of the treatise itself, as they are, you may think, outlandish," the priest was saying.

"It appears to have been written at the behest of that famous emperor of Byzantium, Justinian, whose official biography portrays him as a great man of war and, of course, great law-giver. Matters become more interesting when we read the *Secret History* recorded by that same Procopius who enshrined the emperor as so wonderful a ruler; for in his unofficial work, we see the emperor as of quite literally an unhuman nature. (It is, to me, remarkable, that whereas in the Greek Church the holy angels are sometimes referred to as the *asomatai* or 'fleshless ones,' Procopius's conception of the unclean spirits infesting this lower world appears to have been that they were *akephaloi*, '*headless* ones,' or were beings, at least, of a *plastic* form. I have been much struck by the report in Procopius that says one night, some members of the emperor's retinue observed his *head* to disappear; while Procopius also claims to have learned that a courtier observed the features of the emperor's face to dissolve, and then, slowly, reappear.)"

Mr. Fletcher saw that Geoffrey was listening to the priest with evident absorption. What could the invalid have heard or read that would render him thus attentive to such superstitious fancies, worse than any Papistry?

"However," Trefillan continued, "other sources suggest that it was not Justinian himself who was demonic, but record that, and here is where our treatise comes in, he commissioned the composition of a treatise which would set in order the knowledge of the airy ones, just as the laws of the Second Rome had been codified for the ages to come. This document was duly prepared; by an infidel—who, again, it is suggested may have been something other than human—called Tessaracontapechys of Tiberias. That means 'Forty Ells Long'—surely a curious name for a *man*. This individual is mentioned in the Acts of the Seventh Ecumenical Council, that is, the Second of Nicaea, of which I have read in the history by Hefele.

"The story of the treatise is blank until the time of the iconoclastic dissension, two centuries after Justinian. One source says that the image-hating emperor Constantine, unpleasantly surnamed Copronymus, repented of his persecutions before his death, and divested himself of a number of forbidden books, among which was this very one; but it was not, after all, delivered to the flames, in disregard of the emperor's will . . . Whether or not this Constantine possessed the treatise, it is worthy of note that the book was known to exist at the time, and was of foul repute. But the rabble so often reveal their own meanness by the low regard in which they hold those things that exceed their mean capacities. As a grocer, Mr. Fletcher, no doubt you have often had the same reflection."

Mr. Fletcher looked sharply at the speaker, who returned an expression of innocence.

"Well, we may skip over a millennium until we come close to our own period. As you may have heard, Mr. Fletcher, a rage for Orientalia characterized the age of *Rasselas* and the subsequent decades. Lovers of the exquisite, the ancient, and the curious all demanded that the Levant, the fastnesses of Armenia and Turkestan, and the farther reaches of the East, yield up their hoarded treasures. The name of one such collector may be known to you—the distinguished William Beckford, author of *Vathek*? No? You must read that phantasmagoria someday, Mr. Fletcher, it will transport you utterly from the realm of Accounts Due and Hutchinson's Willow-Root Extract. Beckford, one of the richest men in England in his day, acquired one of the few complete extant copies of the treatise upon which Geoffrey is at work. I have read the record of a rumor that it was the enunciation of magical spells from it that effected the destruction of Beckford's tower at Fonthill!

The book had been stolen by a learned friend of Beckford's, who could not wait to read it; hiding himself in the tower, he very foolishly began to read the Levantine Greek aloud, at random; and then . . . Beckford really rather heartlessly said he wished that he had been there to see the tower fall. I don't believe that this copy was ever recovered. Isn't it a matter for sober contemplation, that possibly several translations of this calamitous work are at large in the world?" The cleric was obviously greatly enjoying his discourse.

"How do you come to have a copy, Geoffrey?" Mr. Fletcher asked.

"He supplied it," Geoffrey said, indicating Trefillan. Mr. Fletcher thought that his friend looked uneasy.

"If posterity should hallow the name of Elias Bewdon Trefillan," the parson said, "it will not be for his evangelism of the Indian, the Parsee, or the African, but for his recovery of that precious manuscript, the most complete now in existence, which has been entrusted to your friend, Mr. Fletcher. It came about in this way. During a time of residence in the Holy Land, I sought an audience with that once beautiful, reclusive woman, Lady Hester Stanhope. Lady Stanhope had settled in the Lebanon during the time of Napoleon, and taken control of the village of Dahar-Joon, which was presented to her by the Pasha of Acre. I visited her at the compound she erected beside some medieval ruins, having at last secured her invitation; for she had little regard for Europeans, and least of all for her onetime compatriots. She presided over her Druses as their unquestioned mistress, and indeed as their Sybil. I waited patiently while she talked through the better part of two days, permitting her to ventilate her views on local politics and to expound the composite religion she had created—a farrago, I may say, which died with her. At length I was rewarded with a view of her manuscript collection.

"O, Mr. Fletcher! What treasures were there! And all, all despoiled when she died. None of them, however, truly mattered to me, save that one only treatise of Justinian. But an American missionary found that her servants had taken all her valuables, save the garments and jewels upon the corpse."

"How did she die?" Mr. Fletcher asked, as Trefillan paused.

"Her dissolution was entirely due to outworn nature. As soon as I heard that she was dead, I hastened from the Anglican mission at

Beyrout, and returned to her fortress. It was in disarray, with thieves and mangy dogs prowling about. However, I was able to trace the manuscript which I desired. Some poor fool of a Druse had taken it without having any conception of its worth, seizing it, I suppose, with a bagful of other things before fleeing."

"So you tracked him down," the visitor said.

"O yes. He was hiding in a leper encampment, clutching his tawdry ornaments about him. He could scarcely believe the evidence of his own eyes, that a Christian would follow him even *there*. But he had more than ocular proof that I was no apparition, for I thrashed the fellow to within an inch of his life. When he perceived, at length, that all I required was the manuscript, and that he might keep his baubles for all I cared, the clown held my knees in gratitude and watered them with his tears. I spurned him and strode from the cursed huddle of tents and vile mud dens."

Mr. Fletcher saw Diana Fieldfare's expression of distaste for the vein of bombast the priest had opened.

"Returning to England, I set myself to find a young man of appropriate scholarly gifts, who should be my partner in the enterprise of translating Lady Stanhope's treasure. I inquired among the masters of all of the Oxford colleges and was told that young Geoffrey Cleeve was the most promising man of their acquaintance."

"Why didn't you translate it on your own?"

"Mr. Fletcher, the book is written in tiny characters, almost impossible for me to read at my age. A few minutes with the *Times* can give me a horrid head-ache. Moreover, although I have some incomplete knowledge of the language in which it is written—a species of medieval Armenian—I no longer can learn a language with the ease possessed by a man of younger years. Geoffrey knew little of Armenian when I first conversed with him, and yet he became proficient within a matter of months. If any other reason is needed, I will admit that I believe that the translating of the manuscript will be the making of the scholar who accomplishes it. To a younger man, with many years ahead of him, let this accomplishment be given. Have I satisfied your inquisition?"

"Might Mr. Fletcher see the manuscript?" asked the young woman, with a little emphasis upon the name.

"It is very old and incalculably precious, Miss Fieldfare. You know that I do not take it from my room."

"Mr. Trefillan copies out portions of the manuscript himself, and gives them to Geoffrey to translate. Geoffrey has never examined the entire manuscript," she said.

"Really?—Haven't you?"

"Well, Wilfred, I've had a look at a page or two. Most of the pages are loose, so—I thought it best to leave the handling of the book itself to Trefillan."

"How do you know he's copying it right?"

"Mr Fletcher—if I might interpose. You may be sure that I am very careful."

"Begging you pardon. But I thought you said your eyes are weak. Too weak, you said, for you to translate it yourself."

"Mr. Fletcher, you don't understand, I perceive, that the mere mechanical labour of copying is a far easier matter than translating. As I said, I am not proficient in medieval Armenian—what languages do you have, if I may ask?"

"Just English, all I need for my line of work," the visitor said.

"As I surmised."

"Look, would you like to hear some of it?" the invalid asked.

"I don't expect I'll make head nor tail out of it, Geoffrey, but please go ahead if you like," Mr. Fletcher said.

"Here, this will give you an idea. It's the bit I've been working on the past few days. 'Of what Powers do we know aught, save those that are of the earth, the water, the fire, and the air? Let all obeisance be made to those Mighty Ones whose strength is abroad in the earth, the water, the fire, and the air. And Their strength is imparted to the Wise that they may prolong their days. But the celestial Hierarchy, and That which made Them, Who have no presence beneath the sphere of the moon, let those called the Faithful adore them, and find their reward when and where they may. In their books they indite of the fleshless Ministers of the Most High, Who adore Him Who became Man (as it is said); let the Faithful, I say, venerate Them; but the Wise would rather know of those puissant Ones whose Thrones are set in the middle air; nay, let them know even of their attendants, the airy Beasts that course among the waste spaces, who scent out blood whenever it is shed, and lie in wait; of them the wise man would know, that he might command them.'"

The woman's face was turned from the man she loved as he read. Elias Trefillan, however, looked on avidly. His face had become flushed, as if he were a healthy young man who had just had exercise.

"Well—it's not very Christian, is it?" said Mr. Fletcher.

The priest responded. "It *is* very Christian in a way. Think of the doctrine of the priesthood of all believers. Some to be priests of the public Christian rites; others not. Every man to make his way to his spiritual goal. That is what Christianity really means: not structures planned in the heads of Pugin or Street, nor the salvation of darkies, nor water poured on infants' heads, nor the relief of widows, nor squeaking organs and illiterate hymns. All such activity only comes between a man and the exercise of his powers—the life abundant."

Geoffrey looked, Mr. Fletcher might have said, embarrassed, but not ashamed.

"We are to become as little children—is it not said?" Elias Trefillan continued. "Now what is the way of little children? Is it not the capacity to become absorbed in one thing, exercising all their powers upon it? Such simplicity! A Spiritual Man does not dissipate his powers upon a dozen different objects of so-called charity, upon books of sermons, or upon slum visiting. He must become *like a little child* if he is to take his kingdom, in all the power of youthful will."

"That is not what becoming a child means, at all," Diana Fieldfare said.

"Spoken like a true protestant!" the priest rasped. "The layman or the woman quite free to correct the professional. I'm sure that you do search out many Gems of Consolation and Wisdom in your Bible, Miss Fieldfare. Pour out your heart upon it, by all means!"

She did not reply. The invalid stirred. "If you people are going to have another disputation about theology, please continue your discussion after I retire. I've been toiling at this thing all afternoon, and I'm *so tired.*" Indeed, Mr. Fletcher thought, his friend looked very weary. The members of the little party went their ways, Diana Fieldfare to her lodgings nearby for the night, the two men to the kitchen with the scraps. Then Mr. Fletcher, with a nod to the priest, excused himself for a walk. Lamps were lit—the little town did not have gaslights yet—and the moon would be full in another two or three nights. He saw no one, and heard little but the pad of a dog somewhere in the shadows. He let himself inside and soon was in his bed, sleeping deeply.

VI

Mr. Fletcher spent four more days in the company of his boyhood friend. During this time, his dislike of the parson became settled; his resignation to his friend's possible decline towards death deepened; his esteem for Miss Fieldfare grew. Sometimes to Mr. Fletcher it seemed that his friend's lot likely would turn out to be enviable, if it were not wrong to feel such envy—Geoffrey would impart to the learned public a treatise of great interest to the learned few. It would be the making of him; and Geoffrey would be famous and would marry Miss Fieldfare. Then imagining their happiness together made Mr. Fletcher more grateful for his own pleasant household. At other times, Mr. Fletcher longed to confront Trefillan, tell him the translation project was surely injuring Geoffrey's health, rather than giving him an object in life, and he, Trefillan, should leave them all alone and go to his own place, wherever that should be.

On the subject of Trefillan's antecedents, Mr. Fletcher had talked once before with Miss Fieldfare. At first, his estimate of the young woman colored, or tainted indeed, by the parson's early remarks, Mr. Fletcher had tried to work up distrust in her confidences, but her transparent sincerity and goodness soon impressed themselves upon him.

He could not help but admire her enterprise. It would not have occurred to him to consult *Crockford's Directory of the Church of England*; indeed, he had never heard of the book. Miss Fieldfare had visited the nearest prosperous parish, and been permitted to examine the most recent edition on hand. On page 624, she found a list of clergymen who had been suspended from, or had defected from, the Established Church since the previous edition. Most of these were named in a list of secessions to Rome—men still persuaded by the case of Cardinal Newman, some of them. A very few others had surrendered their livings in favor of Dissent. Just three names were listed under "Apostasized; Excommunicated." Mr. Elias Trefillan, formerly rector of St. Gerrans, in Knellerbridge in Cornwall, was among these.

"I wrote to the Cathedral at Truro," Miss Fieldfare had said. "As I had expected, the reply to my inquiry was in few words. The bishop does not discuss these unhappy matters publicly, the letter said; he would say only that 'Mr. Trefillan was rebellious and dishonest, and it was to be feared that his infidelity had hardened beyond hope of remedy.' After his return from the African mission, he had seemed to satisfy his peers that rumors of irregularities in his conduct there must be false; but the complaints of his parishioners soon reached the bishop, and this time Trefillan's 'contumacy was manifest,' he said."

Miss Fieldfare had told Geoffrey Cleeve her findings. "But you have seen how strong that man's hold over Geoffrey is. Geoffrey really does seem to need him, somehow; he becomes agitated or despondent whenever I try to reduce Trefillan's hold upon him, whether by argument or—tears." She had looked directly at him, smiling. They were standing outside the house, as she was about to walk home to her aunt's for the night. He asked her if they could speak further "about all this," and she agreed.

Their next opportunity for private conversation came about when they walked to the market square for some shopping. Both were not quite at their ease in thus conversing together in the public eye, since their connection might be open to misunderstanding; but there was no help for it. Diana Fieldfare was determined to communicate as much as possible of her misgivings.

"Geoffrey has never rejected the doctrines he learned from his mother and father, but he stays away from Church, and tells me I make too much of Mr. Trefillan's remarks and of his departure from his curacy—he says probably some of Trefillan's brethren are envious of his scholarly attainment, and so—how easier blacken a clergyman's name?"

Mr. Fletcher considered.

"He seems to know the Bible well, at least."

Now she stared, not in a hostile manner, but in real surprise. "Mr. Fletcher, haven't you noticed how he turns it to his own purposes? Why, just the evening before you came to us, Geoffrey and I had been talking, and I had been urging him to put the manuscript by, at least for a time. Let him take up some work as a—as a schoolmaster if need be. He is wonderful with children and youths, Mr. Fletcher; I have never seen a man who converses so naturally with them, when his shyness or his preoccupation don't interpose themselves. And Geoffrey really was listening to me, and was, I believe, convinced that it was time to put the unclean thing away. And he began to talk with that man. And Mr. Trefillan drew himself up and said, 'Geoffrey, have you never heard what the Blessed Apostle said—"Let us not be weary in our work, for in due season we shall reap, *if we faint not!*"' And I was speechless for a moment. Before I went to bed that night, I found the place—it is in the sixth chapter of Galatians. Saint Paul says, 'Let us not be weary in well doing.' But that man seizes even the Holy Scriptures and impresses them in his own service."

Mr. Fletcher realized that, for a moment, he had not been attending to Miss Fieldfare's words. He had been looking into her face, which was framed with glowing strands of her dark hair, which strayed from the bonnet she wore, as the chilly sunlight kindled them from behind her. Her eyes and mouth were animated by unfeigned expression; and she had pretty, even teeth; and Mr. Fletcher was thinking that his own Sophia would say that it would never do—that Geoffrey should die and not live to marry this fine girl.

Diana Fieldfare turned to examine a cart of vegetable marrows. Mr. Fletcher looked beyond her at the throng of buyers and sellers. They were pressed together closely; once, there was a disturbance of some kind, as people got out of the way of a passing dog, it seemed. Then his gaze wandered to the shop fronts. EDW. BUNYAN GENERAL GROCER might be worth a look-in, he thought, professionally interested. PETTIBONE: STATIONER was next . . . Mr. Fletcher's attention wandered. . . . Across the busy crowd from where Mr. Fletcher stood, stumbling next to a slate wall, was a man, whose halting movement seemed to betoken illness. The man raised his head and looked directly at him. His face was a deathly mask of suffering.

"*Geoffrey!*" Mr. Fletcher cried.

He leapt into the crowd and pushed through to the other side. Geoffrey was gone. Mr. Fletcher looked into the alley nearby. He saw nothing but blank walls down the length of the space between two buildings. He ran the length of the alley and burst into the next street. A few sauntering passersby regarded him, but Geoffrey was not to be seen.

With a rustle of skirts, Miss Fieldfare swept up to Mr. Fletcher. "What is it?"

"I thought I saw Geoffrey! He looked deathly ill."

They looked all around, keenly. An old man and woman went by quite briskly.

The wind moved the bare branches of a nearby oak. Their shadows faded as a veil of cloud passed in front of the sun. The warm color went out of the buildings. "He's not here," Mr. Fletcher said.

There was no one near them now. It was time to return to the market square, to buy the things they had come for, and to walk home.

Before they could turn towards the alley again, they heard a sickly moan.

The man and the woman raised their eyes. In branches high, high above them the dark shape of a man was caught. Its back had been turned to them, but as they stared, it twisted itself around and a white face looked down at them. Mr. Fletcher sprang for the lowest branch and began to haul himself up into the tree. Twigs scratched his face. He strained upwards—then he stopped; only grey sky showed in the branches above him.

"I looked away from him to you—just for a moment. Then he was gone," said the woman. She considered. "I think we should buy what we need and then return to him. I believe we will find him at home," she said with an effort.

VII

When Diana Fieldfare and Wilfred Fletcher had returned to the house Geoffrey Cleeve rented, they found the invalid cheerful from a good afternoon's work of translation, although tired. The priest was reading a book. They said nothing about the vision in the town. After an early supper, Mr. Fletcher expected that Miss Fieldfare would tell Geoffrey about what they had both seen. But instead, she took the lead of the conversation and guided it deftly into paths of reminiscence and anecdote. Glasses were filled, unusually, with wine. Soon Mr. Fletcher was in his element: the youngest of three sons, a tradesman with a hearty regard for his employment, he loved his brothers well, but found no little relish in relating incidents which they, had they been present, might not have greatly enjoyed hearing.

Mr. Fletcher's eldest brother was a country lawyer. "He's a *fire-breather* as prosecutor, Henry is. Once—I was a lad and he let me sit somewhere in a corner—there was some chap charged with stealing a dozen hogs. Brodick was his name. My brother was shouting at that jury like a patent medicine man at a fair. Oh, you should have seen him. You'd have thought Magna Carta was in danger, the way he carried on. Made out that stealing pigs had always been considered a very bad thing to do in this island. As indeed it is. 'Gentlemen of the Jury,' says he. 'Think now what this man did. He trespassed upon the private property of a most respectable citizen. Then he did *steal* not one hog, but twelve hogs! Not only did he steal twelve hogs, he stole twelve *fat* hogs! Twelve *fat* hogs, *exactly the same number, my Gentlemen of the Jury, as I see in the box before me!* Hee-hee!—But didn't the man *get off*, too!"

"Now you must let me say something of my father," Diana Fieldfare said, when their mirth had subsided (although Mr. Trefillan's laughter seemed a little unnatural). "He is a rural curate—in Little Madeley. He is such a man for taking pains over his sermons. I do believe he has never read the same one twice. I see him now, with his Greek Testament and his Hebrew Bible before him, and the volumes of the Caroline divines and Waterland, Bethell, Wall, and Jones of Nayland on shelves all around him. Why, at this moment the dear man may be writing his next sermon. I must tell you I too, that for all his learning, he cares most for his people, and generally, I do believe, takes great care not to reckon without their understanding. He speaks up so that one and all can hear him, too, except for two deaf old men. On one hot Sunday morning, it was just a few years ago, he was preaching from the Book of Joshua, about the fall of Jericho. (I remember his next sermon was about Achan and the false Israelites in the camp—oh, how he made our blood run cold, when he described the discovery of the deceivers!) But he told how the Israelites marched about the walls of the city, blowing on their trumpets. And he had a *schoffar* which had been sent to him by a missionary in Palestine, a great trumpet. And he said, 'Those trumpets no doubt looked something like this!' And he raised it to his lips—and at that moment, Mr. Decker's donkey thrust in his head through the chancel door and burst into the most dreadful brays! What an uproar from all of us in the church! I do believe the smallest children thought the church walls were going to fall upon us! And didn't my father laugh the loudest of any of us!"

Then Geoffrey Cleeve looked over at the priest. "What about it, Trefillan? Don't be left out." He poured more wine into his empty glass.

"Since you honor me—yes," he said. "I have been thinking of my years in South America. Yes, I myself have been a missionary, Mr. Fletcher. True, the white fields of the Lord's harvest I long ago left to other reapers, returning to these shores—this was at the time when you were at university, Geoffrey." His attention centered, for the most part, upon the invalid, the priest related some of his adventures.

"I journeyed to that distant land, not only in the interests of my Church, but to follow certain threads. The Mother Church was very far away, Geoffrey, and so I was able to despatch reports from the Orinookoo that painted pictures of multiplied conversions, although I more often went among the savages to learn than to evangelize. After all, scholarship has its claims, something you will understand even if many do not. I have contributed a paper or two to journals of folklore. In time, I became accustomed to many things an Englishman would abhor."

Mr. Fletcher felt it was his turn to say something with an air of assumed innocence. "The diet, I suppose you mean? Manioc, isn't it?" (He had remembered the word used by a missionary who had spoken in his church once.)

"Ah, yes, quite so. Manioc, yes. I see you have read some books of travels, Mr. Fletcher. I trust my own story doesn't sound like travellers' tales? There are, I trust, no discrepancies in the details?" Beneath the clergyman's bantering tone was a suggestion of irritation.

"No, no," the other mumbled, wearily.

"I lived among the people for some time. From time to time, I was able to send reports of conversions home. I told how an ancient woman, on her deathbed, renounced her witchcraft, with great sobs—the account has since been reprinted many times as a tract of a missionary society. Would you believe it, I receive a royalty cheque of a pound or two a year, to this day! I will admit to this little circle that I consented to write according to the conventions established for this type of literature. On the spot, though, I found my theme of conversation with her must largely be that of the torments that awaited her after her death if she did not tell me all about her little ways, for some of these people know things about the prolongation of life, for example, or the enshadowing of one will by another, that are very curious. Yes, Geoffrey, I see you are interested. I ensured that I should know what she knew. Then, by all means let her be baptized, if she liked. . . . Her death was impressive. Once she had burned her spirit bag and so on, which she thought fit to do before her Baptism, the villagers rounded upon her. They had feared her before. Now that she had renounced her evil arts, she was thrust out of the village, and went to live in a hut in a clearing a mile or so away. I happened to see her the last of anyone. She was set upon by a dozen wild dogs. What a clamor was then! A primordial *Nunc Dimittis!*"

The invalid giggled, then blushed. He did not look well, Geoffrey thought. The young woman's face returned no expression as the priest spoke. Geoffrey, had he looked, would have known that she was angry. As for Mr. Fletcher himself, he had never cared for worldly wit in a clergyman, but he supposed such a way of talking might be ordinary in social ranks above his own; and he was not sure what a "*Nunc Dimittis*" was.

"—She was an old woman, Miss Fieldfare, very old, and there was *nothing* I could do to rescue her, I assure you.—At length, my researches in South America were complete. I threw up the mission and roamed from the muddy banks of the Orinookoo to the jungles where once Aztec priest-kings calculated the infinite cycles of their calendar, the mathematics of which drown our own paltry 'B.C.' and 'A.D.' in torrents of time. I'm afraid I had to pay my own way back to Britain—yes, the bishop had decided he didn't care for the advancement of knowledge, he wanted souls—so I resumed my connection to the University, Geoffrey; where one day I would find you employed in learning. I found friends there. One of the colleges agreed to sponsor my researches in the Ottoman lands. This helped me repair my reputation with the bishop, who promised me a parish, if I were interested, when I should have returned. I travelled by way of Belgrade and Semlin, staying at Pera, thence to Smyrna, and so to Beyrout. Near Sidon it was that I recovered Lady Stanhope's manuscript, Geoffrey."

"Look, I say, could we all see a specimen, Trefillan? You showed me a piece once, and I'm sure we would all like to see it." And he rose to his feet.

"No, it isn't necessary for you to get up. I will bring one of the fragments." He looked into Mr. Fletcher's eyes and glanced away from Diana Fieldfare. "The manuscript is exceedingly precious, and as fragile as it is precious. You will forgive my offering only one specimen." He slipped into the dark hallway that opened upon the sitting room. When he returned, he bore a narrow, flat black leather case between his hands, his left hand supporting it, his right spread across the cover of the case. Mr. Fletcher thought the man had never looked so priest-like. A table had been cleared and Mr. Trefillan placed the case on it, and carefully raised the cover of the case. Brown with antiquity, the fragment lay on a velvet backing.

"There is, of course, much more," the priest said. "Many months of work lie ahead of you, Geoffrey, as you know. But you progress very satisfactorily."

So this was a piece of that ancient book, the visitor thought, that had come from such a distant land; that Miss Fieldfare did not like; that Elias Trefillan cherished, and claimed would save the invalid's life, by giving him a supreme object of effort; that his friend sometimes regarded with fascination, and at other times loathed. The brown bit of cloth or hide, with black ciphers still visible among the wrinkles and wear, and other pieces like it, all extracted from the booty of a desperate thief hiding among the deformed inhabitants of a lepers' village, now rested under the roof of a house in one of the lanes of a town in England. Suddenly it was more than Mr. Fletcher had any liking for, and he told the priest, shortly, that he was going for a walk, late as it was.

Again, lamps flickered in the cold night breeze, and the full moon cast dark shadows on the pavement. Few lights shone in the shuttered houses as he passed by. Even Mr. Fletcher couldn't help fancying, like many another man so circumstanced, that it was as if somehow the populace of the teeming earth had been snatched away, and only he of all mankind was left. What if, inside those houses, even the ones with illuminated curtains, no man nor woman nor child dwelled? But such odd notions were much more in Geoffrey's line than his own. There remained something of the child about Geoffrey, although Mr. Fletcher was not sure he could put a finger on it.

Perhaps it was being married, he thought after he had walked fifty more yards. Or loving. Diana Fieldfare was younger than Geoffrey, but she seemed more adult than he; her love was a woman's love, but Geoffrey's had something unmanly, childish, in it. It was good, Mr. Fletcher supposed, if a man retained something of the boy, but yet he should be a man, too. It might be that Geoffrey loved Diana Fieldfare in his way, but the work of loving her as wife lay ahead; at present, he seemed to love her as sister, friend, even as mother.

The night really was rather windy. How it whistled round the corners of stone buildings and along the uneven pavement. It brushed against him like a vigorous, questing animal. Indeed, as he looked along the street ahead of him, Mr. Fletcher thought he saw shadows passing, low and swift. Shadows, but no bodies to cast them! Such a sensation of horrid dread passed over the pedestrian as formerly he had never known save in rare nightmares, unless in very distant childhood. Without conscious decision, he turned and began to walk very rapidly back to Geoffrey Cleeve's house. Worse and worse!—As he bent his steps that way, he saw the phantom shapes hastening ahead of him. But he knew no one in Croatley with whom he could stay, other than the inmates of that house, and Miss Fieldfare; and he desired very much to get inside, with locked doors and drawn blinds screening the streets from him.

VIII

The priest's screams were over already when Mr. Fletcher bounded up the stone steps and through the open doorway, through which light poured into a street where frightened neighbors were gathering. A man who now stood among the others there had opened the door, but had been unable, for fear, to enter the house.

It was subsequently that Wilfred Fletcher was told about those hellish screams, which had not only awakened Geoffrey in the extremity of terror, but had wakened everyone in the environs of the house, save for a deaf old man who slept through the entire night. A police inspector from Wroxsleigh, who wrote to him a week after his return from Croatley to his own village, related to the grocer, as a person concerned in the strange events, what he had garnered in his interviews with the people of the neighborhood.

When Mr. Fletcher, however, commenced his search of the house, almost maddened by his apprehensions of what the beasts—wolves, call them—might have done, the house was almost silent. No one was about on the ground floor, but on the first storey, Mr. Fletcher found his friend in a state of nervous collapse. From another room close by came monstrous growls.

Mr. Fletcher was to live another forty-two years. Before the cool summer morning in which he died in the presence of his youngest daughters, Alice and Diana, he would read of tremendous machines of war that rolled and crushed over stark fields denuded of every living thing; he would see them, in the swirling masses of grey images that were projected on a snow-white screen. He would read about poisonous gases that crept into mud trenches, and he would see ruined men who had been returned to their home shores, men who would never draw an even breath again. He would lose his son Arthur, a father himself by then, blown to bits in France; and Rosamond and his own wife would die in the influenza epidemic that followed that Great War. And the worst moment in all of those years would be the one in which he heard the postman's step outside his door, and knew, with inexplicable and immediate certainty, that the man bore news of Arthur's death. But even harder than rising to his feet and walking to the door to answer the postman's knock, was walking from Geoffrey's room, now, to the priest's room.

The door was closed, but those beasts which sought the man's life had not been thwarted. Mr. Fletcher opened the door. A lamp was burning. Smoky shapes darted in the room, tumbled, the warm light passing through them. They pulled at the body that lay by the bed. It flopped and fell back again and again, and the shapes nuzzled it and turned it over, seeking. Mr. Fletcher knew no Latin; he had never read of the ghosts encountered by Aeneas, who craved blood that they might speak. Three years later, however, Mr. Fletcher was to gasp, shocked, when, in church, from the lectern the parson read of the destruction of a queen of Israel, and how the dogs licked her blood.

Mr. Fletcher turned away from the room, shut the door, breathed deeply a few times, and went to his friend.

Geoffrey had revived. The two men eventually crept into the street, where the frightened bystanders let them pass without interference. The invalid, supported by his friend, brought them in time to a house where lived a spinster named Elizabeth Clara Monance and her married sister's daughter, Diana Fieldfare.

The press made capital of "The Croatley Horror" and moved on after a few days when no further horrors were forthcoming.

We, who read the record of the events of those days, may be told in a few lines what was pieced together, and inferred, only over time by Diana Cleeve and her husband—a man who preferred, for his part, not to think of those days often. These particulars she communicated to Mr. Fletcher and his Sophia, on the occasion of a visit to Bigglesfield some months after the conclusion of the events of this narrative. Those particulars are, briefly, these: Mr. Trefillan was a practitioner of unholy disciplines by means of which he sought to prolong his life, and, indeed, recover more and ever more of the vigor of youth. He was an ancient man when he first discovered that it might be that a man could draw life from another, for many years, if he overshadowed him in childhood, dominating his will. Trefillan knew Geoffrey's father, a bitter church architect, and through him became acquainted with the architect's imaginative only child. The boy began to learn scraps of vile magic from the old man, scraps eked out with Trefillan's own inventions. Trefillan began to grow younger; the boy sickened. The hold he had over the boy became stronger when another boy, Wilfred, was brought into the "club"—"web" is a better word. But Wilfred's father broke off the boys' friendship and threatened the old man who, he knew, was seducing them spiritually, although he did not understand the manner nor the aim. By then Trefillan had established an invisible and immaterial link between himself and young Geoffrey Cleeve, however, and continued to draw some vitality from him, even when half a world away, seeking the furtherance of his forbidden knowledge and power. What cost, in declining perception of the distinct reality of others' natures, may have been his? Indeed, what loss of intellectual keenness?

A great surprise awaited Geoffrey when Diana Fieldfare, clearing out the priest's room four days after his death, discovered that "Lady Stanhope's Manuscript" hardly could be said to exist. There were but a few brown scraps, scarcely enough, it might be, to be worth bringing to the attention of scholars; and the sorrowful old prophetess, wearying in her self-imposed exile so far from England, knew that. They were, indeed, of a magical character, the one-time translator acknowledged; but Trefillan had augmented them with copious inventions of his own. It were a hard matter to judge how clearly he himself knew his outpourings to be sheer fantasy. He had evidently sat at his desk composing the passages of "Armenian" that he would, the next day, give to his *protégé* to "translate." In Elias Trefillan's scheme, the scholarly edition would never be written; the "manuscript" was little but a device by which the old man—who grew younger by the month—poisoned the invalid and made his life his own. Geoffrey had become incapable of noticing Elias Trefillan's resurgent vitality, as his own diminished. Diana Fieldfare had suspected that some evil connection existed between the two men, and had watched for it to betray itself.

We may ask: Did Trefillan ever know that the few bits of Lady Stanhope's manuscript, brought to England by him, were indeed the remnants of a genuinely magical treatise, and that those avengers, who horribly feasted upon his lifeless body, had been awakened and drawn from the place where they were, by the activity of a malign mind—Trefillan's, not Geoffrey's—upon the fragments of the accursed treatise? How much of the "pedigree" the priest propounded for the treatise was real? Perhaps the day came when even he could not have said. He had spoken of the beasts of the air; had he known, only at that last intolerable moment, how very real they are? Until that moment, perhaps the power of his mind had become so narrowly focused a beam of light—a light focused upon himself and the flow of life he drew from another spirit—that all else was darkness to him.

Did fragments of the treatise—whatever its source—somewhere survive the burning, by Diana Fieldfare in the presence of the man she loved and his friend, of the pieces Trefillan had possessed?

The reader must be content to let these questions remain unanswered.

However, he may like to know a little of the further histories of the principal actors, other than Elias Trefillan, who have figured in this history.

Geoffrey Cleeve was to become a private tutor in ancient languages, resident in Cambridge, for eight years; he never held an official position with that University, but candidates for Holy Orders especially found him a patient teacher. He was never strong, although he died the father of one child, who died in infancy. Four years after she first donned widow's weeds, which she put away after six months, Diana Cleeve married a Norwegian scholar-pastor, a relation of the famous Nicholas Grundtvig. She had met Thomas Aagard at the home of a friend, the sister of a Cambridge scholar of the Lutheran Reformation. Two children were born to them.

Mr. Fletcher and his wife attended the wedding of Diana Cleeve and Thomas Aagard in an ancient stave church forty miles from Christiana. They listened appreciatively to Pastor Aagard's carefully-enunciated English, and marked his own pleasure in listening to his new wife's hopeful Norwegian.

Mr. Fletcher wanted to see how the Christiana grocers managed things; but Mrs. Fletcher insisted they see the fjords.

Powers of the Air

A diarist in southeastern North Dakota wrote:

April 25, 1934

Last weekend was the worst dust storm we ever had. We've been having quite a bit of dirt blowing every year since the drouth started, not only here, but all over the Great Plains. Many days this spring the air is just full of dirt coming, literally, for hundreds of miles. It sifts into everything. After we wash the dishes and put them away, so much just sifts into the cupboards we must wash them again before the next meal. Clothes in the closets are covered with dust.

Newspapers say the deaths of many babies and old people are attributed to breathing in so much dirt.

May 21, 1934

Saturday Dad, Bud, and I planted an acre of potatoes. There was so much dirt in the air I couldn't see Bud only a few feet in front of me. Even the air in the house was just a haze.

The newspapers report that on May 10 there was such a strong wind the experts in Chicago estimated 12,000,000 tons of Plains soil was dumped on that city. By the next day the sun was obscured in Washington, D.C., and ships 300 miles out at sea reported dust settling on their decks.

Ann Marie Low: *Dust Bowl Diary* (University of Nebraska Press, 1984). Quotations used by permission.

Today North Dakota and most of the adjacent states are part of Flyover Territory: an immense expanse of prairie stretching eastward from the Rocky Mountains to the much more densely

35

inhabited regions of eastern Minnesota, and reaching south into Texas and north to the Canadian border and far beyond. The jetliners cruise along five or six miles above, and the passengers, thousands of them everyday on scores of flights, gaze for a while at the hazy land below, or, more often, at masses of rounded icebergs and snowplains—in truth, the upper surfaces of huge cloud blankets—and then go back to their magazines, or their naps, and settle in for another two or three hours.

Gazing out at the dense, luminous clouds of the wettest summer in a century, I found that I was remembering an account I'd heard, of that parched era which people in this part of the country speak of as the Dirty Thirties. Some fifteen years ago, during my year as vicar of St. Mark Lutheran Church in Norby, North Dakota, one of my oldest parishioners told me about a strange experience that had occurred to his son, who was a college student at the time, preparing himself for a career as a high school teacher.

Orel Vinje's story took me back to the days before I was born, when electrification and the radio were still new to many Dakotans. His son Pete Vinje, then twenty-one years of age, was returning to college for his last year, hitch-hiking and walking to save money. The Depression was over, but the rains still weren't coming. Thousands of square miles lay defenseless beneath the sun, and the winds came day after day, night after night, whirling the topsoil all the way to the Atlantic seaboard, maybe the hugest patch of fog, brown fog, that had ever been in the world. So sometimes Pete walked along the dry dirt roads and couldn't see the burnt-up cottonwoods along the occasional shrunken rivers, unless he was within half a mile of them. Some days were much worse. It all seemed to rise before my mind's eye as Orel told the story, although he was not an exceptionally orderly narrator.

He said that young Pete sometimes read as he walked, waiting for the next farmtruck to come rattling along enabling him to hitch a ride for a few miles to the next town. What was he reading? Orel told me I'd be surprised: psychology. An unusual topic for the reading of a strong young Plains boy at that time, especially one with no yearning to get away and find a place for himself beneath the bright lights of some big city a long way away.

His son had had some educational psychology, Orel told me, but was eager for more exotic material than the classroom-oriented fare. The teacher's-college library had some volumes of Freud and Jung, and others, and Pete was working his way through them. There probably weren't very many people reading Freud or Jung in North Dakota at that time. Mr. Vinje said that, during his visits home, his son would sit up talking about his reading for hours after Ida, his mother, had gone off to bed. Orel, tired from a farmer's hard day, listened without objection, and also, he freely admitted to me, without much comprehension. If a young man went off to college, it was to be expected that when he came back home, he'd have learned things his mother and father had never heard of.

Like, I suppose, a great many young readers of psychology in those days, Pete had, it seems, been much taken by the idea of the struggle, often not recognized as such, between children and adults, and even moreso, no doubt, by the idea that hidden physical desires underlie a great deal of human behavior. Orel seemed just a little embarrassed when he mentioned this. It was clear to me from what Orel said, that Pete was ready to use these ideas, so conventional today, at the first opportunity, to interpret others' conduct.

Anyway, there he was, walking east along some road in the middle of the state, the poor harvest in, the winds of autumn coming across the endless level plain and growing stronger, unnoticed by him, his attention all on some case study illustrating the structure of the unconscious, perhaps. He who runs, or walks steadily anyway, may read, on those empty level roads. Before he turned a page, however, Orel said, Pete would reach down and shake the dust off one of his pants legs, and then pause to rub the printed surface against the trouser leg, wiping the thin film of dust off. The two open pages would have become dirty in the few minutes that Pete held them open.

On one such occasion, he looked around him, and saw that the grey-brown air was dark; he checked his watch: this wasn't the onset of evening; clearly the wind had risen, and was carrying a heavier load of soil. He thought he should have been able to see some trees off to the left, along a meandering little creek, but they were no longer visible.

He looked at his pocket watch. Night would be coming in a few hours, but he wouldn't be able to see very well long before then, if the wind continued to mount, creating a true ground fog of dirt. As it was, he'd been walking since six o' clock that morning, when he'd left a farmhouse a couple of miles outside of Dexter. He would look for a place to spend the night. From earlier experience, he had no doubt that he'd find hospitality. Perhaps he'd take the harmonica out of his rucksack and some grizzled old Norwegian farmer, who still spoke English hesitantly, would get out an old violin. The wife and maybe a few older children and a couple of laborers staying the night would listen appreciatively.

Orel Vinje said his son had to walk a long time before he came to a farmhouse with lights on. Pete might have passed one or two dark houses; sometimes people gave up and went to California to get away from the empty sky and the dust. I've seen the foundations of some of those old places. I'll find myself thinking of the darker words of the Psalms—"Let their habitation be desolate; and let none dwell in their tents." Or Isaiah: "It shall never be inhabited, neither shall it be dwelt in from generation to generation . . . But wild beasts of the desert shall lie there; and their houses shall be full of doleful creatures; and owls shall dwell there, and satyrs shall dance there . . ."

But Pete saw a house with light in its windows. As he approached the house, he looked at his watch again. Although it was only a quarter to four of a late September afternoon, twilight had fallen.

Orel Vinje paused in his narration to sip coffee. Then, before going back to the story, he talked a little about the drought of 1929-1936, a great trial; there just wasn't enough moisture in the soil to let the plants take root and hold the earth down, and the wind erosion was severe. The extensive shelter belts of trees planted in diagonal rows that we have today to break the wind were still in the future. Orel sighed. "Pastor, it was a miserable time, not all the time, but for days at a stretch you couldn't keep clean, you'd head for bed at night and there would be collections of black dirt in all the creases in the bedsheet. Ida used to cry sometimes, it was so upsetting.—You could get used to being dusty, at least I could, but not to eating dust. Your pigs, or if you had any, cows, were prone to respiratory infections. You'd look out the window or step onto the porch, making sure you shut that door behind you, not that it helped that much, and look out and couldn't see anything but brown out there."

Then Orel went back to his story.

Pete could tell that the rising wind would last a while. It was good that he had found shelter. A few hundred yards from the house, he was startled by something that leaped past him—a bounding tumbleweed.

It turned out, Pete had told his father, that only three people lived in the farmhouse, a couple and their daughter, who was around fourteen or fifteen, he supposed. It seemed to be a big house for three people. He never heard that there were any brothers or sisters who'd moved away or had been carried off by illness; there were just the three of them. He told Orel that he doubted that they'd built the house themselves. It was his theory that they'd *found* it; some family couldn't stand it any more, and left the house for whoever wanted it, human or animal. Orel Vinje told me that, at that time, you could offer a fine big house out on the prairie for sale for almost nothing and not get a buyer.

He digressed again for a moment.

"You were losing money you could be earning by the work of your hands somewhere else, if you sat home waiting for someone to come along and buy your house. Your land might not bring more than a few dollars an acre. The best houses in a town such as Norby might bring a few hundred dollars." I knew that old-time Dakotans relish the pleasure of holding forth on property values past and present, so I steered him back to his son's story.

"Pete said they weren't much of a family to look at. He admits that, as soon as he saw the man and his wife, he felt like turning around and walking off into the dust. Not that they were abnormal, physically really bad-looking, but the man and his wife, when they came to the door, were something more than unfriendly-looking, and also seemed jumpy. The man did have an ugly scar on one side of his face.—Pete says the only time he ever heard the man laugh was when he explained how he got it. He said he'd been drunk one dark night and gotten scratched by a she-devil named Barb Wire.— Pete couldn't tell how old they were. As for the daughter, at first she was as shy as a doe, he said. I asked him if she was as pretty as a doe, too, and he said, no, she was as plain as plain. She had an old-country name, Sigrid."

During his two days there, nearly all of the work that was done in the house was done by the girl, with Pete contributing some, too, and feeling much more awkward about it that he usually did when he put up with a family. He couldn't get comfortable with them. Because of the wind and dust and the time of year, little was done outdoors other than the pumping of water for the chickens and the pigs twice a day. Orel said, "The husband did that much. He took his time about it, too, though he always came back inside coughing and spitting, right on the floor, and blowing the dustcake out of his nose and wiping it on his sleeve. The wife sat and did very little, so far as Pete noticed.

"But now here's what happened," Orel said. Just as soon as Pete stepped over the threshold, there was a loud BANG! above his head off to the right. Nothing was amiss that he could see, but what disturbed him very much was that the man and wife pretended not to have heard anything; yet he'd seen them flinch. At that point he hadn't seen the girl just yet. Because of their odd manner, he found that he was reluctant to ask them about the noise.

He sat down across from the man of the house, who mumbled, in response to Pete's query, that he was Jens Somebody—Orel didn't remember that last name. His wife was Louisa; she'd been born in Springfield, Illinois. "Pete told me you could tell a lot from just that fact. The poor woman grew up in a well-settled state that was known around the world, not just for its agriculture but for manufacturing. And somehow she ends up married to some Norwegian immigrant and stuck out in the middle of nowhere. I'm sure that's how it must have seemed to her, anyway. Not being used to it," and Orel Vinje grinned at me.

The daughter came into the parlor from somewhere, and Pete had a look at her. Just a plain pioneer girl, looking like someone out of an old picture, he thought. Barefoot, braids.

Jens commanded his daughter to go to the kitchen and bring some coffee. Pete was facing away from the kitchen. There was a tremendous crash. He spun around, expecting to see the girl standing in the midst of a mess of shattered crockery. She was halfway to the kitchen, frozen in midstep. Then she strode solidly forward. At Pete's side, Jens screamed at the girl that she had better not drop any more dishes or he'd whip her. Pete was shocked by the obvious unfairness of the implied accusation; the girl had not been in the kitchen when the noise occurred; moreover, there was hatred and fear in the man's voice. Louisa's face was turned away from them.

Pete got up to help. But the kitchen floor, although gritty, showed no signs of an accident. Sigrid opened a cupboard and removed some cups; both cups and plates were neatly stacked.

In the next room, Jens was swearing and cursing his daughter for her clumsiness.

Pete had said to Jens, "She didn't drop anything, sir. Everything is all right."

"She cleaned it up fast," Jens growled. Pete declined to quarrel with his host within minutes of his arrival.

Then the two men talked, off and on, about predictable topics, the weather, crop yields, the impossibility of paying taxes to the United States government when your land wasn't producing and your animals were sickly, and the like. Pete told Orel that he didn't think Jens knew very much about homesteading. Pete had met bitter Norwegian immigrants before, men who had come to the States "expecting the ground to plow itself," but he didn't think that the man's anger was solely due to disappointment with the land. "Pete said he never did get to the bottom of that family. You'll see why," Orel said.

All the time that they talked, Sigrid busied herself with household chores. Pete said that he could see her making a good wife for somebody if she only weren't so plain and shy. Or was it shyness? As the evening drew on, Pete had told his father, he felt rather that she was preoccupied. He could have believed that she was writing a novel in her mind.

Pete was directed to an empty bedroom. An old blanket to lie on, another one to cover him, and a musty pillow met his sleeping requirements. Pete was used to family prayers before bedtime, but Jens didn't say a word about that.

He didn't sleep well. The wind moaning along the walls was part of it; like most people, he often didn't sleep well his first night in someone else's home. Once he awakened in the middle of the night and heard softly-spoken syllables coming from behind one of the doors in the hall opposite his room. He made his way very quietly closer to that door. It was Sigrid praying, urgently, although

41

there was no desperation in her voice. Well, somebody in the family was religious, Pete thought, and went back and lay down again.

The next morning, Sigrid lit a fire in the stove and fried eggs. Pete sat at the kitchen table, a nice oak one, he thought. He was not looking at any particular thing; an abrupt movement attracted his attention.

"Now here's what he said happened, and I believe him," Orel told me. A trivet sailed across the room and smacked against the wall under a John Deere calendar. No one could possibly have thrown it! Jens looked angrily at his daughter and his wife, and neither spoke.

"Then, Pete said, a light went on in his brain," Orel continued. "He called it a *poltergeist phenomena*. He said it was really exciting to see something like that, and really fascinating when you looked at it from a psychology point of view. In one of the things he had read there had been an account of poltergeist phenomenas. They were supposed to happen when there were disturbed teenage girls around, he told me." Orel shrugged. "I thought surely there's no such thing, but Pete said he had read about it in a psychology book. These things are on record.

"So Pete put it together like this: the girl was mad at her momma and poppa, as who could blame her, but she couldn't show it; 'plus,' he said, 'don't think I'm vain, Dad,' but she was attracted to him, and maybe didn't understand her female urges, you know, and all this was making her tense, and somehow that made these weird things happen around her. Did you ever hear anything like that?

"Anyway, now that he had a theory to fit what was going on, Pete didn't feel as uneasy as he would have otherwise. In fact, he settled in to watch what was going to happen next."

Pete found things to do to help the family that day, minor repairs which he would have expected Jens could have undertaken when they were first needed. Two or three further strange incidents occurred after breakfast, Pete had told his father.

That afternoon, the mother was in a bedroom, presumably sleeping, and the father had gone outside. Sigrid came up to Pete. The young man thought perhaps she was going to make a declaration of love!

"Begging your pardon, mister, are you a *Bible-reading man?*" she inquired breathlessly.

Pete faltered. This wasn't the question he had expected. "Some of it," he said.

"Do you go to church often?" she said.

"Well, I suppose so," Pete said. That was true enough when he was at home with Orel and Ida.

"What's your favorite part of the Bible? There's the Old Testament and the New Testament."

Pete guessed then that she wanted him to read to her from the Bible; she was illiterate.

Compulsory schooling was the law of the nation, but school superintendents across the state suspected that children were kept home to provide labor on farms, their names never appearing on school enrollment lists. Pete reflected that not only was she illiterate, she was bound to be terrified by the poltergeist activity, however little she showed the fact; she had no idea that she herself was the cause of it.

"You know, those noises, the things flying around—you shouldn't be afraid," he had told the girl as she stood there in her faded calico dress and bare feet.

"I'm not afraid," she said. "Never was, after the first few times." He believed her; but he went on reassuring her, anyway.

"I think they'll disappear when you're a little older. It's just a kind of funny mental thing."

"I don't understand, 'mental thing'," she said.

"It's just really a part of nature," Pete said, "just a part that we don't understand. We're learning more about things like that all the time. Someday people will go to the—someday people will have people who can help them so that the noises stop right away, talk it over . . ."

He didn't want to insult the poor girl by plainly stating that she was emotionally disturbed and was causing the disturbances, and he knew he couldn't explain psychology to her in terms she could understand. What she "knew" about the world she probably gained from attending some sectarian conclave somewhere, some "Chapel" where the pastor, likely self-taught and self-anointed, ranted about the Whore of Babylon and the One Hundred and Forty-Four Thousand. ("Now Pete never heard such things when he was in church, but he'd read novels about crazy revivalists and had what he thought was a pretty accurate idea of what you'd find in these little chapels around," Orel remarked.)

Pete went back to poking with a broom handle in the chimney, which he'd been trying to clean when the girl approached him. The fireplace smoked badly. As he pushed at a clump of soot, he brooded on the way Sigrid's mother ignored her and her father treated her like a slave or a draft animal. He became very angry.

"I don't know how you stand it, the way they treat you," Pete said abruptly.

"They don't ask anything much of me."

"Even if that were true—the way they ask it! How can you stand it?"

"It's more a matter of how can they be so unhappy. But they'll never be happy till they come and lay their burdens at the Mercy Seat," she said simply.

In the Lutheran church, back then or now, the "Mercy Seat" isn't an expression we use very much. But Pete had said to the girl, "Well, until they do, I don't know how you can stand it. Don't you feel like telling your father—" Pete cut himself off.

"You shouldn't talk like that," Sigrid said. "God give us our parents, me same as you. And where would it get me, if I was not to forgive them?"

"Well, I think—"

But Pete was cut off a second time; a black load of grime had come loose and fallen down the chimney, covering his face and shoulders with soot and dirt. He backed away from the grimy cloud. He couldn't speak for coughing.

Sigrid laughed. "I never thought to see a black Ethiopian in this house!" she said. "And he can't talk civilized!" Her tone of voice invited Pete to join in her mirth, and he soon found he couldn't help doing so.

"That was a mean trick to play, though," she said.

Pete asked what she meant, croaking. But before she could answer—

"What's all this?"

Jens stood at the door. It infuriated him to see his daughter talking with Pete, and very likely he blamed him for the sooty mess, too. Pete braced himself: in so tense a moment as this, poltergeist

44

activity was likely to occur. He almost seemed to feel a prickling, as of imminent lightning—and it was puzzling; he realized that he did not feel that the threatened explosion would precipitate from the girl, or himself.

"What is it?" Pete gasped, looking at the girl, feeling that pressure.

"You *feel* it too! They were here when we took the house!" Sigrid said eagerly.

"What are you two talking about behind my back?" shouted the father.

Orel said that Pete told him that at this point, he was completely confused. His feelings insisted that the phenomena were directed against the girl more than the rest of them, that even the terror of the father and the mother was meant to crush the girl, and yet surely the only possible explanation was that the girl herself was the cause of the poltergeist outbursts. That, Orel said, is still his view.

Jens growled at the girl, "You'll answer me, you'll answer me."

"Father! Please let him alone. You know that nobody has said nothing wrong. We should just pray that God will defend us from all our adversaries, like I've said before."

Right then seemingly something huge threw itself against the side of the house. Pete saw nothing but the grey-brown sky through the window.

"I've tried to tell Dad. Prince of the powers of the air, it says in the Bible. Powers of the air. They try to frighten us," Sigrid said to Pete.

"Liar, liar!" screamed her father. "It's the wind!" His features relaxed slightly. "Wind. Never *seen* such a place for wind—"

Then the flame in a kerosene lamp flared wildly. The glass cracked.

Something seemed to seize Pete by the leg and throw him to the floor. Jens stared, panting, but Sigrid crouched beside the young man. "All right," Pete said. "I don't feel hurt."

Next, the mother screamed from her room and came running. "Something ran across the bed," she sobbed.

Jens ran out of the room. The front door banged as Jens flung it open.

"Pete doesn't know if he ever came back," Orel said, concluding his narrative. "Jens was still gone the next morning, when Pete left. Pete promised to send a doctor for Sigrid's mother, who was in a bad way, and to let somebody in a position of authority know that the father was missing. Before he left, when morning came he and the girl looked all around for him, but not a sign. He says there was a tremendous amount of banging and other noise all that night, including yells from inside and outside the house, although just the three of them were there. The dust was something awful. They had to hold pieces of cloth torn from the sheets over their mouths and noses all night long. Sigrid didn't pray aloud, but Pete saw her close her eyes sometimes as if she was praying; he's sure she was. He says that at the time he felt that she was the only thing protecting them from going crazy or . . . or worse. That's what it felt like, he says, although that seems strange, since she must have been the one responsible for all the phenomenas.

"Along about five o'clock, the wind died down very suddenly, and by seven they could see the sun for the first time in two days. Sigrid's mother was asleep. Pete says he gave Sigrid a big hug and went off. He says he'd have said they should write letters to each other, only she couldn't write, no doubt.

"Well, that's his story," Orel had concluded. He'd sat there with me in the church basement after the quarterly voters' meeting, and told me just about the most remarkable story I'd ever heard. I sometimes considered asking Orel for his son's address and phone number. It would have been interesting to hear the story from his own lips. Pete was a school superintendent in Iowa, not far from retirement. But I didn't ask Orel, and I heard he was dead and buried two years later.

Unless you're forbidden to do so, you have to pass a story such as that along. A few years ago I related it to Father Paul Heitkamp. We may stand on opposite sides of the Reformation, but he's a good friend. I told him I hoped I'd not embellished the story too much, and asked him what he thought.

"It was when you mentioned the 'Ethiopian,' that I made a connection to something. How's your patristics, pastor?"

"*Athanasius contra mundum.* 'He who will not have the Church for his mother cannot have God for his Father.' And mostly a lot of

Augustine," I replied. "But courses in church budgeting and pastoral psychology didn't leave us a lot of time for the Church Fathers."

"Athanasius—you're right there. Listen to this." Fr. Heitkamp had taken down a heavy grey book from one of the shelves in his office, where we were sitting comfortably.

"*On the Incarnation?*" I asked, puzzled. That was the only thing by Athanasius that I could remember, that and that he didn't write the Athanasian Creed.

"No, not *De Incarnatione*, but the *Vita Antonii*, the Life of Antony," he said. Listen to this passage: *The devil could not bear to see his spiritual resolve*—that's Antony's resolve; he was the first great Christian hermit; a great ascetic of the Egyptian desert. . . . *He caused a great dust cloud of thoughts to rise in Antony's mind. But Antony held his ground against the tempter's wiles . . . He advanced against Antony, creating great disturbances by night, and striving to keep him from his prayers all day, no doubt to terrify him into losing faith. He took the form of a woman to try to seduce Antony, but Antony extinguished the tempter's fiery darts by meditating on the excellence of the Saviour. . . . At last, the Dragon took on the appearance of a black boy, and essayed to reason with him, and flatter him. But Antony demanded who he was, and the devil shouted, and departed.*" He closed the book. "See the connection?"

"No," I said.

"Young Vinje was tempting the girl to hatred of her parents, wasn't he? That would have been the speediest way to her spiritual downfall. Not that Peter was the devil or possessed by a devil. He didn't know whose hands he was playing into. But I was reminded of the passage. There she was, the young girl; with a vocation to the spiritual life, could it but have been realized. But she is out there in the 'desert,' with no one to instruct her accurately. She was the object of a great deal of violent persecution from our invisible enemies. I'm from the old guard, and we still believe in them. That young lady seems to have understood much about prayer."

"I have to admit, I thought the poltergeist theory was the key, Father."

"Perhaps you had a little too much psychology at seminary, and not enough patristics," he said.

The Ergushevo Icon

I think I could speak for most reporters when I say that we have a great capacity for taking an interest in things that people are doing and saying, while feeling little emotion about those things. In any event, a religion reporter rarely feels that he or she is close to historically important events or exciting occurrences. Bishops' promulgations of a committee-written statement on peace and human rights or pronouncements of denominational vice-presidents have to be reported, however predictable. Church-funded seminars on "God/dess sprirituality" were stimulating or weird twenty years ago. But not in the mid-1990s.

There have been a number of stories that I wrote up as heart-warming human interest stories, but in the process of making my notes into a feature of the right length, I myself felt mostly a concern for my craftsmanship as a reporter, not a personal involvement. A reporter comes on the scene of, say, a church's outreach to refugees or illegal laborers or its efforts to help victims of a fire or one of our California earthquakes, and right away, that reporter starts framing the story for other people, and not for personal reflection. The reporter's ideal of objectivity and impersonality becomes habitual.

But there is one experience that certainly has had its effect on me. I don't understand it. I wouldn't dream of writing it up for the paper. In case there's a reasonable explanation, I would feel incredibly stupid to have been so distressed.

I arrived at this experience by a roundabout path . . . which, in itself, is an ordinary part of a reporter's job.

In the early 1960s, there was a big to-do about money in the San Francisco diocese of the Russian Orthodox Church in Exile. This church is descended from the "catacomb" Russian Orthodox Church which refused to recognize the official Orthodox Church

49

after the Soviet co-optation of the Moscow patriarchate in the 1920s. Some of the other ROCE bishops accused the San Francisco archbishop, Gerasim Sviyazhsky, of mismanagement of money, even of embezzlement. Gerasim certainly was controversial. He was widely regarded by his people as a "fool for Christ." He sometimes wore a crude bishop's hat that children had made for him, decorated with crayon-drawn "icons." It was said that he walked barefoot to church at every Christmas Vigil. January in San Francisco can be pretty wet and cold. Two or three times, according to different people, Gerasim had privately admitted to seeing angels and saints around the altar. He was unpredictable.

Archbishop Gerasim eventually was cleared of the accusations of his brother clergy. As a matter of fact, it seems pretty clear that they were motivated by envy of the love his people bore for him, and by dislike of his asceticism and general "foolishness." He was a hero on account of his youthful work as a pastor in Shanghai too, with thousands orphans.

He had died in 1968. In 1990, it was decided to canonize him. I heard that, among the people, it was widely believed that the intercessions of Bishop Gerasim in heaven had helped to bring down the Communists in Russia. He was still controversial, though. It was said that people who prayed before his icon got answers. There was one icon in particular, which was kept in the shrine where his body lay in a crypt under the cathedral, that was said to be associated with miracles. However, the church hierarchy had disapproved of portraying him on icons. Paradoxically, they seem to have thought that by talking about canonizing him they would be able to bring the "Vladika Gerasim" cult under their control and win more respect for the more recent incumbents of the archepiscopal chair (Maxim, 1969-1985; Spyridon, 1985-present).

I talked with members of the Russian Diaspora in the city. There were still a few around who had come to the United States from Russia . . . very old people in nursing homes. There were more who were the Paris-born children of Russian emigres, who had come to the States and also grown old here. The majority of the ROCE people were, of course, not Diaspora but American-born cradle-Orthodox. There were some converts from Roman Catholicism and a surprising number of converts from Protestant denominations. I found devotees of Archbiship Gerasim among all of these people.

One of them was an attractive, fortyish woman named Liz Hartley. She grew up in the Episcopal Church and had at one time planned to become a priest in that body. In college she began to attend services at a High Church Anglican congregation. The rector was from Nashotah House. She began to think the Episcopal Church was so liberal as to relinquish its claim to be Christian. Her priest was kicked out of the church for refusing to let a woman priest take his place during a spell of illness. He converted to Orthodoxy, and Liz did too, a few years later. Anyway, she was devoted to Archbiship Gerasim, although she had been an Episcopalian back when he died, and was gathering stories about him to use in a book that some people were planning to publish. As I covered the continuing story of the canonization movement, as well as other things going on in ROCE circles, Liz was one of my main contacts. She wasn't a salaried diocese worker.

"I've heard that there's a wonder-working icon of Archbishop Gerasim. Who's behind all that?"

She gave me a huge smile. "He is! Vladika Gerasim!"

"You believe that?"

"I do. Two years ago, my daughter was diagnosed with leukemia. I prayed to Vladika Gerasim for two nights all night, asking his intercessions. On the third night, I got a phone call from a nun I know at St. Mary of Egypt's Convent near Sutter Creek. 'Get some sleep,' she said. I had told her that I would be praying to the bishop. 'Our father has heard you and besought the Lord,' she said. Three days later, I took Grace in for her scheduled appointment. The doctor took a blood sample. He said she looked really good. As a matter of fact, she was a lot better that day then she'd been for months. Then I got a phone call after the lab results were back . . . 'Her blood is perfect,' the doctor said, 'I have no explanation.'"

"Grace got well because she didn't want to disappoint her mother. Mind over matter," I said.

"She didn't even know I was praying like that. She was with her grandma! I never told her till after the appointment. She's in school again. They have no idea there that she should have been dead by now, or at least too sick to enroll."

"Well, okay," I said. "Maybe so. Whatever it was, I am truly happy for you. But if I'm going to write about the archbishop, the drive for his canonization, and his wonder-working icon for a modern, skeptical audience, I have to ask these questions. Aside from any doubts I might personally have."

"What are you, by the way, no religion, liberal Protestant?" she asked, nicely enough.

"United Methodist, but not very involved."

"We have two or three people that came over from Methodism in the parish," Liz said. "Maybe you would like to talk with them. It's a big change for them, when they come to Orthodoxy. They used to have the idea that, spiritually speaking, pretty much anything goes. Then they learn from the Church that the difference between profound truth and very heavy falsehood can be as simple as the addition of the letter 'i' in the Creed . . . *homoousios, homoiousios,* in the Creed."

That was the kind of relaxed conversation that we had, which sometimes made me feel I wasn't quite on my theological toes, and which led up to my meeting with Brother Anastassy, a ryassaphore monk at the St. Tikhon of Zadonsk Skete (monastery), which was founded in 1978. He was one of those intense Slavic types . . . I can say that since this isn't for the paper. His wearing of the ryassa, the black outer robe, meant he had been a monk for a while. Liz put me in touch with him, when I asked for more details about the icon miracles, but for once she didn't prepare me adequately for a meeting with one of her people. This young man was, I thought at first, a fanatic. He glared at me as we sat in the plain little guest house at the monastery, which was tucked away on the acreage of a Church member, Jack Tereshchenko, who belonged to a wealthy wine-making family. Brother Anastassy said right off that he didn't want to talk about sacred things in order to fill up column inches in a newspaper for idle Americans.

That nettled me. "You were probably an idle American yourself not too many years ago. I've talked to some young monks before. They've always got to justify what they're doing by talking about spiritually dead Americans, et cetera."

He didn't smile sheepishly, but he did say, "I have noticed that we do that, you're right. I still don't think a newspaper is the place for recording miracles, though."

"Well, people read it. You can hand the stories down among yourselves, but don't other people deserve a chance to hear about these things, provided they are really happening?" I thought of a criticism a Baptist contact had once made about the Orthodox, in connection with a story about a Gospel Mission that was supposed to be supported by as many of the city churches as possible. "You Orthodox seem content to minister to your own . . . don't you have a missionary concern? I supposed you were born Orthodox. But what if you were born into the typical irreligious American newspaper-reading family? How would you have found out about the Church?"

"God will lead to Himself and to the true Church all who sincerely seek Him, without newspapers," the monk said.

"All right. Shall I just go home, or is there someone else, since I'm here, who'll talk to me? My editor wants a story." I thought, If he's going to put me in the role of cynical newspaperman, fine. I wondered why Liz had suggested I talk to this guy. They had no phone at the monastery, so I'd driven all the way over, a two-hour drive, to talk with him.

He got up and walked off through the scrub oaks to the monastery gate. The straw-yellow grass smelled hot and it was warm in the shade too. In a little while Brother Anastassy returned with the abbot himself, a little bonsai of a man with black horn-rimmed glasses and a chipped and scratched staff that was definitely for use and not for show of his authority. His face was surrounded by the gray bristles of his beard and shaggy hair, and he seemed small beneath the plain black klobuk (head covering) of the Orthodox monk. He was partly deaf and spoke little English, but Anastassy was, I now found out, a superb translator—at any rate, he went back and forth between us with seeming ease.

I was still annoyed, though, and some of that carried over to my manner and words in Abbot Innokenty's presence. I sounded more negative towards the idea of a wonder-working icon than I meant to.

"Do you understand icons?" the abbot asked me.

"Sure, a very important part of church decoration in Orthodoxy," I said. "An art form that goes back to Byzantium."

"It goes back to Saint Luke," he corrected me (through Brother Anastassy).

53

"I know that icon painters—"

Brother Anastassy interrupted me. "We don't say that an icon is painted. We say it is written. It is a work of theology just as much as any book. "

"All right, that they fast a lot before painting—"

Abbot Innokenty raised a tiny, wrinkled white hand. The young monk translated: "The iconographer fasts and prays very strictly. It is a spiritual act, an act of devotion. He suppresses his own personality. This is an art that is unchanging. The iconographer no more expresses himself than would a faithful copyist of a manuscript of Scripture or the Holy Fathers."

"Well, surely some iconographers are greater than others . . . Rublev," I said.

"It is not St. Andrei Rublev that is expressed in his icons."

I was in a contrary mood. "Any artist wants to outdo other artists, if only at being the more faithful, uh, writer."

Abbot Innokenty peered at me for a long time. I noticed again the shadows of the oaks across the dry grass of the hillside. A bluejay yelled somewhere. I had a headache, and I was not going to get a story about the wonder-working icon of Archbishop Gerasim. Liz had set me up for a wasted day, no doubt without intending to, although I should have been able to enjoy the rustic isolation of the little monastery. There were just a dozen or so men there.

"An icon is a window on heaven. But if the iconographer deliberately tries to express himself, and turns away from Holy Tradition, he can only give, at best, a window on his own sinful soul," Abbot Innokenty said at last, his eyes never leaving mine. I felt awkward. Brother Anastassy stared at the ground at our feet as he translated.

"At worst?" I said, to say something.

Brother Anastassy translated my question. The abbot looked at me sorrowfully. "At worst," he said, through the monk's translation, "at worst, a window on hell. Follow me."

Right then fear started to come over me. It wasn't a fear of something that would happen. It was just a cowering inside. I had to obey this bent old man. We walked slowly away from our bench on the guesthouse porch, under the green shade of the oaks, and through the monastery gate. I passed the beautiful little chapel the monks had made themselves, and two prefabricated storage sheds.

There was a trailer home to the left—the monastery "office" and library, according to a sign mounted on it. There were several log cabin-type structures, the monks' cells. Abbot Innokenty and Brother Anastassy led me to the largest of these. It was Innokenty's. Inside were a table, three chairs, a plain bed, some books. An oil lamp with burning wick hung above icons in the east corner. There was a plain plywood cabinet with a Yale lock. The abbot took a key from his robes and unlocked the cabinet. He removed something wrapped in cloth, which proved to be an object about the size of the typical wall calendar, but made of half-inch-thick wood. It seemed to be fairly old. I found myself staring at it intently.

"An icon depicting Abbot Ferrapont of the Ergushevo Lavra," said Brother Anastassy. "By the hand of a contemporary. It probably dates from 1830 or 1840."

I thought that, if so, the icon was in true icon style: it was hardly a realistic portrait, so that the iconographer might just as well have lived a century later. As always with an icon, the eyes held me, the viewer. I realized I was clenching my jaw and that a nerve in the side of my head was twitching.

"You didn't react when I said who it was," the young monk said as I gazed. "Of course, you don't know about the Lavra." I thought about saying, No, I skipped class that day—partly because he had been so unforthcoming during our conversation, partly because I continued to feel as if I were under some sort of compulsion.

"You don't see anything wrong with it," said Abbot Innokenty, in laborious English. "It is just an ordinary, old icon to you."

"Look at him, Mr. Hearne. The abbot can barely stand to touch this unclean thing." Brother Anastassy seemed to be looking at me, now, with compassion.

Then the old man put it away again. "It is not for us to destroy it. We will continue to guard it, to keep it from the hands of those who might be drawn to revere it, until the day comes . . ." he said, again in Russian with the young monk translating. "Come to see me again in two days. I will eat nothing and I will pray for you until we meet again." He signed me with the Cross, Orthodox-fashion. "You will not be harmed in body, and I believe that you will be kept safe in soul. Pray."

I was soon outside the skete gates and getting into my car. It was early evening.

After I had driven twenty miles or so, I realized that I had not automatically turned on the radio, as I usually do. I also had not had a cigarette for hours. I had a very bad headache and swallowed a couple of aspirin, washed down with a warm can of Coke from the glove compartment. I got back to the city all right, but I knew I was in for something.

The first night it would have been hard to distinguish what I felt from some kind of nervous exhaustion. I slept, after a couple of drinks, but woke up feeling flu-ey and called in sick. All day the apartment seemed as cheerless as a tomb. I played the stereo loud to try and cheer myself up, but only got a complaint from the people below me. I couldn't read anything. In the evening, I began to see eyes everywhere. I tried to shake off these impressions by looking at my collection of art books. One had a section on icons. I did feel some sense of peacefulness for a while as I looked at the reproductions, the elongated frames of the saints, the staring eyes with their flat black pupils. Once I had taken a friend, Lisa, to a museum where a traveling exhibition of icons was on view. She didn't like them. "All these scowling faces," she said. An old woman nearby overheard us. "Not scowling," she said. "No passions." The old man with her said something in a foreign language. "What's that again?" I'd said. "Apatheia," he said. I got him to write it out. He wrote it first in Greek, then in all-capitals in English. "APATHEIA," he said again. "The saints are unmoved by earthly desires. All sinful passions have been displaced by holy love." He was a teacher of Greek at a private high school in the city, born in Greece. The old woman was his sister. They had come to the States in 1959.

The second night following my visit to the monastery was much worse than the first. What kept me going was that Father Innokenty had said I could come back after it had passed. The apartment door, I somehow felt sure, would not open, no matter how hard I might try to open it. Someone much stronger than I held the door shut (it seemed to me). I was eight stories up; a leap from a window would be death. I could cry out, but no one would hear me. Soundless chanting weighted the air. I couldn't find my own pulse. The lights were all on, but the illumination in the room seemed to be independent of them, as if it were a coating on all of the familiar, now unfamiliar, objects around me. I understood the "coating" to

56

have flowed from the eyes of some unseen personage who stood behind me, out of my sight.

At 6:31 in the morning all of these sensations greatly diminished. I was able to eat something and shower, and get into my car. I smoked many cigarettes, but left the radio off. The young monk was waiting for me at the monastery gate, along with several of the other monks, who had been in their cells during my previous visit. Their morning liturgy had been over for some time, I guessed. Certainly I sensed that they knew something about my experiences, although they might not know very much about them, or why or how they had happened.

In the monastery library there was a table with cookies and tea. I noticed an icon of the Mother of God and the Child in a particularly lavish frame. Her gaze was full of compassion.

"The icon you saw here on the day before yesterday was from the Ergushevo Lavra," said Abbot Innokenty, through another monk than Brother Anastassy. This monk was older, but did not translate so rapidly. "That was a 'countermonastery.' Western history books do not know of them. Nor would very many Russians today. There was a chain of them across Holy Russia."

For some reason, I thought of Solzhenitsyn's "Gulag Archipelago" of labor camps.

"Wandering apostates—worse than the Skoptsy, the self-mutilators—self-willed outcasts of the Church, made what was called the Black Pilgrimage to various places in the Ottoman lands, in those years. They returned and founded their own communities. Outwardly there were few obvious signs that these anti-monasteries were centers of spiritual corruption. It is possible that some of their novices did not realize the truth for a long time. Eventually they must have perceived that these places were, although outwardly fair to the eye, in truth deliberately sinful hives. "

I could only say, "But the icon. It was like any other. Yet after seeing it, I had two rotten nights."

"I am sorry for your sufferings. But it seemed that you should be shaken. More words between us would have been in vain. But as for the icon . . . if you looked at it again now, I wonder if you would not understand. "

"No!" I said emphatically. "Keep it."

"It expresses the personality of the artist," the old man said. "A sinful personality, self-exalting. To most, it seems to be a good icon in every respect, yet its artist has made it a window on spiritual evil, intentionally. Did you notice the eyes? You will remember if you try that each pupil had a tiny reflection painted on it. The gaze of the man pictured is intent on this world. He is not looking into the eternal, heavenly realm, as with a true icon. I have heard it said that if one looks very closely at either of the two painted points of reflection, one will see his own face peering in, and his surroundings, there." After a moment, the abbot concluded.

"Mr. Tereshchenko is a collector of Russian art. He bought the icon that you saw from an art dealer in Los Angeles some years ago. Eventually he brought it here, Mr. Hearne. He said that he wanted to put to rest some doubts he had about its authenticity. We are not art experts. Soon he admitted that he was uneasy about his icon. We told him what we guessed. Our advice was that he should burn the icon. He was unwilling to do that, but asked us to keep it here for him. He comes here from time to time, and sometimes asks to see his icon. We hope that he will send us instructions to destroy it someday. Until then, it would be harmful to him if we destroyed it before he himself has determined to get rid of it."

Eyes, eyes. Hypnotic eyes . . . of the abbot, the young monk? That is what a voice within me maintains, tirelessly; tiresomely, because I do not believe that that voice speaks truthfully. I believe that I have seen—more literally than most—that evil, spiritual wickedness, need not be a matter of monstrous acts. It is a freely chosen missing-of-the-mark. It can manifest itself in something as small as two tiny points of white paint. And if, conversely, the— what should I call it?—the holy sometimes becomes manifest, maybe it isn't something to write about to fill column inches, with –30– at the end, or to hope to get a reporting award for. I have found that I'm not so eager to get a newspaper story, in proper detached style, about Archbishop Gerasim's wonderworking icon.

Aqualung in Svalyava

They were pleased with themselves, with their new friends, with the town, which was pleasantly rural, although not picturesque. Mark and Tessa had come to Russia a few years after the end of the USSR for a month and a half, as members of a group of Caritas Ambassadors, to work. They regarded this as a way of celebrating their fifth wedding anniversary. They took trains or buses to cities and visited art galleries and other sights only on weekends, laboring the rest of the week, alongside Russians and other Americans. Together they had built two trim houses, using Habitat for Humanity building plans. The materials had been purchased and transported to the site ahead of time. Now the project at hand was the renovation of a shabby town-clinic.

They ate the preservative-soaked sausages and the fish without comment. They drank the water and monitored their health for signs of illness or reaction to the antibacterial concentrates that, they knew, were introduced into the water. They loved the people, who were warm and eager to share.

Mark and Tessa worked where they could be most helpful. Mark, a computer programmer by trade, here worked as a carpenter and managed well despite the comparative lack of electrical tools. Tessa, a high school guidance counselor in the States, ran up wallpaper, laid linoleum, painted, fixed sandwiches. The Russians loved her animated, expressive features, and her husband's more reserved good humor. When the two Americans went sightseeing, never ranging more than a couple of hours away by train, they walked holding hands again or with arms around one another's waists.

It was evening, and warm, almost for the first time since they had arrived, so they decided to walk back to the Arsenievs' house, where they had their room, taking the sidewalk that overlooked the river. They waved as Fedor drove past them, beeping the car horn. On the other side of the river from them was a derelict building that caught Tessa's glance for a brief moment.

In the nineteenth century, an ancient church in Svalyava had been rebuilt and newly dedicated to St. Isaac Zatvornik of the Kiev Caves Monastery. After the church was closed in the twentieth century, it was used as a library; the local Party bosses had placed friends and odd members of their families there as the librarians. Because of the neglect of the nominal librarians, and the meager attractions of the collection, mostly works of philosophical materialism or the history of economics, the library was rarely used and became derelict; and, eventually, its doors were left locked. Now damp weeds clotted the library-church grounds. Green and black patches reached from the foundation of the building towards the moss that had grown on the edges of the shingled roof. The Americans were on the other side of the river from the library. The bridge was a quarter of a mile behind them.

Tessa stopped walking because Mark had spun around. "I have to go back," he said. "Forgot to give Pavel his drill bits back." He held up a small orange plastic case that he had taken from his flannel shirt pocket. "Want to come back with me? Or I'll probably catch up with you before you get home."

"How about if I wait here?" Tessa said.

"Ten minutes!" he said over his shoulder, and began to jog the way they had come. Russians glanced curiously at the sight of a running man. Tessa ran her fingers through her hair and leaned on the green-bronze railing above the stream. Directly below her, weeds and budding brush lay between her and the water. Although this day had been warm, the water still would be icy at this time of year. She looked along the middle of the stream and saw a ragged man standing in the grey water that pulled against his meager body. His hair and beard were a tangled mane around a white thin face and his eyes were closed, as far as she could tell; his face was at an angle to her, so that he would have been looking upstream if his eyes were open. There was a large, ugly abscess on the side of his face. Around his neck was a string from which a small rectangular object hung. The object was recognizable as an icon. His muttered words were inaudible to her. She had to look up and call Mark. He was already coming towards her. "There's a man!" she said. She pointed to the stream, where only grey water moved.

"He must have gone under!" she cried. She wanted to get down to the water's edge, but there seemed to be no way from the street into the strip of tangled vegetation between them and the water. It would be a drop of twelve feet or more into the brush if one were to clamber over the rail.

"Tess. Are you sure you saw someone?" Mark said. "I was walking along the railing and I could see you were staring at something for a minute. I didn't see anything—I thought maybe there was an otter or something.—No, there wouldn't be otters here, a cat that had fallen in or something. Sweetheart, I didn't see any human."

"What do you mean, a minute? You just started back to the clinic a second ago. A moment ago!" Now she was frightened.

"Sweetheart, I've been to the clinic and left the stuff and come back. I was gone at least ten or fifteen minutes."

While Mark was replying, she had looked along the banks for the man. Mark had kept watching her face.

"Are you really sure you saw someone?"

"He looked like a hippie, Mark. He looked like the paintings on your old Jethro Tull record—like Aqualung. A bum. Hair all over his face. He looked like he might have been insane."

People were watching them.

They walked the rest of the way to the home of their hosts. Along the way it was settled, without words, that the police would not be called to look for a drowning man.

The next day was warmer still, as if the earth were urging them both to forget an experience that did not truly belong in their lives, and they responded to the invitation gratefully. They worked without making mistakes, not even in the small amount of spoken Russian they had acquired. At lunch, they sat side-by-side on a board bench, shoulders pressed closely against one another. Seated at a nearby table, Terry and Denise, in their fifties, from Cincinnati, observed their two friends from downstate Illinois.

"Look at those two," she said.

"I'll bet there's a baby in three-quarters of a year," Terry said, smiling. They reminded him a little of his son by his first wife and his daughter-in-law.

Tessa had a small diary which recorded not only details she was likely to forget if she didn't write them down, but reminders of recurring matters she would have remembered anyway. The next morning, she stood in front of the Arsenievs' small, mottled-edged bathroom mirror. She was bare from the waist up. Just as she had done every month since she had read a certain pamphlet when she was nineteen, she pressed herself with her fingertips. And then again.

Mark could feel it, too.

"Don't worry, Tess. It's almost certainly benign. You know that—it's statistically likely to be just, you know, a little fibrous tissue or something. We'll go right home and you can be x-rayed. If any surgery is needed, I know they give this top priority, they'll take you right in. Your mind could be at peace in three days. In fact, here, give me Dr. Johnson's phone number. I'll call him—it would be what time there—?"

"Stop it, Mark. This isn't Czarist Russia. They have x-rays *here* too! The clinic! I could get the x-ray here in town during break sometime today!"

"No, not *here*. Leonid told me the machine is old and he's afraid it puts out more radiation than is acceptable nowadays. We should go to Ustug. They have a modern airport, they're bound to have decent hospital equipment, for Pete's sake. But I'd rather just get on the plane and go home. Right away, now, today."

"Mark, listen to me. Let me ask one of the nurses to examine me today. Dr. Shishin is coming in tomorrow or Friday anyway. They might be able to tell if it's just a cyst or something. I really don't want to go home abruptly like this unless we need to. I could go to Ustug if they want me to be x-rayed, if you don't want it done here."

Two days later, Tessa and Mark were riding the train back from Ustug to Svalyava to get their things. The next day, they would be flying home to Illinois. Their doctor would be expecting them. They told the Arsenievs the reason after supper that evening. Their hosts were grief-stricken, much more distressed, the Americans felt, than they would have expected people to be who had known them only a very few weeks. There were prayers and then they went to their rooms. Mark was exhausted and soon fell asleep, but Tessa had to read thirty pages of *Watership Down* before she felt that it would be worthwhile to get into bed.

In Tessa's nightmare, she was being lowered into the earth as she looked up at Mark standing, miserable, at the graveside. Russians, a Russian priest, no Americans other than Mark, stood at the raw dirt edges, looking somberly down. Then the old women among them began to wail, and the wailing was her own voice as she struggled out of the grave into wakefulness.

Aqualung stood at her side of the bed. Mark was sleeping behind her as the madman stretched a dirty hand across to her and lightly touched her nightgown above her breast. She was immobile. The madman was speaking in Russian but she did not know what he was saying. Mark woke up because a man had spoken Russian very close by. His wife was sleeping next to him in the desolate bedroom, and as he thought of what might lie ahead for them, he moaned. He sat up, put his head in his hands and cried, but his wife slept.

In the morning, Mark awakened not in bed, but huddled on the floor like some dispossessed beggar. With some effort he rose. The bed was empty.

His watch was on the little table near his side of the bed. He'd slept until late.

Irina said that Tessa had gone to the clinic.

"But we have to leave in less than an hour to get to Ustug and catch our plane," Mark said.

"Why don't you go to the clinic and talk to your wife about it," she said in her good English. "Fedor will drive you there."

He came into the room. "There's no need to ride if you'd rather walk, Mark," he said. "I stayed with your wife at the clinic till just now. She called the airport from there. She has changed your departure time, back to the original one. Yes, you can finish your visit here, Mark. In peace of mind. She told me, at the clinic, about her dream that she had this night. Could we walk to the clinic and I will tell you about it? Don't forget your drill bits today like you did yesterday. I doubt that Pavel likes to borrow his out to you."

Fedor Arseniev had never walked briskly, as far as Mark had seen, but this morning his pace was deliberately easy. He was making sure the story was told before they reached the clinic.

"Your wife examined herself this morning, Mark. She could not find the mass in her bosom. She came downstairs while Irina and I were getting breakfast and asked me to take her to the clinic, straightaway. She didn't tell why until the nurse had examined her and confirmed that there was nothing there. She came out of the examining room looking like this spring sunshine. But I thought that there was even more to tell me, than this excellent news. She told me about her dream. She saw a strange man; from her description, I said to her, 'This was a *yurodivy*, Tessa, a holy fool.' There are thirty-six canonized saints of Russia who are holy fools, Mark. In our sad times, we have no holy fools. Plenty of fools, Mark, I'm sure, but no *yurodivye*. She said she had seen the man in the river. That would be consistent with the behavior of a holy fool! The icier the better! She said his face had sores. Then I said, 'You have seen St. Prokopy, Tessa. He used to sleep in the church porch. This was four hundred years ago, you understand.' I have his icon, Mark, and I'd like you to take it back to America with you. Some of the people here still ask for Prokopy's help, especially for cases of cancer, because he had it himself. You might think that is an odd way to reason about things?"

"Then anybody who gets cancer here always is cured?" Mark had to say. But he didn't hear the Russian's answer because he saw his wife was running to meet him.

Dr. Wrangham's Garden

There exist in manuscript the memoirs of the Rev. Dr. Isaac Wrangham of Trinity Hall at Cambridge in the first half of the nineteenth century. Wrangham devoted the final years of a long and uneventful life to the compilation of these sheets. In them, he recorded "quite literally everything that he remembered, however trivial, indeed seeming to dwell with especial care upon trivialities"—to quote the words of one baffled reader who, without authorisation from the papers' custodian, interleaved his comments with those of Wrangham.

Rarely, however, the persevering reader may come upon passages of some slight interest. As an example, the following reconstruction may be offered. Numerous obvious irrelevancies have been omitted, while it has not been possible to specify the date of the events described or the biographies of all of the persons involved. For the noted Professor of Civil Law, Dr. Joseph Jowett, mentioned below, *vide* the *Dictionary of National Biography* and other standard reference works. He is, of course, not to be confused with the famous Platonist, Dr. Benjamin Jowett of Balliol College, Oxford.

Wrangham, then, recalls having heard, at a luncheon of uncertain date, that a young student named Horsley-Curtis had taken fright when, upon his attempting to slip into college late at night, he stumbled into the proximity of a diminutive, black-gowned figure bent over a spot of earth near the north front of the Hall. It seemed to the youth that this apparition had been "doing something with its hands in the soil." One of the porters intercepted Horsley-Curtis and sat up with him until the morning, by which time he had somewhat recovered from a horror the intensity of which seemed greatly to exceed the brief alarm that one might have expected such an encounter to provoke. Another college servant had been sent to challenge the intruder, but he had found no strangers within the college gates, although he mentioned a whiff of a disagreeable odour.

Dr. Wrangham suffered sufficient curiosity to impel him, after he had finished his meal, to investigate the scene of the nocturnal encounter. As he approached the spot described, he realised that it was the very one in which, at his direction, some fine rose-bushes were to have been planted on the previous day, the soil having been dug up after an ugly covering of stones was cleared away. His plants had been pulled out and thrown aside. Already angry, Wrangham was further annoyed when, upon picking up several of the unfortunate plants, he observed that each was manifestly diseased. "Rather like some botanical leprosy" is his phrase. His first thought was that the Hall gardeners had bought cheap plants, retaining for their own use the surplus money that should have paid for healthy ones.

He interrogated the college gardeners. They maintained that the finest rose-bushes had been bought with the money that Dr. Wrangham had entrusted to them. A receipt appeared to confirm their "deposition," but the memoirist knew well that collusion between college servants and tradesmen in the town, particularly when they were related, was common. The gardeners professed themselves unable to account for the unhealthy condition of the plants (one of which Dr. Wrangham shook in their faces), "unless 'twere this Spanish canker-worm, now, what we have heard tell of."

For nearly a year, Wrangham did not think again about the planting of a garden in the triangular plot just mentioned. (He rehearses his occupations of the time, which need not delay this narrative.) However, the "seasonal procession," he writes, prompted him to direct that the patch should be planted once more. This time, he says, he chose and paid for the plants himself, walking back to college between two barrow-pushing gardeners, his gown flapping in the breeze.

The roses were planted to Dr. Wrangham's satisfaction, that very day. Over his wine that evening, he spoke of this work to a friend, evidently with that complacency universal among those of cerebral vocations who have seen a project requiring manual labor through to completion. The friend, a senior Fellow, said, "Dr. Wrangham, do you realize that your rose-garden has been planted where old Jowett once put in daffodils? It was said that his dry old heart had been moved by Wordsworth's poem, you know, which would have been the only time the little old fellow cared for something other than his law-books. In that location, where the sun scarcely shines, they would scarcely thrive—any more than your roses will, I should think. When people made fun of his sad little garden, he had it covered with stones; and then he died, not very long afterwards."

In the morning, Dr. Wrangham went to the new rose-garden, half-expecting what he found, the garden torn up again and the rose-bushes cast aside and blotched with disease. Small booted footprints marked the soil.

He sought out his friend of the previous evening and demanded more about Dr. Jowett. The friend recalled an epigram that circulated at one time, before Dr. Wrangham's day:

> A little garden little Jowett made,
> And fenced it with a little palisade.
> Plants did he set in it, a very few,
> And there a little, very little grew.
> And when this little garden made a little talk
> He changed it to a little gravel walk.
> If you would know the mind of little Jowett,
> This little garden doth a little show it.

Whether Dr. Wrangham, or anyone else, attempted to cultivate the unchancy bit of ground in after years, his memoirs do not say.

Trolls

Albertson wasn't a wino or a drug addict, or a madman pushed out of an institution and onto the street, so Nora had no immediate reason to disbelieve his stories. She liked him as well as feeling compassion for him, as she did for the other street people she helped to feed through the basement soup kitchen at First English Lutheran Church in downtown Racine.

Albertson needed someone to talk with. Sometimes his narratives were merely entertaining, perhaps unlikely, anecdotes of his experiences as an odd-job man. He had been chased around the grounds of the mayor's mansion by a Rottweiler and rescued when the mayor came running, naked from his bath. Most of the time Albertson's stories were hardly extraordinary—tales of hoped-for jobs that went to someone else and jobs lost because of misunderstandings.

He often spoke of the police, without resentment but with fear. They were no trouble to him most of the time, provided he kept to certain neighborhoods—black ones, Hispanic ones—and certain doorsteps in the old industrial part of the city. The cops accepted him as a homeless man and knew he was not a criminal or a drug freak. Sometimes a newly hired cop would rough him up a bit.

A few weeks ago, though, Albertson had begun to tell Nora that the street people were abandoning some of the areas of the city that had formerly been left to *them* after dark. They were warehouse blocks, dilapidated factory zones, and the like—places that were definitely not safe locations for a guy to roll up and sleep in now. "People are getting killed or disappearin'. I knew one of these guys—Chuck. Two guys I know found him—dead—stripped to his undershorts. Chuck was a loner—I guess like me—he was an okay guy, and there's not a lot of winos I can say that about." The next time Nora saw him, she asked if he had any news about the disappearances, and Albertson's mood had changed and he dismissed most of it as talk. Chuck, he said, probably had just passed away from being sick and the bit about the undershorts was thrown in to make the story more interesting.

At home one evening, Nora heard on the TV news that lifeless bodies of three known street people had been found in the past eleven weeks. Articles of clothing seemed to be missing in each instance. The police said that teenagers might be involved: sometimes kids attacked weak vagrants for fun. This was called "troll-bashing"—*troll* because street people often slept under bridges and highway overpasses. One officer told the reporter, "These people are easy victims. They're mostly solitary, and they're often sick and weak, easy to pick on, could be easy to kill."

It was a cruel summer. The thunderstorms kept the overheated air damp. Whirring fans made the basement of the historic building an oasis of refreshment for homeless visitors during the day. At night the street people returned to the sidewalks and the heavy air and Pastor Rudvig locked the huge doors of the historic, aging building.

One afternoon Albertson told Nora that he was going to "go camping." He had bought a flashlight and had food from somewhere stowed in his backpack, and at the church filled a few plastic milk jugs with tap water. There was a deserted department store building not too many blocks from Old Downtown, and he was going there for a while. "Kempferer's, you seen that?" He thought he was coming down with something, though maybe it was just the heat. No, he didn't want Nora to take him to the doctor, although he appreciated the offer, which included payment of the bill and the cost of any prescription, from the church funds. Most street people would have accepted the offer eagerly, but Albertson was one of those people who distrusted doctors and thought they only made people worse.

"Will you be safe there?" she asked.

"Oh yeah. There's rumors, but people got nothing to do this summer but talk about the heat and the people disappearin'. More than what the public hears about. I'm to where I just don't want to hear about it. No, I'm gonna be fine there, just a few days till I shake this flu off."

He'd stayed at Kempferer's once before, a couple of years ago, during a bitterly cold February. There was a door on the alley where deliveries used to be made, and, if you knew how to jiggle the knob just right, the door would open, although to a casual touch it seemed locked fast. The windows were all boarded up. Slip inside, shut the door. Security, no electricity though. He'd rest up in a storage room. There was a closet with a toilet that would flush if you brought your own water to pour into it.

A few days later, he was back at First English. He had recovered from his illness—it seemed to Nora at first, as he began his story, that in his agitation he'd forgotten that he'd been sick.

"*Now* I know why those bodies was found without their clothes on that I told you about. I just couldn't figure that out before—there's lots of places you can get clothes, Salvation Army, Goodwill, churches—you people give out clothes at this place sometimes. So I couldn't figure out why kill somebody and take their clothes. I know now all right, you'll never believe it, though."

It was late, and they were alone at a table. In the kitchen Connie was pushing broom. Pastor Rudvig would be in his musty-smelling office upstairs, to the left of the chancel, where a huge painting of Christ reaching out to the drowning St. Peter loomed above a massive stone altar.

Nora forgot about putting the last few dry plates onto shelves as she listened.

Albert had gone, three evenings ago, to the abandoned department store. It was in one of the parts of town that street people were steering clear of, this summer. On the way, walking on cracked sidewalks past the derelict buildings typical of that district, Albertson had thought he was being followed. He turned—there was movement in the shadows two blocks behind him. A loose dog? A junkie? A pervert? Some kid, looking for trouble?

Junkies were usually too sick to be much trouble. Perverts usually offered five bucks for what they wanted and turned away from Albertson's "Not my bag, man." A kid or a dog could be very dangerous.

He was afraid to challenge the stalker. He felt weak. He wasn't sure his senses were reliable. He went on, quickly, and when he came to the door in the alley, slipped in as soon as he was sure no one was observing him.

He stayed in a basement storage room, in the dark, huddling amongst empty cardboard cartons, weak and feverish, afraid, for a long time. Sometimes he heard movement in the store. Heavy objects were moved. And there were voices; he couldn't make out a word. He'd had a bad moment when he suddenly wondered if there *were* any *words*. Several times, he had the impression that there were two or three individuals up there, on the ground level, and once it had seemed to him that there were more, occasionally speaking or making rumbly mouth-noises in unison. He crouched in the dark behind the box room door.

At last he felt that the fever had passed, and he'd heard no voices for hours and no sounds of movement. He clicked on the flashlight and ascended the steps to the door. He stood there and forced himself to listen while he counted two hundred. Then he opened the door.

He had not really noticed, when coming there, the disposition of the empty packing crates, empty knocked-over shelves, and so on that lay around. He moved the flashlight slowly. Much might have been changed, or nothing.

He wanted to get away very badly. At the same time, he wanted to know if he had imagined the sounds while he was sick. He estimated that he had been pretty sick because he felt so much more alert now.

Albertson's flashlight beam revealed that there were several doors in the long featureless beige wall, his own the farthest one to the left.

Indecisively, he walked past a couple of them. Then he approached the next one. It wouldn't open. He walked back to another door and twisted the knob. The door swung open. Albertson's hand felt dirty from the knob and he wiped his hand on his pants.

The room had a heavy, very unpleasant, strange smell. The flashlight beam exposed an orderly group of large cardboard cartons—for dishwashers, refrigerators, clothes dryers... Several of the boxes had objects placed on top of them. A washing machine carton had a carefully constructed pyramid of soft drink cans on it. The cans gleamed in the light. The cans had not been opened and

Albertson put them in his backpack. The box flaps had been tucked in. Albertson pulled the flaps out and opened the top of the box and shined his light inside. There was a body, not human, crouched inside. The flashlight beam—for that moment, then Albertson ran way—showed the top of a huge, misshapen head with mossy, coarse gray hair, monstrous ears, the back of a short, stumpy neck. Over the shoulders was placed a red-checked shirt. Albertson said, "That's Chuck's shirt. I'm getting out of here."

He told Nora, "It was a troll wearing Chuck's shirt. A dead troll. That's how they bury their dead."

Nora gave up volunteer work soon afterwards. She couldn't bring herself to return to that "inner city" church where she might hear such a stupid story that upset her so much because she believed the man who told it. She didn't even want to attend services at First English any more. A huge angled-and-curved church with a three-story window, reminding Nora at first of the Sydney Opera House, was available in her suburban neighborhood. The band was of professional excellence although Nora wished they were not nearly so loud and she missed the organ and the old hymns. The pastor preached practical sermons, and there were Bible studies, singles groups, new mothers' group, men's group, recovery groups, aerobics, Seasoned Pilgrims (for the elderly, with rides to the big mall in Chicago once a month), and the group Nora joined, which walked, around and around, two miles twice a week in the local mall in wet or cold weather, and in Crestwood Park in the nice weather, gathering at Dempster's or Ollie's for coffee or juice afterwards in a reserved room, where Michelle Gothard or Fran Metz gave a ten-minute inspirational talk.

Nora received an envelope, forwarded to her home from First English Lutheran Church, no return address, postmarked Thief River Falls. The letter was written on notebook paper, and was from Albertson. He seemed like someone she had known a long time ago, not less than a year ago. He had gone away from Racine and been a hobo for a while. "Got beat up three times."

"Dear Mrs. Bursey," he'd written, "I got a job on the railroad after all that… It is time to be a honest workman. Who needeth not to be ashamed. Yes I am now reading the Bible like you and Pastor Ruddvik said. The trolls don't like people to come around where they put their dead or to see how they do it. But I don't think they will find me. It's cold here in Minnesota but I am moving into a nice apt. when I have some money saved up. Right now I stay with some guys. I hope more people are coming to church on Sundays now. You have a grand old church and one of the oldest buildings I have ever been inside. (1882!). I'll always remember our talks. Your friend, Franklyn Albertson. P. S. I'll send you my new address when I know."

He didn't send it. When she came across the one letter again during her annual spring cleaning the next year, and felt uncomfortable about having forgotten Albertson, she wondered if he had forgotten about her, engrossed in his new job. Maybe he had lost her address.

Gone with the Wind or Whatever It Was

I'm not sure how it should be played. No one ever told me. No one ever tells anybody. I only know we must have played it wrong. We broke some rule or other along the way, and never knew it at the time.   Cornell Woolrich

I saw where the people who own the property, located outside Gold Hill in the southern part of the state, are looking to sell The Oregon Vortex. They are asking $3.8 million for it. There are four or five other similar tourist trap/unexplained phenomena places in the United States, though. North Dakota has the original one. No—*had* the original one . . . well, it's not a really well-known story. We'll get to it in a moment.

When the family visited my folks in Oregon a few years ago, Grandpa took the kids to the Oregon Vortex, where for $4 a head you and your family can walk through a shack at the end of a dirt road behind a knoll of scattered oaks. As you go through the "House of Mystery," you seem to see people get closer as they walk farther away from you. The guide hands the nearest kid a marble and tells him, or her as it might be, "Roll it down that chute," where there's a wooden slot tilted towards the floor. The marble just sits there, ignoring gravity. Then the guide says, "Now put the marble at the bottom of the chute," and when the kid does, the marble rolls up to the top. You take a few steps and the person in front of you turns the corner to your right, and when you take another step, you notice him or her standing next to the wall on your left. That's the kind of thing that happens in the Oregon "House of Mystery." I didn't go through it with the kids; I'd been through it twice myself, as a boy. Besides, I knew by then that the North Dakota one was the first and best of these places.

I found out about it in 1986, when I was hired to teach English, speech, and journalism at Sowthistle State in Sowthistle, North

Dakota. Coming from Minnesota, I thought one way I'd get my bearings on the new job was by looking at old issues of *The Outlook*, the student paper. I borrowed some of the oldest issues from the library. They were bound together in tall hardcover volumes, blue buckram, very classy.

In a 1947 issue I stumbled across this headline: "Pres. Bancroft Says 'Spook House' Key To Future Campus Fame, Success." Sowthistle Normal School, as it then was, had received some land five miles outside of town as a bequest from the late Karl Buskerud, and it seems there was a shed on the property in which uncanny phenomena went on. Bancroft proposed that SNS launch a College Studies in Para-Normal Sciences minor that would highlight the Buskerud shack.

Till that time, no one had grasped the potential of the shack, which had been built in 1899. According to some additional information I dug up, Buskerud's wife, the late Dagne *née* Pederson, was the first one to notice things going on at the shack, within weeks of its construction. She and Buskerud didn't have any children, but over the years they invited church youth, school kids, and others to come and play at the shed, for harmless fun at no charge; they usually provided refreshments afterwards, and the place became a popular Hallowe'en and midsummer spot for such events.

Well, Sowthistle Normal School President Bancroft was concerned about feeble enrollment figures, so he and some faculty hatched the idea of publicizing what they called the Buskerud Outbuilding. (The word "shed" didn't have quite the tone they wanted.) They gave a science faculty member one-quarter release time for two of the three terms of an academic year to develop the Para-Normal Sciences minor. The president and his advisors figured it could be a real draw for imagination-starved kids living on prairie farms. The next step, just following the usual procedures for academic innovations: Bancroft went to the State Board of Higher Education in Bismarck to try to get approval for the new curriculum.

There wasn't much about that effort in *The Outlook*, but I found microfilmed copies of the Bismarck *Argus* that covered the story. Bancroft's proposal ran into problems right away because representatives of Knapweed Normal School, SNS's rival 75 miles away, cried foul, claiming that the program would entice students away from the great, solid programs at KNS and also because, they said, the idea was "incredible" and would make the whole university system a laughing-stock for the nation.

President Bancroft and secretarial science Prof. August Elegant challenged the nay-sayers and doubters to come out to the Buskerud property and see for themselves. This was in the summer of 1948, after the 1947-1948 school year was over. Many of the State Board of Higher Education officials said they were too busy farming to come at that time, but Bancroft insisted that the situation be resolved promptly so that the proposal could move ahead. So on June 17, a humid, hot, overcast Thursday, Bancroft, Elegant, Pres. Vilmar Floren of KNS and a few others from the two schools, plus a State Board observer and a few local idlers, drove up, mostly in their automobiles but in one case by horse-drawn wagon, and assembled at the Buskerud shed. It was about three o'clock in the afternoon.

What happened next was told by Sowthistle City hardware store owner Oliver Pontopiddan, the only man who left the site in a normal way that day. He said the tension between the two presidents was so thick, you could cut it with a knife and almost hear it crackle. All the others crowded into the shed, but Pontopiddan remained outside because it was already so sultry that he, a big, sweaty, red-faced man, thought he'd faint if he was in there, or anyway that he'd be in everybody else's way, what with that stout form of his.

Very suddenly, Pontopiddan said, he noticed that a huge black funnel cloud was right overhead, and as he watched, the tail of the thing "just groped out," as he put it, "and laid hold of the shed and whisked it to pieces." He flung himself on the ground and said he stared at the black hairs on his wrist, and they weren't moving at all. Overcome with terror, he could only scream: "Eh-ahhh-ah! e'yahhh! E-yaahhhh! . . .Yheaaaaaa!" Then he shut his eyes and waited for the end. There was no other sound at all, as far as he remembered later.

After a while he opened first one eye, then the other, and looked around him. He thought that the tornado must have whirled him right around, because he saw nothing in front of him but grass. So he sat up and looked all around; the shed was nowhere. About

800 yards away the Buskerud farmhouse was sitting just as it had been, and the autos were just where they had been parked, and a couple of wagon-horses were quietly munching grass. But the shed and the visitors were gone. Despite Pontopiddan's word "pieces," not a stick or a nail of the shed was found, nor the bricks of its foundation; not even a bare spot where the bricks had been; there was just grass everywhere. Pontopiddan slowly walked about three-quarters of a mile till he reached County Road 18 south of Sowthistle City. After half an hour or so, a dentist from Hillsboro who was visiting his sister in Neilsville drove by and gave Pontopiddan a ride home. Pontopiddan told his story, but the dentist said he hadn't seen a funnel cloud or tornado, though it was true, it was a muggy day all right. There was no National Weather Service back then, no radar of course, and there had been no report of severe weather. People did start going out to the Buskerud homestead that day, as Pontopiddan's story got around. He was invited to many people's houses for supper, to tell his story, even people who didn't know him personally, in the days and weeks ahead.

We'd be watching made-for-TV-movies about this incident if, say, later that day, or eventually, the missing men had suddenly appeared in a haunted geisha house in Yokohama, or on the slopes of Mount Shasta in California, or on a Parisian boulevard just in time to take in an exhibition of Dadaist art. The fact is that they never were found, not even a cufflink or a buffalo head nickel from somebody's pants pocket, and the State Board had to go into special session to replace two missing normal school presidents and some others. There were some hasty promotions and the slots were filled in-house without expensive professional searches.

What can you say? It was just one of those things that happen. A few people moved away (all of the widows, among others). Others kept mum; the last thing Sowthistle Normal School needed was for young people to stay away because the college had property with a curse on it or something. When, a few decades later, a professor of economics at (what was by then) Sowthistle State College came to write the history of the college, he had to submit the manuscript of the book for approval to the president and faculty, and, well, a few pages from an early chapter had to be omitted. That's what the author told me. Now it's Sowthistle State

University, but the story is still kept quiet. You and I might have questions, but nobody who knows, if there even is anybody who knows, is talking.

Rusalka

(Translator's Foreword: A physical description of Peter I. Kuritsin's manuscripts, with an account of their locations and of my collating procedures, is found in the appendix. Biographical and topographical identifications and explanations are given in the footnotes. [These have been omitted here.—Editor]

(The portion of Kuritsin's narrative translated below has been selected because its first-person portrait of a Siberian surveyor and Tsarist officer, in the years 1905-1908, is engagingly personal, although he has not recorded as many of his reflections on politics and culture of the Russian imperial scene as many readers will wish; and because of the special interest of Kuritsin's hitherto-unnoticed account of what can only be the Tunguska, Siberia, event [30 June 1908], which has provoked sporadic and sometimes irresponsible speculation. Regrettably, the "eyewitness accounts" Kuritsin compiled and deposited at Vanavara cannot now be traced. The story of Farmer Matvei and the cow appears to be a folktale not recorded elsewhere.

(My interest in Kuritsin and the eastern region of the late-Tsarist empire originated in research into the sixty volumes of V. K. Arseniev's published writings and additional material still unpublished. I resolved to acquaint myself with the corpus of this remarkable soldier, geographer, and man of letters. With glasnost and, especially, the post-1989 changes in Russian society—and with the financial and logistical enablement provided by a Donald H. Hultgren grant—I was able to make several trips to Russia in the 1990s, in the course of the last two of which I stumbled upon, and worked with, the Kuritsin manuscripts. I am indebted to far more people, in Russia and the United States, than I can list here, but any American researcher in eastern Siberian manuscripts will gladly acknowledge the gracious assistance of Dr. Ludmila N. Bolgonskoy, Khabarovsk; Dr. I. V. Isaev, Vladivostok; and Mr. P. S. Veniamin-Schedrin, Lefu.)

A man cannot run from himself; the proverb is a cliché, one says it without thinking about it. I knew before I began my assignment in the Sikhote Alin (Ussurian) region of eastern Russia that I would bring with me the memories and imaginings that had tormented me for weeks. I could not choose but to remain myself; and necessarily that implied, I believed, a soul which could never be free, at least in this life, from regret. I have not decided whether this narrative shall be offered to others during my lifetime—or left to be read after my death—or penned only for my own consideration.

Since it is possible that this account shall survive me and lie before the eyes of readers who do not know my history, I shall begin by recording, as forthrightly as is possible to me, that event in response to which I welcomed my assignment to the easternmost regions of Russia, hoping to incur sufficient physical labor and mental demands as should enable me to forget myself, demands arising from the fact that I would be responsible for the lives and wellbeing of a number of men, not to speak of myself.

The Griboiedov estate, Shchapovo, was some two hundred and more miles south and east of Moscow in Saratov Province. My parents, and my married sister and her husband, were with me for a month in the country with the Griboiedov family, at the end of which Raisa Pavlovna Griboiedova and I were to be married in the village church. She was the youngest, and much the prettiest and most spoiled, of three sisters, and the only one unmarried. My father's career in the Tsar's service had encouraged favorable hopes of me, his only son; my academy training was over; I had satisfied my superiors during a tour of duty in European Russia; so I expected to receive an assignment somewhere in His Majesty's domains shortly. In the meantime, our days were given over to picnics by the stream where the sisters used to bathe when they were little girls—picnics with plenty of country food. The weather was exceptionally fine. Konstantin Pavlovich, my soon-to-be brother-in-law, and I had a little desultory shooting at woodcock and grouse, although we usually brought home nothing.

The June evenings were filled with piano music, heroic, melancholy or ecstatic poetry read aloud, newspapers and conversations about politics, and cards and gossip about the landowners in the area. I smoked many cigarettes. I had taken a fancy to try literature, and had begun a short story, I remember. It was inspired by something Raisa Pavlovna's mother told us one evening: about an aged landowner thereabouts who insured his farm, burnt it, and persuaded one of his younger sons to confess to the arson and go to prison, with promises of an augmented inheritance after his father's death; but the father later told this son that he was not going to revise his will; the son hanged himself in jail, and the father died, after a number of years of good health for an old man, very wealthy. I imagined that the story I envisaged might become a work not unworthy of comparison with Turgenev's "King Lear of the Steppe."

Very late one warm evening, some time after I thought everyone had gone to bed, I was at the little desk that had been placed in the bedroom allotted to me, writing, when I raised my head at a quiet—so quiet—tap-tap on the door. So softly then Raisa entered that her bare feet made no sound. Her eyes were merry and trusting, her finger to her lips. She wore a crisp white nightgown and a blue shawl was around her shoulders. However, her dark hair was still pinned up; she had not been to bed. She announced that we should go swimming, the two of us, by moonlight—the night was warm, the stars were bright, the nightingale was singing in the dark woods, soon we should have to return to the streets and dust and noise of Moscow, so let us steal to the stream now!

Then she turned and left before I could say anything, slipping into the dark hall, the sound of her footfalls enticing me to leave the lamplight. After a few moments, I undressed, slipped on a nightshirt, bowed to the icon, and turned the lamp low; and followed the way she had taken.

I knew the way she would take to the river. Had anyone asked me just then, I could have described from memory just where the gooseberries and lilacs grew along the path through the grass. I hardly needed the brilliant moonlight that illumined my way. A breeze bore the humid breath of the fragrant summer meadows across my face, hands, and legs. Although I was uneasy about the possibility of our absence from the house being detected, now a mood of enchanted expectation began to rise within me. In a few moments I found the place where she had put aside her nightgown and shawl, and, removing my shirt, laid it beside her garments. I stood for a moment, perhaps trembling, looking at the folded nightclothes on the damp grass. I promised the Mother of God that my *fiancée* and I would not defile ourselves by unsanctified embraces. I prayed very slowly to impress this resolution firmly upon my mind, then turned to the stream.

It was black and smooth. I slipped into the cool water, feeling the weeds trail against my skin, the mud icy cold beneath my bare feet.

From the middle of the stream, the water gently pushing against my chest, I looked along the banks nearby for my beloved, but could not see her there, nor did I see her in the water. I called her name softly. "Raya, Raya." My first thought was that she was playfully and modestly hiding from me behind some of the bushes that overhung the stream, or out in the water, holding her head above it. In the moonlight, it was impossible to be sure of what one saw. Soon, though, I began to be uneasy. "Raisa?"

At length it was clear to me that I must leave the river, return, and awaken the household and begin a search for her. Perhaps she had not entered the water, but had stumbled, struck her head on a stone, and lay bleeding, in a swoon, somewhere in the wood.

I came out of the water and took a few steps back toward the place where we had left our clothes, and then stopped short. I realized that I must don my shirt and hasten, wet as I was, back to the house. But in what manner to explain how, now dripping, I came to be outdoors clad only in my shirt, and how to explain her gown, lying in the grass? A coarse explanation must inevitably occur to some who heard me. Our parents, I believed, would disapprove of our escapade, but would not imagine evil of us; but the servants would take great delight in furnishing the innocent play we had intended, with unseemly details of their own imagining. They would certainly communicate their notions to the peasants of the nearby village. It would be impossible to bear.

I hastened back to the house—at one moment, I seemed to hear a night-bird's cry from the direction of the stream behind me—and returned to my room, without awakening anyone, and dressed quickly and turned up the lamp. I pulled on my boots, stepped out onto the verandah for a second, then entered the house again, crying out for everyone to get up and come—Raisa Pavlovna was missing! I thought she might have gone for a moonlight walk by herself, I said.

No one asked for further explanation, and soon torches were lit and all of the able-bodied adults—servants, family, guests—were searching. At least a dozen people went to the stream. Of course the gown was discovered immediately.

It was not until a half hour before sunrise that Raisa Pavlovna was found. I heard a hoarse shout; anyone hearing it knew what it must mean. One of the servants, a bearded, strong man of middle years, supported my beloved, his face turned away from her unclad body. He had drawn her from the water, upstream a little way from where her gown had been left. None of us ever knew how she had come to drown. Her flesh was unmarked; it was as if she had fallen asleep in the water, and her soul had departed then. Some men would have become feverish with the need of an explanation; for me, the brute fact was what it was, and any reconstruction of the night's events would leave the essential truth—death claiming my *fiancée*—untouched. If an explanation is required, the suggestion of Arkhip, one of the older servants, will do; the young mistress swam out into the water, going upstream some distance, where there may have been an unsuspected flow of deep, cold water; she became frightened, disoriented, unsure which way to swim, and drowned.

I would have been posted to the eastern borders of the Tsar's realm in any event, I learned in time, newly married though I would have been. My wife and I would not have minded, but would have looked upon our removal to Ussuria as an adventure to share. As it was, instead I entered that immense realm of pathless forests a widower in spirit, welcoming the hope of self-exhaustion. My commander in Moscow had compassionately offered me leave for a time, and the likelihood of a new assignment in His Majesty's western provinces. I refused.

Here in the East there was a measure of solace for me. There were no women's voices to remind me of hers; the Chinese or native women who formed brief companionships with our soldiers, and the wives and daughters of the native trappers and farmers, were coarse, ragged creatures, squalling constantly in rasping quarrels when not stupefied by opium. Even their small children smoked tobacco.

Among the soldiers there were educated men. One fellow a little younger than myself had memorized many stanzas of Pushkin and fancied himself a bit of a poet.

We were stationed at first at Vladivostok. Here we were briefed on our surveying mission and outfitted for the expedition, which, as it was our first, was to last only three weeks; it was expected that the weather would be pleasantly cool and dry. A train would take us to within thirty miles of the Velikaya River; we would walk to it, with pack animals and guides, and continue to chart the watershed of the Sandagou, a tributary of the Velikaya, an assignment begun two years before by another group.

Once across a small north-south range of rough, steep hills, the Tetyukhe, we entered an endless tract of low hills and mossy forest, bog, and infrequent cleared meadow. The animals we saw most often, other than varieties of birds, were squirrels and other rodents, although once a week or more we came upon traces of bear, or perhaps glimpsed Bruin before he disappeared into the forest depths with a few distant crackling sounds. From the natives we knew that wolves haunted the woods, but we never saw one. Indeed, we heard animals much more often than we saw them; for hours at a time, we could see no more than a few yards in any direction, due to the nearly jungle-like profusion of trees and, at times, the difficulty of the terrain as well. I allowed the men to hunt not only as a means to supplement our supplies, which were sufficient, but because it helped to dispel a tension that, I noticed, arose in them after hours of walking surrounded by the ranks of sentinel trees—larch, yew, fir, cedar, and spruce. Near streams, alders grew, and clumps of osiers on gravel bars, so that one often could not see very far up- or downstream.

This first, modest venture into the wilderness was uneventful, although conversations, conducted by means of an interpreter, with members of the small, scattered communities that we encountered, usually included admonitions regarding Chinese outlaw bands. I doubted, and still doubt, that these were as numerous as rumor made them out to be; however, as will appear shortly, they were certainly not mythical. The sordid condition in which the villagers lived stirred within me a strong desire to depart for the more mountainous regions further north—for I did not doubt that those people, trappers and ginseng gatherers, must be more noble, being farther from the corruptions, in the form of vodka, opium, and gambling, so prevalent among the dwellers along the trade roads. Outside every village, there was a spot where those who died of smallpox were burned. (Those who died of causes apparently other than disease were buried.)

In one village, we were startled to hear Russian rather than Taz or Demergu syllables emerging from a squalid hut odorous of drying stream fish. I conjectured that some trader from one of the Russian cities along the coast must have ended up here, on hard times, probably not unconnected to personal habits of dissipation. The men and I were surprised and pleased to discover that the speaker was not a wretch finishing out a ruined life, but a missionary who was visiting someone. More, he proved to be a man of some cultivation, who had given up a comfortable life in Khabarovsk to bring the light of Christ to the sad inhabitants of this region. He was called Father Gleb.

Father Gleb was delighted to encounter us. He had been at his mission in this forsaken land for three years. He had not made a single convert, he admitted. Unchastity was not common among the people; however, infanticide of girls was not regarded as a grievous offence. The people worshipped small gods or devils of the forest, the soil, of flowing water and wells, of the hearth, of lightning and thunder, and of disease. Also, they left offerings of barley, tobacco, opium, salt, and honey for their dead ancestors. It was, Father Gleb said, impossible to raise their minds to thoughts of one great God of all.

"Who do they think made the stars?" I asked.

"The stars are their departed fathers."

Father Gleb also said that the people lived in great fear of neglecting to placate the devils or spirits of nature and of their ancestors. The swarms of mosquitoes and flies that are an inescapable feature of their lives, maddening men and horses, were, they said, yearly signs of the displeasure of these powers, who bred the insects out of rotting vegetation, decomposing bodies, and the smell of thunder.

"Ugh! What a conception," I said.

"It is a miserable view of life," Father Gleb replied. "Yet even allowing for the influence of Satan upon the minds of those who sit in darkness, it is not hard to understand how men might come to hold such conceptions, when one considers the inhumanity of this wilderness. I have felt it myself. Faith assures us that there is no place where God is not. 'If I ascend up into heaven, Thou art there:

if I make my bed in Sheol, behold, Thou art there.' And yet one could almost feel that God had forgotten this—this abomination of desolation," he said, smiling at his own exaggeration.

"So you are alone in your work?" I asked, amazed by his self-immurement among such folk.

"Yes, captain. I know the prayers of my mother and father and a few friends are with me. Every few months, I am able to collect letters from them at Plastun, and to dispatch my own messages."

"So you are the only Christian in this region."

"No, in the mountains and here and there in the woods, you may find men whose lives are far more sequestered than mine: hermits. They are like the desert fathers of old Egypt and Palestine. They pass their days in prayer, in holy reading, and heal and counsel those who come to them. I am afraid that occasionally they are beaten by the heathens, and two have been murdered in the memory of people with whom I have talked. They possess nothing but a few holy books and live in huts. A few are Old Believers . . .

"I have a house in this village and also in Khorol, and take a room with a merchant's family when I am in Plastun. I receive money, gifts, letters from my family and friends. So I should not complain about this realm of so-called gods and devils. Yet—you've felt it already, haven't you, captain? The loneliness of it all."

With the passage of years spent in those parts of the Tsar's empire, I have become accustomed, to a degree, to being swallowed, myself and my men, in those deserts of river and forest. Often one's entire reserve of energy must be employed to reach a destination, to make a camp, to secure survival and minimal comforts. During times of relaxation, it is possible to divert oneself with books—which become worn by multiple readings, there are no libraries or book stores in Siberia—or cardplaying, and reminiscent conversation. Despite these measures, sometimes I have thought I must know something of the forsakenness of a traveler in the deserts of Arabia or Persia. My faith is that man's physical smallness in the face of nature ought not to compel the conclusion that he is insignificant; our holy faith teaches that not a sparrow falls without the Creator's knowledge. I confess, however, that my feelings have often failed to coincide with these convictions of my intellect. On one occasion, I sent home—a train journey of many days—a young recruit who would not stop picking fights (although he was a slight man and was always beaten); I believed that his pugnacity was due to his uneasiness in the face of those wild mountains and limitless forests that stretch, seemingly, to the furthest points of the compass.

We completed our first three weeks of surveying, returned to the railroad and journeyed to Khabarovsk. The snows began. We spent the winter in studying geographical reports and charts there, in various soldierly exercises—marksmanship practice, drill, calisthenics, and the like—and fulfilling duties of other kinds. Three times, the men and I served as a fire brigade. Even so, I had too much time on my hands, and sometimes images arose in my unoccupied mind; especially of a woman's hand beckoning from dark waters, then submerging. These may have been daylight echoes of dreams, or perhaps the dreams followed the phantasmagoria of daytime reverie. On cold, clear days, it was possible to ride along forest trails outside of the town. Children of the region played on the frozen river. It disturbed me to see them on the ice, but I knew that it was perhaps two feet thick and there could not possibly be any danger.

With the arrival of spring, we set out, very eager to escape the stale air and routine of town quarters. The train stopped; we removed our sleds and equipment, led the horses from their car, and stood watching as the train moved on. The horses' breath was smoky in the still air. This time, we would be on our own for several months.

The headman from the village of Kisi met us, and guided us there, where we would have a supply cache. I left one man to keep an eye on things; he would be relieved, eventually, by another of the men, in turn. We were cautioned, as always, about Chinese bandits. "Hungry in the springtime!" said the headman, who knew a little Russian. He said that the bandits were inactive in the winter, when the villagers were apt to be at home; they preferred to raid in the warmer months, when many of the villagers would be in the woods or clearings, fishing in the streams, or away on trading expeditions. Indeed, the vagrant traders were good game for the bandits. One of my men, Kyril Ilyich Prokhorov, smiled, hefted his carbine, and said he fancied a bit of bandit hunting. Poor man!

Our first encounter with Chinese raiders should have been a great success. We had good intelligence regarding the whereabouts of a band of half a dozen men, and had stalked them for two days. At last, we came up with them. They seemed to have realized we were on their trail, but did not know how close we were. They had hidden, as they believed, in a gully. This should have been perfect for us, having them trapped there. I positioned men such that we had the gully surrounded. The fierce little outlaws, however, were not minded to surrender to officers of the Tsar. Two or three of them slipped out of the gully, hidden by bushes and trees, outflanking us; how they coordinated their fire without calling out to one another I do not know, but suddenly they were firing on us from two sides. The men panicked and began returning fire without having targets. The Russians were shouting, but the Chinese betrayed their presence only by their rifle fire. I saw Prokhorov step forward from the cover of a tree, then, at the report of a rifle, fall to the ground. He had been wounded in the neck. Bending over him and examining him, I saw immediately that he was beyond help. However, I stayed with him, trying to assure him that we would treat his wound as soon as possible, while scanning the woods for sign of Chinese. Occasional shots rang out. After a while, it was evident that the bandits had escaped. The men gathered again. None had been hurt but Prokhorov. He remained alive and conscious, although his loss of blood was great, and, when the shock subsided, his pain became severe.

We had heard from the headman that a holy hermit, such as Father Gleb had told us of, lived nearby. I sent Sviridenko to locate the hermit's dwelling and see if the man were there and able, perhaps, to help us.

We were able to get to the hermit's cabin, made of logs, before nightfall. He was a middle-aged man, spectacled, heavily bearded, rather dirty. I forget his name. He examined Kyril Ilyich and said he could not help his flesh, but he would try to comfort the man as the moment when he must give up his spirit approached.

He had been reading, he said, a book of curious consolation, which had been given him by an Old Believer once. It was a badly-printed, tattered volume called something like *The Teaching of Our Holy Father Among the Saints, Philoxenus*. He read aloud to the dying man as we all listened, our hearts heavy with the knowledge that our comrade would not live till morning. "Hear what our father says, my son. 'At the baptism of Christ, the waters were sanctified. The dove descended and the Jordan blazed with fire. Many waters cannot quench love, saith the Wise King; but now the Jordan becomes purified by divine love and by divine fire that banisheth away every impurity. The waters in which corruption bred, become the fountain of immortality.' Be comforted, my son. Remember your baptism. If thou hast shown mercy unto man, that same mercy shall be shown thee there. If thou hast shown compassion to an orphan, compassion there shall deliver thee from want. We are inflamed with joy when we hear that there is eternal light there, where the souls of the righteous rejoice. Enter into thy inheritance in Christ, redeemed soul, and cry: Alleluia."

The dying man was still; at some moment, as the holy man read and prayed, he had breathed his last.

Thus the first report I wrote that year contained my acknowledgment of a death that had occurred because of my failure to secure the safety of my men. Eventually, my men were questioned by our superiors in Vladivostok, but no negligence was attributed to me at that time. Perhaps I was not responsible for Kyril Ilyich's death. That was not the way it seemed to me then, though I was, of course, relieved to be exonerated.

After Kyril Ilyich was buried—near the holy man's cabin, since no train would come to our district for several days, and we were miles from the railroad then, making it impossible for us to bring his body to the Russian cemetery in one of the cities—I decided that we should continue our mission. This, I realize now, was a mistake. We should have gone to one or other of the towns in the district that were within a days' tramp for us, where I could have allowed the men a couple of days to drink and gamble. I do not approve of these things, but it might have enabled the men to mourn their dead companion, weep, toast his memory, and bid him farewell.

As it was, the morale of the little group did not recover at all rapidly after Prokhorov's burial. The men did not seem to have the heart to tell merry tales any more or to sing as they tramped along. In the evening, they turned in early, morosely drinking their tea, smoking only one pipe, if that much, or if they told stories, these expressed the less cheerful side of the Russian imagination. Dobronravov, who had a fund of Russian folklore at his command—he had had one of those great old nurses, as a boy, an old woman who couldn't read a word, but could tell enough stories to pass a long winter—Dobronravov didn't have the heart for lively stories like "Maria Morevna" or "The Fire Bird." He told legends about holy men subjected to atrocities, and the fates of those who persecuted them; or mournful tales about rusalki, beautiful drowned girls who lured men to share their fate beneath the waters; and tales of the Black Death. One I remember was this: a peasant was fishing from a river bank. He saw a little boat coming towards him with a bent-over hag poling her way across. He rose to offer her his assistance getting out of the boat and onto shore. When he had placed her on the land, she said to him, "You have been kind to an old woman." She indicated a birch broom lying in her boat. "Choose: shall I pass on, or shall I stay and sweep?" The peasant laughed. "God bless you, grandmother," he said, "sweep, if you have the strength." That was the wrong thing for him to say. Everyone in that district died: she was the Black Death.

We were often many miles, so far as I know, from any other human soul. Swallowed in the remote depths of the forest, we should have avoided such grim stories; they were bound to play upon our imaginations. I found myself unable to rebuke the men; I believe now that I was more afraid of silence than uneasy about the campfire talk.

It was during one of those summer nights that I awoke, and found that something had occurred that I was not able confidently to explain. I knew I had been dreaming, but it did not seem to me, when I thought over the matter, that the dream had been terrible or sad. Whatever my dream may have been, I found that my pillow was wet—more than wet, I should almost say damp through. I must have been weeping in my sleep. It was a warm, humid evening, indeed, but the floor of the tent, my blankets, and the like, were dry. Insects hummed and rattled outside the tent. I saw that the flap had been disturbed slightly, which would permit insects to enter and attack Gantman, who remained asleep rolled in his blankets. I got up and adjusted the flap, and turned in again. For some time I was unable to sleep; I was troubled by a sense of loss and loneliness, presumably the effect of our situation in the crowding forest.

However, despite the cheerless atmosphere of our camps, and more accidents than I would have expected to afflict us, inexperienced though we were, we completed our assignment and were settled in for another winter in Khabarovsk by the second week of October. Later that month, we reported for inspection, official deposition, etc. I suppose the life became somewhat dull, but I believe that all of the men, as well as myself, were relieved to be in the city, like men who have made a long sea journey and come to a port—noisome as ports usually are, they are welcome havens after a lonely sojourn.

One incident from this second winter in the Primorsk Kray must be mentioned. Gantman, whose spirits had seemed especially depressed of all of the men, and who had complained of vague apprehensions of danger, deserted. (He had earlier applied for leave, but I had told him outright that there was no chance of this so soon.) I have never heard what became of my tent-mate, and hope he prospered somewhere. He was a good man, if a little fanciful; he had told me once that he felt it was unwise for us to camp anywhere near a stream, and that he sometimes woke in the night, sensing that there was someone in or near our tent. I imagine that I disturbed him, too, with my restlessness; the fact is that I hardly ever slept through an entire night. I woke from vain dreams of the past, or visions of stifling embraces, not rarely, and, once awake, found my thoughts turned often to that summer night a year and more before, when I lost all I loved. On these occasions, dawn often found me still awake, for I was unable to divert myself by a forced consideration of the minute details of our assignment.

My superior officers did not appear, at that time, to blame me for Gantman's desertion, and assigned a new recruit to us, Daniel Aleksandrovich Shchelkalov, to replace him. He began to study and drill with the others that winter. In his naive exuberance—he had enlisted in hopes of exotic adventures, and to get away from the tyrannical "old man"—he brought life and cheerfulness to our little group. He was an ugly little blond boy, self-confident in excess of his capabilities, but yet willing to learn. I was delighted with him.

Once, when we were in the Ulunga wilderness, in the midst of one of the worst spring fogs I have encountered, unable to go anywhere and beginning to imagine Chinese bandits preparing an ambush, Shchelkalov lifted our spirits with an amazing, continuous flow of ludicrous songs, stories, and dances. (That lad must have had Cossack blood in him—to see him dance on one leg was a spectacle!) He told one story that he said was well-known in his district, so many hundreds of miles from where we were, the story of Matvei and the cow. Since I have not seen or heard it anywhere else, I record it here. Perhaps it will be of interest to some collector of the stories of the people, should he see it:

Every morning, farmer Matvei, who lived by himself, milked Marfa, the cow. Every morning he heard her moo as he approached the shed, where he kept the milking pail. One morning, her moo sounded odd. When he entered the shed, he saw that she had the pail on her head. He removed the pail and asked her how she had managed that, but of course she couldn't answer him, but only looked at him with her long-lashed eyes. He forgot about it, and went to milk her the next morning, suspecting nothing, until he heard that odd-sounding moo again. She had the pail there again. Farmer Matvei decided to put the pail up on a high shelf where the cow couldn't reach it. But in the morning, there it was on her head again. Shchelkalov told how on subsequent mornings, as the pail continues to appear on his cow's head, the farmer takes it into his house and puts it by the door; on the table; and under his bed. Each morning, however, it's back on the cow's head. At last, the farmer climbs into bed at night and puts the pail over his own head. He hears wild laughter and pulls off the pail. A little black goblin is standing at the foot of his bed pointing at him and roaring with laughter. "I've been putting the pail over your cow's head! But she didn't look half so funny as you do!" The farmer jumped from the blankets to grab the goblin, who leaped to the floor and disappeared into a crack between the boards, and was never seen again.

Shchelkalov was steady enough except when he was carried into giddiness by his own torrents of nonsense, which needed no drink to bring them to overflowing. In the woods, or toiling up a primitive mountain trail, where carelessness could result in one of our pack horses losing its footing and tumbling into a stream, he was as reliable as any of the men. Once, though, he said, quite unaffectedly, that he possessed the second sight. One of the men had not heard this expression and said, "What, the evil eye?"— belief in which is by no means unheard of among our Russian soldiers. I believed, and still believe, that they were good men, every one of them, even Mihailov, who went on the spree more than once in Khabarovsk, or during our rests in villages such as Lazo and

Plastun. He caught an infection from some prostitute in one of these places; eventually, he had to be discharged in disgrace, and I do not know what his later life was.

Nevertheless, I do not believe the men were malcontents. If they appeared before officials and answered certain pointed inquiries, of which at the time I knew nothing, during our third winter in Khabarovsk, that was only their duty. I do not suspect them of offering false information against me. I was greatly surprised when I was called to a session of my commanding officers, who said that they had decided to re-assign me. They said that they had not been perfectly satisfied about Gantman and the loss of Prokhorov, and that my men said I was subject to fits of melancholy during which my morose behavior and inadequate orders depressed them and led to delays. I admitted that we had not completed our most recent assignment (surveying the region around Lake Bikin); I could not well deny the fact.

They pressed me and I acknowledged that I did not sleep well, and I said also that in the woods and along the marshes, where the shadows of the leaves or grasses move and whisper ceaselessly, it is difficult not to imagine certain presences.

"Your man Murminsky says that you confided to him that you have sometimes fancied there is a woman—but perhaps not a woman of natural flesh and blood?—in the vicinity of the camp— particularly, I believe he said, when you are near rivers or streams? He said that you used the word 'rusalka.'" The speaker, Colonel Nikolai Petrovich Pisemsky, looked at me closely, his eyebrows raised, his expression not hostile, but stern.

Painfully, I admitted this. "But, sir, ask the men. They will tell you that it is easy to imagine things."

"Captain Kuritsin, what you say confirms our judgment that, while you are a conscientious and knowledgeable officer, you ought to be given a new posting. Perhaps the change will liberate you from these delusions. This decision, you may as well know, was made before our deliberations of this morning. You will report to Col. Basmanov at Myakit, Atka District, on the eighteenth of this month. That will give you two days to get your papers and equipment ready."

I could only salute and depart for my rooms. When Pisemsky named my destination, a sensation of dismay coursed through me.

It was a region that was a byword for remoteness and harsh winters, over a thousand miles from the ocean winds that tempered the season in the Sikhote Alin.

As I walked up the stairs to my quarters, however, I considered the possibility that there—in new and even more inhospitable surroundings, where, perhaps, I should find myself drawing upon all my powers in order to survive—I might elude the thoughts and surmises that troubled me. When I went to bed, sometime after midnight, I was feeling more cheerful than I had felt for many days.

Regrettably, after my departure from Khabarovsk, and many hours before reaching Myakit, a mood of self-pity settled upon me. I was certain that senior officers in the region who had heard of my father were comparing me to him: I was to be the feckless son of the accomplished father.

After I reported in Myakit, however, and received my new orders, my mood of self-pity was transformed almost instantaneously into profound alarm. I had expected to be assigned routine duties in that undistinguished outpost of the Russian empire; instead, it was to be merely the first stop of many on my journey west into the most isolated and even unknown region of Russia, central Siberia, that "vast, roofless prison," as someone calls it. When my commanding officer, Colonel Basmanov, saw my expression of dismay, he seemed to take pity on me. He assured me that I should not regard my assignment as banishment; the region to which I was sent was rumored to possess reserves of gold, coal, and iron, the latter two of which would be needed if the Motherland's war with Japan should revive. He said that the region had been only minimally surveyed. There was a real need for the work I would do.

"The region of which you speak, sir, is uninhabited save for wild tribesmen and convicts! Sir, please, can there be any mistake?"

He assured me that there was no mistake. I would not be alone; as in the Sikhote Alin, several men would accompany me. We were to write our reports in the prison town of Chambe. After two years, we would be eligible to apply for three months' leave. The Machakugyr and Shanyagir tribes were hospitable and it would be easy to find skilled native guides to hire. These reindeer herders, though poor, were hardy, intelligent, and friendly. Some of the prison guards at Chambe, he said, had formed liaisons with tribal girls. It was possible to enjoy some of the comforts of a household, which, however, need not detain one when the time came to leave.

I could only conclude that my senior officers had decided to dispose of me, either because of my personal inadequacies, or—the thought was a new one—because of envious spite directed against my father, to whose generation they belonged for the most part. To this day, I am not sure that there were no "considerations" at work in my new assignment.

The journey to Okhchen was wearisome. The terrain was mostly flat, and the railway was surrounded by dark conifers, which were cut back from the tracks at a distance of fifty to a hundred yards, to reduce the chance of fire caused by sparks cast from the locomotive. We crossed many bridges. At least the weeks-long train journey ended, and from Okhchen, I and the men who drove the supply wagons journeyed over a rutted road. The horses were sometimes in danger of injury. It took us a week to reach Chambe; we forded several streams. Daniel Aleksandrovich Shchelkalov had been commanded to accompany me, which lends credence to Pisemsky's protestation that my assignment was not just an excuse to get rid of me, as Daniel Aleksandrovich was a competent surveyor.

Before we saw it, as we emerged from a spruce forest—late in a warm afternoon of early June, 1908—the wind brought the smell to us; the odor of woodsmoke, of cooking, horse- and cattle-dung, and something worse, the smell of filthy human beings.

The village was a large stockade inside which were the prisoners' barracks, the somewhat more tolerable residences of their guardians and of a few sable trappers for whom Chambe was a trading post, a few military offices, and a couple of taverns. There was a small wooden church; I never saw the priest, but heard that he was often drunk and persecuted his wife and children. Most of the construction of the village was the work of the convicts. Those who died thus, as slaves, of typhus or exhaustion, were buried off to the left of the road as one approaches the stockade, so that the convicts with life sentences had plenteous opportunity for reflecting upon the destiny that must eventually come upon them; that was how their katorga would end. Bodies of non-prisoners who died at Chambe were buried some distance further away, as if to permit

97

them to sleep out of sight and hearing of the village. There was a small and rather pretty chapel, as I discovered a few days later, surrounded by trees. Aside from occasional pleasant rooms within a few of the buildings enclosed by the stockade, the chapel was the only spot of beauty, almost of decency, in the entire place. At a little distance from the log walls that surrounded the village, a few conical native huts were scattered. From white birch poles in front of them, white strips of cloth fluttered, either to attract benign spirits or to frighten off harmful ones.

I was fearful of the convicts at first, not because of their crimes, but because of the almost inhuman appearance of some of them—women as well as men. Their clothing was rags; they were dirty and, I was sure, lousy. The men's scalps and beards were tangled. The faces of men and women were burnt dark from exposure and showed the marks of hunger, suffering, and, as I was sure, of depravity. A few of these criminals stood erect, but many of them slumped or limped from ill-usage and hopelessness. They lived without children. If, despite the surveillance of the guards, a woman became pregnant and had a child, the infant was given to one of the tribal women, with a small stipend. The only children in the place, those of the priest and of the owner of one of the taverns, were kept indoors most of the time.

The prisoners were employed as lumber gangs. During their summer sojourns in the forests of the region—which were as vast as the sea—they slept on the ground or in the most rude of shelters. In the winter, I was told, the men spent much of the time fishing through holes in the ice over nearby lakes. This was not an activity to keep them occupied—they continued to work in the forests except during the days of most severe cold; but the fish they caught were an important part of their diet, without which they would have been very hungry indeed. They split wood for fires and tanned reindeer hides, with which their own moccasins and leggings were made, although they first had to make a set amount as trade objects for traffic with the local tribesmen, who supplied the raw hides, and also brought reindeer meat and yoghurt, which were consumed by those residents of Chambe who were not prisoners. In the cold months, some of the educated prisoners—criminals or political exiles—mounted theatrical performances. Women worked in the camps, too, but the sexes were strictly segregated. Women were the water—or ice!—haulers.

Consciously, I set myself to find things of beauty on which to rest my eye. The woods here were low and dark, and exclusively coniferous, cheerless and unwelcoming, and scrawny in comparison to some of the giants of the Sikhote Alin. The wildflowers were already gone when we arrived, and in any event were tiny. So I turned to the skies and their denizens, the birds. Although I had been told that I could expect a few weeks of warm summer days, the nights were nearly always chilly; however, I became aware, indeed, of the heavens as I have never been before, at least not since I was a very small child. The skies of day were sometimes of a melting warmth and loveliness; at other times, clouds mounded and not a breath of wind stirred till thunder broke forth and lightning and rain came down. At night the stars burned brightly. High in the heavens, Arcturus looked down upon me in friendly wise, but the scales of Libra, low on the western horizon, suggested I had been weighed and found wanting.

One night at the end of June, after the men and I had spent a week surveying the taiga and had returned to the village, I went off by myself. As I studied the heavens, unwelcome footsteps hurried up to me. Daniel Aleksandrovich said, a little breathlessly, "Sir, who was that who was standing here with you just now?"

"I have been alone until your arrival," I said, coldly. I had no desire for any company but that of my own thoughts. For some time, I had found that while I could enjoy company during the day, it had become displeasing to me after nightfall.

"Sir, someone stood beside you—I should have said he or—she—was embracing you."

"Your eyes were playing tricks on you."

"No, sir, with respect, I'm sure someone was standing at your side."

"Very well, Daniel Aleksandrovich, will it make you happy if I say I had an assignation with one of the women prisoners? We had just managed to pick open the lock on her leg irons. After you leave, we will pick the lice out of one another's scalps."

"I apologize, sir."

"How do you come to be awake at this time of night, anyway? One sleepless Russian soldier is enough for this little rural Paradise."

He said nothing for a moment, then: "I'm sorry, sir, it will sound mad, but I was dreaming of you, sir. I dreamed that you were drowning. I awoke and looked into your room and saw you weren't there, and came looking for you."

"That was kind of you, Daniel Aleksandrovich. However, as you see, I am quite dry, and as I will not be able to sleep this night, I will not accompany you back to our quarters. Perhaps in future, if you awaken from a dream about me, you should just go back to sleep. Haven't you a sweetheart you could dream about instead?"

"Dreams may tell the truth sometimes, sir. It's happened so, in my life, more than once."

"Is this your second sight? Now back to bed. Thank you for your concern, but I am quite well."

Shchelkalov headed back in the direction of the stockade, as I thought. I was not inclined to linger at the meadow spot where we had talked, and was vexed that my sequence of impressions and thoughts had been interrupted; so I walked on, into a small wood, the sort of place where I might have hoped to find mushrooms when I was a boy. There was no trail that I could see, so I picked my way, stepping over fallen branches, around shrubs and clusters of nettles. The stars and the light of the moon provided adequate illumination. Perhaps my conduct would have appeared, had anyone seen me, to be that of a sulky truant.

I was getting quite wet from dew and had some scratches across my face and hands. I seemed to be the only moving thing under the watching sky. Eventually I emerged from the wood by a good-sized stream. The night was becoming chilly. A devastating loneliness swept upon me.

"Eh, what's the use," I muttered. I didn't know why I said this. I replaced the pipe I had been about to fill. I stared at the black water for a long time. In two hours, it would be dawn.

"A man could slip into the water, the little waves would close over him, his body would be found after sunrise," an inner voice suggested.

After a while, I stepped to where the ground became soft under my boot sole. There was a little space where few plants grew out of the mud, although tall, dark blades grew on either side of me. I could hear soft sounds of a small animal or two moving in the water.

I listened for several minutes. Then I began to call, in a low, quiet voice, "Rusalka, rusalka. Rusalka, rusalka."

The moon seemed to stand near my shoulder, listening. There was no sound of breeze. I called again. "Rusalka, rusalka." Now it was as if I were speaking shut up in a room, although I had no roof above me, everything was so quiet.

I continued to stare towards the middle of the stream. Something white showed and disappeared.

I stepped forward, into the yielding mud; another step. "Rusalka," I said. The mud released a rank odor as I disturbed it.

Water was flowing over the tops of my boots. I reached forward toward nothing.

"Rusalka."

A white woman-shape rose from the water, a cold, dripping hand took mine, drew me further into the river. Streaming over my shoulders, the moonlight shone in the glittering eyes and hair. I heard a hoarse shout behind me, which seemed to come from a great distance away, my eyes held by those other eyes. I was drawn closer, into an embrace I could not and did not want to escape. The cold water was up to my waist, my chest. Lips sought mine.

Then Shchelkalov tried to thrust himself between us, groaning, his struggles splashing water in my face. He pushed or fell against me. I did not know where I was for a moment—water filled my mouth, nostrils, eyes—I leaped up through black water, gasping. Shchelkalov seized me about the chest and, straining, drew me to the shore. Our breath came in deep gulps.

"Merciful God save us! Captain! What was it?"

I felt as if I could not remember any words.

"Captain! From a distance, it seemed to me a woman was leading you into the water. But as I ran up to you, she—it—it was less and less distinct—grey—like smoke or cobwebs!"

I had to keep my eyes turned away, staring at my feet. The face seemed to be burnt onto my eyeballs. I was afraid to look even into his eyes because of those other, glittering eyes.

Yet, as I sat with my back against a tree trunk, and my breathing quietened, the world seemed to form around me again, and the face to recede. That face and form were becoming a memory, not an image that had possessed me. I was exhausted, yet also felt strangely lightened.

I slowly rose to my feet. For a few moments I looked at the river. I began to walk towards it. "Captain!" Shchelkalov stirred behind me.

"It's all right now, Daniel Aleksandrovich," I said. I walked into the water, up to the tops of my boots; paused; went forward a little further, then moved on until the water was at the level of my shoulders. I counted fifty. I turned and began to approach the river bank again. And then a searing light in an instant bloomed in the sky and the river seemed to burst into flame for a moment beneath it as a terrible explosion sounded. Daniel Aleksandrovich and I both cried out.

I hastened to the shore. The leaves were agitated in some unnatural breeze that coursed through them for a few moments.

"God help us, what was it?" he said.

We stood by the river bank for perhaps the quarter of an hour, listening intently. Thousands of stars that might have been created just then blazed in the dark vault of the sky. For a while there were no sounds at all, not the least sound of a nocturnal bird, no sound of insects. These gradually emerged as the sky brightened by imperceptible degrees. Shchelkalov and I at last began to theorize. Could a vast ammunition dump have exploded? But there was no such stockpile for hundreds of miles. Had a brief but violent thunderstorm passed by? We could not believe it. Shchelkalov asked if a fiery mountain, a volcano, might have erupted somewhere. It is a sign of how shaken we both were that this seemed to us a possible explanation.

We were not to learn anything until several days later, when a trapper of one of the Tungus River tribes came into Chambe. His narrative was so astonishing that the whole village was filled with wonder. The trapper told of the sky tearing apart before dawn—of a tremendous noise, of choking heat that ignited cabins and killed reindeer (though he knew of no human beings who had been killed). He said that he had been told of hills whose trees were pushed over flat as if by the violence of the gods. The man was a convert to Orthodoxy, but I could see that he was struggling against the superstitions of his people about Ogdy, their sky god. Indeed, as I have since wondered, perhaps there was some truth in their sky god; that he was a shadow of the Creator, cast upon their hearts.

Now, as I write, some twenty years after the events of that summer night just before dawn, still no one knows what that Visitor was—meteor, comet, or some phenomenon of nature never before recorded? Few Russians have seen the vast tract of desolation that that "angel of death" passed over, and the tribal people are afraid to go there; it remains taboo.

For me, that summer brought the beginning of a new peace. It is as if the light from the sky shed light into my soul as well. The stories of the Visitor that we began to hear as the brief summer continued filled me with new emotions, as I heard of men, of women and children, shaken, terrified, and in some few cases, impoverished by the catastrophe. I remained a surveyor; I worked in that region for two years, before being called away to new duties under new superiors. Much of my work was done in the winter, when land that was almost impassible mud in summer was frozen hard, to the depth of four feet or more. During those two years, however, in addition to my official duties, I found occupation among some of the tribal people who needed not only supplies that the Tsar could provide these forgotten subjects, but the reassurance provided by a recorder of their tales who did not believe they had been punished for their neglect of pagan pieties. I have recorded their eyewitness accounts and deposited them at Vanavara.

"Why seek ye the living among the dead?"—I have learned to cherish these words of the Easter Gospel.

Among the living, the distraught people living north of Chambe, as well as in my official work, I found that I could surrender the dead. With a heart that was learning peace, I considered, deliberately, the events that had occurred during and after the summer when I was to be married. I began to realize that, in my confusion and embarrassment on the night when she drowned, and in my youthful inexperience of life, I had not rightly mourned Raisa Pavlovna and relinquished her to heaven. That failure, I believe, rendered me susceptible to forces that prey upon the faithless and despairing.

Have I acknowledged to anyone, before writing this account, that I never till that summer of the Visitor had had a panikhida, a service of "eternal memory," for her?

Shelter Belt

Jeremiah did not think about the sky, but he felt its immensity and depth whenever he stepped out of the small house, whether alone or with his mother. When he was in the front yard—a small space overlooked by the dark rectangle of the picture window, and bounded by a scruffy low hedge—he felt the sky invite him to step onto his scooter and dash up and down the cracked cement path that connected the front steps with the graveled street. When he reached the street he would want to leave the yard and propel himself along the hard earth of the street's edge until he came, a few hundred yards from home, to four mailboxes mounted on a wooden post. The lady in the blue shirt and dark blue pants who drove the mail truck would turn around after she filled the mailboxes, because the street ended there. Beyond the pavement was a field of black dirt that went on as far as an unpaved county road, which ran at a right angle to Jeremiah's familiar street, and which Jeremiah could not see, though in summer he sometimes stood looking at the long, long strip of dust that followed a speeding truck that he could hardly see or hear.

When he had pushed closed the second mailbox from the left, Jeremiah would turn and look at the other houses. He wondered who lived in them.

When he stepped out of the back door, he saw a plain yard with a board fence at its furthest extremity. In the fence there was a gate, which obscurely troubled him. Beyond the fence, grass and weeds grew, and then a shelter belt of trees stood in the way of his vision. The windbreak of American elms, Chinese elm and ash stretched as far to the right and to the left as he could see when he stood looking at it, the closed gate in front of him. In the summer, the shelter belt was a sighing wall of moving green leaves that reached up to the sky, and so Jeremiah loved it. In early October, only a few

105

shriveled and brown dry leaves remained, and the sky showed through the upturned branches. The sky weighed upon Jeremiah's spirit for months, until the trees were clothed with green again.

Television was in the house, the smell of food, and his mother's bedroom, and his own. Next year he would start school. The bus would come right to their house, Mother said.

A window was set in the east wall of Jeremiah's bedroom. It looked upon the side of the garage, and there was a sandbox that he rarely played in. But from the north window, Jeremiah peered through a white plastic telescope that was set on a table. He looked at the shelter belt.

His mother asked him, "What's your favorite thing, Jermy?"

He named a television program, but, without his being aware of the fact, it was the shelter belt that engrossed him more than any other thing.

He liked Nicole, the young woman he stayed with while Mother was working at the variety store in town, but, though he could not speak to himself or others of this, he knew every moment with Nicole was a suspension of his real life.

So the boy grew, and secrecy he did not intend grew within him, secrecy that was filled and shaped by the wind and the strip of trees. His mother read to him in the evening, sitting by his side on the sofa. He liked television, but when his mother read to him, he was deeply happy. Hers was the only articulate voice that spoke only to him. He was absorbed—not so much by the stories she read to him, about a Little Engine That Could, or Peter Rabbit, or Three Bears, but by sounds that she wonderfully shaped in her body, the same body that had carried him for nine months in darkness and warmth, and that he remembered. His mother's voice was the only voice that he loved.

Yet he listened also for another voice, a wordless voice that he did not think about, but listened for, perhaps listened for most keenly when he slept, the wordless voice of the wind in the branches beyond the back yard fence.

It began to happen that Mother did not always read to him in the evening, after dinner and wash-up, after television, and the things that were done as bedtime approached. Sometimes Mother said that she would read to him tomorrow, and she did read to him the next evening, nearly always, if she had said that she would. And some evenings, she read to him more than ever. Jeremiah knew now, though, that reading time might happen or might not happen. Mother was silent most of the evening on some days, now, and Jeremiah played with toys on the living room floor, and was cheerful because his mother was there, and let him have two cookies and milk sometimes now, which was a new thing.

One morning, Mother told Jeremiah that she would pick him up at the same time as always at Nicole's house, and they would go home and have something to eat, but then, after the news, she was going to take him to Nicole's again, till almost bedtime. Then she would be back for him. She told him why: she was going to have dinner with a young man named Daniel, who owned the store where she worked. "I'm going to have a *date*, Jermy," she said, watching his eyes closely and smiling.

Jeremiah liked Daniel, and he liked going to church with Mother and sitting between her and Daniel on the seats that were long and hard. There seemed to him to be many people in the church, including at least five children. Jeremiah heard a man at the front of the room reading from the Bible. Mother read to him from the Bible at home, sometimes, too; "The Lord is my Shepherd, I shall not want. Blessed are the meek, for they shall inherit the earth. And the greatest of these is love."

"Daniel likes this psalm a lot, Jeremiah. Do you like Daniel?"

Now Mother would sing songs from church sometimes, when she was taking care of things at home. "Sweet hour of prayer, sweet hour of prayer, that bids me from a world of care," she sang softly, folding towels.

And yet, the boy heard fewer words addressed just to him; and that other voice seemed bolder, as he lay in his bed. He knew that the leaves would soon all have fallen from the shelter belt.

One Saturday afternoon, Daniel's truck was parked on the road in front of the house. He had lunch with them. Then the three of them sat on the cement block that was the back step. The sun was bright, but the air was chilly. Daniel and Mother were sitting close together, and Jeremiah was on the edge of the cement. After a few minutes of listening to them talk to each other, and experimenting to see if he could find an angle for sitting that was ample enough to be comfortable, Jeremiah stood up. The adults stood up, too, and went inside. Mother held the door open for the boy, but he said he was going to stay outside for a while. Mother's warm right hand cupped his cheek for a moment and then the door closed behind her and Daniel.

He looked at the yard and at toys he had left lying on the brown grass, then at the fence and the gate. He walked to the gate, which he had never opened before. A horseshoe-shaped latch was, unexpectedly, easy to raise, and the gate moved outwards at his push, obstructed by burdock that grew close. Jeremiah looked unhurriedly and saw that there was a little path or trail off to the side a few feet, which might lead through the burrs.

He left the gate resting not quite closed, and walked to the path, which he saw did provide a way to pass through the tough, dry weeds. Every few yards, he stopped to pull the bristly gray weed heads from his sleeves and pants legs and from the shoelace knots. He became expert almost immediately in applying just enough force to pull the burrs loose, without pinching them so tightly that the sharp tips broke the skin of his thumb and forefinger. He threw each one far away.

The ground rose just a little, and Jeremiah stood and looked back. He had never seen his house from such a perspective. He could see the entire fence that bounded it on three sides, and part of the road on the side furthest from him. He could not hear or see Mother or Daniel inside the little house. He turned away from the house again, and there was the shelter belt close in front of him. He was under the branches of a tree. Now he was aware of the wind that had been sounding in the branches all the time he had been outdoors. He listened to it.

"Jeremiah? Jeremiah?" It was his mother's voice from a distance.

He stirred and rose up in the bed, where he had been dreaming of the shelter belt. Mother had called to him as he stood there listening to the wind. He knew that he had heard her voice in his sleep. He settled back into the blankets, sighed, and slept again.

The time came when Daniel was at the house every Saturday afternoon, and sometimes he followed them home after church on Sundays in his car; he always offered Jeremiah the chance to ride home with him, and Jeremiah liked and trusted his smile. But he rode home in the car with Mother.

On Saturdays, Daniel had lunch with them, and then did things like cleaning dead leaves out of the gutters that hung from the eaves of the house, or raking leaves with Jeremiah and his mother, or splitting firewood that had been dumped by the sandbox. In the evening there was dinner and a fire in the little fireplace. Before dinnertime, Jeremiah found himself on his own. He was drawn to the gate, the path, and the wall of trees, trees that were bare, now, and that bore the voice of the wind. The boy could almost understand that voice, now.

He had begun to explore the shelter belt, stepping around fallen branches, looking at holes that had been made by small animals he never saw.

On a Saturday afternoon in early November, when the sky was steely, dry, and cold, Jeremiah, in a padded jacket, penetrated more deeply into the trees than he ever had before. He was not very interested in passing through the shelter belt; there was nothing beyond it but a band of grass a few dozen yards wide, and then, behind barbed wire, a rutted field with wheat stubble on the other side. Not interested in the grass beyond the trees, or in the stubblefield, Jeremiah could stay inside the strip of trees and, so far in his explorations, never come to the end. He understood that the wind was inviting him to keep walking, so that he could discover a secret thing.

To reach it, he would have to negotiate the worst patch of burdock that he had encountered under the trees. There seemed to be no trail around it. He stood in front of it and thought for several minutes; then he remembered that there was an ancient shell of a car, abandoned in time too distant to be meaningful to the boy, back in the trees some little distance behind him. He returned to it and found a sharp edge of rusty metal, so corroded that, by working it back and forth, he was able to break off a piece. He tried it on a bit of dried fungus nearby. He sawed the fungus loose from the dead branch in a moment.

With the jagged edge of his improvised knife, Jeremiah began to cut through the burdock stems that had obstructed his way. An adult would have been surprised by how quickly the stems parted as the small boy began to cut his way through the barrier. He was oblivious of the sticking heads now. Soon there were many of them clinging to his arms, his legs, his back and his shoes. Numerous scratches on his hands, even his face, did not deter him. He obeyed the voice.

Then he was free of the mass of weeds, and in a sort of small open space. There was a depression of a few inches, and the boy began to dig, at first trying to use the piece of metal, then digging with his fingers. The gray soil was dry and powdery. He flung handfuls of dry dirt off to his side. His fingers touched something hard. He stopped digging and raised his head, and looked about. The trees stood all around and the wind said that he had done what he was expected to do. Jeremiah scratched soil loose from the object; it was a piece of dry, white bone. He knew that. This was what was left when something died. What animal was buried there? What part of the animal had this been?

Jeremiah walked straight home. The piece of bone was in his jeans pocket. As he walked, he realized that the wind was trying to tell him something about the bone, something he didn't want to know. He walked faster, trying to listen just to the sound of his own footsteps that cracked twigs, that rustled in dry grass. His footsteps made sounds that were good to hear in the midst of the trees. Then he heard an airplane, too, buzzing louder and louder, drowning out the sound of the wind.

He found the place where he had entered the shelter belt and stepped out beneath open sky. The plane was droning loudly quite close overhead, catching the sunlight and reflecting it brilliantly, and now turned gracefully away, at an angle, towards the east, as if someone in it had been keeping an eye on him till he was almost home. He waved at it. Then he put his hand on his pocket, feeling the bit of bone.

He pushed open the back door with his left hand, his right still in his pocket.

Mother and Daniel were sitting at the kitchen table. "Jeremiah," she said. "Daniel and I would like to ask you something." They were smiling. He came to himself and returned their smile. "Would you like to have a daddy?"

"All right," he said, uncertainly. Then: "Oh boy!"

At that moment she noticed: "Jermy! You're *covered* with burrs!" And she and Daniel burst into laughter, and then Jeremiah broke into laughter, too.

He put the piece of bone on the ledge of the north window. A few days later, his mother, cleaning the room, noticed it, and asked him what it was.

"Just something I found in the shelter belt," he said. He had forgotten about it.

"Do you want it?"

"Not really," he said.

From that time, when Jeremiah listened to the wind in the branches, it was only wind. He liked the sound. He imagined that he could hear it when he lay in his bed, the windows shut, the darkness warm, and the sound of a woman's voice, singing softly, coming through the two-inch gap that was always left in his bedroom doorway. He liked the sound of the wind, which was the sound of wind, not a voice.

The Allegheny Exception

with Adam Walter

I emerged from the cool interior of Berglund's Hardware with its pervading fragrance of planed lumber. I was turning towards the high school two blocks away when Prof. Dennis Jesperson appeared, lunged, and grabbed me by one arm.

"Kellett! Come with me. Get in." He hauled me towards his Ford.

I found my voice. "Prof. Jesperson, I'm on my lunch, I have to be back at the school in a few—"

"Let's go. I cleared it with your principal. Get in! I'll explain on the way."

The State U campus kept to itself on the other side of the meandering brown Lidger River. Jesperson drove fast toward it. The bridge said *ahhhh* as we rushed across it.

"You say it's okay with Snodgrass?"

"Yes, he's getting someone to cover your afternoon classes. Now listen to me—"

"He told you where to find me?"

"Yes. Listen. You know I have fourteen guys working for me. And of course the grad assistants, who don't know really what's going on. And neither do you. You know we started out that this was war work, but that didn't pan out. Yet the government has kept funding us. It's actually called Operation Uncertain—more descriptive of their attitude, you understand, than of the work."

"I see."

"Yes, it's what you'd call quasi-military." He turned onto Campus Drive, rolled past Old Main, and swung the Ford around back of the Rangell Lab, a two-story red brick building. "We'll go to my office."

He unlocked his door. Its window was frosted glass. The door was numbered 21, but there was no other identification. We stepped inside. Plenty of light came through the south-facing windows. Jesperson didn't flick the light switch on. He sat down and motioned to the chair on the other side of his desk.

"Okay, this is why you're here. In a moment I'm going to ask you to do something that you'll think is a little goofy. So why do it and why ask you? Answer: I want to see if you hear what I hear, but I didn't want to ask someone else on the project. Why? I don't want any of these guys to think the prof is going crazy."

The tension in his face and voice was controlled but unmistakable.

"Well, any questions?"

I paused. "No, I guess not. Look, Prof. Jesperson, you know I owe you a lot. I never would've finished college if you hadn't got the assistantship for me. And I wasn't exactly, ah, qualified."

"You did a fine job teaching basic classes, Paul. You needn't thank me. And if that was an investment in the future, then I'm sure it was worth it. You're a good teacher, I know."

"Thanks. Well . . . let's go ahead, test me or whatever it is."

He got up and I followed him down a corridor to a windowless, unmarked door. He unlocked it. Inside was the principal lab for the "Operation." I saw nothing that I hadn't seen before. To me, it was just a lab with machines I couldn't hope to fathom—bulbous metal-and-glass hulks, bizarrely shaped conductors, and the like. Though I had taught remedial science classes at the university, my major had been English.

"Come over to this corner." I stepped to the northwest side of the room. "Now, do you hear anything?"

I stood still. "I hear: the forced-air system. Some humming from over there"—I gestured towards a group of machines— ". . . Some people just walked past this room . . . No, nothing unusual."

"I didn't think you would. Now do this." He cupped his hands behind his ears, his expression completely serious, and so it didn't even occur to me to grin or laugh. I did as he said.

"Well, the air system sounds louder, of course. Like there's a steady high wind. I'd say that actually the humming sound is less noticeable now. . . . There's a sort of rising and falling whispery sound."

"Good. Keep listening, Paul."

I stood with my ears cupped for another couple of minutes. "No, nothing else . . ."

"Right. I didn't expect anything. Now step over there"—he gestured to the northeast corner, where a wooden ladder leaned against the wall under dead fluorescent lights. I repeated what I'd just done.

"Air system . . . humming sound. Should I be hearing anything different?"

"So, nothing different there?"

"No."

He stepped over to where I stood, his expression stern. He cupped his ears for a few moments.

"No, I don't hear anything either."

I waited for him to say something more. After another moment passed he turned and headed for the door, opened it, waited for me to step through.

"I'll drive you back to the school. Thanks, Paul."

"Aren't you going to tell me what I was supposed to hear?"

"No . . . no, I don't think I will just now. But I might ask you to try the experiment again sometime. Can you come right away, if so?"

"Well, yeah, if you square it with Snodgrass."

In the car, Jesperson said, "I might call you up or come by your place even in the middle of the night. Paul, it's important. It's important to me."

"Sure. I'll come."

"Don't mention this to anyone. If your principal asks what was up, you can think of something."

I relieved Mrs. Sammons, who had passed recent issues of *The Saturday Evening Post* and *Collier's* to the eleventh graders. They seemed to be on good behavior. I decided that Jesperson would tell me more if and when he felt that he needed to.

Mine was a third floor apartment on Catalina Street. I had a bedroom, lavatory without bathtub, and a small sitting room-kitchen with fridge, and my own exterior wooden stairs. In warm September weather such as we were having now, I sometimes pulled a kitchen chair onto the landing and sat looking across the rooftops and trees of the flat Midwestern town. The tallest structures were, naturally, the grain elevators and the water tower. The water tower was closest, six blocks away on the far side of the railroad tracks. The sun went down and a feeling of contentment settled on me; I had washed my dinner plate and the pan in which I'd fried some eggs, and I was well ahead on prep for the week's classes. If I turned to look into the room, I could see on the kitchen counter wall a warm glow from the tubes in the back of the radio, which played softly. The cloudless sky, flushed after the sun's disappearance, and, on the stair rail close by, a cold bottle of beer imparted their contributions to a sense of well-being. Warm yellow light drew my eye to windows in houses here and there. Birds were settling down for the night and a mother in the street was calling her kids inside. In a few years I'd probably be teaching one or other of them. So I said a small prayer, that they'd be reasonably well-behaved. "Classroom management" took it out of me at times. In this, my second year of teaching, I was often tired after a day in class, even if it'd been an uneventful one—as today, except for the curious run out to the university, had been. I dozed.

A knocking at my hallway door roused me. Orange light still lingered in the west. "Mr. Kellett! Telephone for you," called my landlady, Mrs. Friend. I followed her down the carpeted stairs to her phone. I hardly ever received calls, so she didn't mind.

"Hello?"

"Kellett. This is Jesperson. Listen, can you see the water tower from your place?"

"Yeah. Why?"

"I want you to look and tell me if you see anything. I'm standing at the pay phone on Main now, looking at it. I think someone's walking around up there."

"Professor, shouldn't you be calling the police? It's probably a kid on a dare or—Why call me?"

"I need to know if you see anything. I'll stay on the line, you go look."

I laid the receiver on a crocheted doily atop the mahogany telephone table. "Mrs. Friend, may I leave this here for a moment and run up to my room?"

"Of course, Mr. Kellett."

I ran lightly up the stairs, moderating my footfalls so as not to disturb the other lodgers, slipped through my open doorway and out onto the landing. My eyes took a moment to adjust to the dimness. The lights of Main Street shone behind the water tower, itself a dark bulk. I stared for a couple minutes. Once I thought perhaps I saw movement, but perhaps not. I might have seen an intervening branch move in the breeze, or a bird coast by, or only some subjective flicker.

I went downstairs again and picked up the phone. "No, I don't see anything, but then I'm on the other side from where you are on Main. Do you still see something?"

"No, not now—Thanks, Paul. Look, you probably think I'm out of my mind. I'm not. Sorry to bother you." He hung up.

I stood there a moment then asked Mrs. Friend if I could make a local call. "That's fine, Mr. Kellett. Would you like for me to step into the next room?"

"No, thanks, it's nothing too personal." She had a directory on the table beside the phone. I turned the pages till I found Jesperson's number, which I dialed.

"Hello? . . . Mrs. Jesperson, hi, this is Paul Kellett. Is your husband in?" Of course, I knew very well that he could not be home yet. "Do you know where I could find him? . . . Okay, thanks."

She thought he was at the university. I hung up and returned to my apartment. Why had Jesperson been downtown? Except for a few cafés and bars and the Hub department store, everything would be closed now. He'd seemed agitated, nothing worse. But: might he be mentally unwell? I'd never observed even a hint of instability in Jesperson. I'd seen him every so often since graduating and landing a teaching job in the same town, and he seemed to go on from month to month unchanged. I knew that a secret element remained to his work, which was funded by the Department of Defense— originally the Department of War, of course.

I walked out onto the landing. Above the town lights, the sky was dark, the constellations spread out and easy to identify in that clear atmosphere. I felt a warm breeze. The radio continued to play quietly. From somewhere below me I caught the smells of a cigarette and a family's dinner of fried food. I settled into the chair again and thought things over.

117

I knew that Jesperson had gained brief notoriety researching hitherto-unidentified properties of solar radiation. He had come to State University from a government installation in Brooklyn when coal deposits fifty miles away had been found to bear evidence of possible solar abnormalities hundreds of thousands of years old. How that might tie in with military work, and then some ongoing national security angle, I didn't know. I used to joke about it with fellow students at the university, how the Reds were probably snooping around, etc. The fourteen men who worked under Jesperson lived in town, and two of them did some science lecturing. Eight of the men were married, and there were eleven kids among the families. All these people seemed ordinary. When asked about why the hush-hush stuff, the men would say something like this: "I think it's just left over from the war. When we get our new contracts each year, they have the same security oath as they used to. They could just as well take it out, far as I'm concerned, but" (shrug) "it's their call."

I puzzled over the incident that afternoon—Jesperson asking me to listen for something in the lab. Maybe he had already tried it on one of the lab men and he, like me, hadn't heard anything. Or maybe Jesperson thought the sound was something his colleagues would be used to but I wouldn't. I really didn't know anything yet. I told myself that if Jesperson tried to involve me further, I'd insist on an explanation.

With that settled in my mind, I slouched back in my chair, linked fingers across my stomach, and gazed at the cozy lights of the town below me and the unimaginably distant lights in the sky. I thought: I should take my telescope out of its box and set it up on the landing. Once again I became drowsy. Somebody began honking a car horn close by below. Irritated, I stood and lifted the chair to take it inside. Turning my head towards the interior of the apartment building, my sight swept across trees, elevators, lights, water tower. My eyes flicked back to the tower. Had there been another movement there? I didn't see anything now.

Knocking again woke me. The room was dark.

"Mr. Kellett? Are you awake? Mr. Kellett?"

"Yeah—yes, I'm awake. What is it, Mrs. Friend?"

"Telephone call for you—Dr. Jesperson. He seems upset."

"Okay. Be right there." I wrapped myself in a bathrobe and once again followed her downstairs.

Mrs. Friend, wearing a robe of her own, disappeared into her kitchen and shut the door. I picked up the phone. "Sir, what is it? It must be the middle of the night—"

"Kellett, listen, you have to get out of town—right away. You'll come with me and Margaret."

"What are you talking about?"

"You have to trust me. You have to go, now. Tell your landlady there's a family emergency."

"Look, sir, I'm not going anywhere, and I think you should talk to someone about these—weird panics or whatever it is. I'm sure I can't help."

"I'm asking you to trust me once more, Paul. I promise I can justify this."

"When?"

"I'm going to come by your place in a few minutes. I don't like taking the time; if only you had a car. Anyway, get a few things together and we'll be there right away." He hung up.

I looked up his number again, not remembering it from however long—a couple of hours?—it had been since I'd used it to call his wife. There was no answer.

I had no doubt the Jespersons would arrive in a few moments. I could stand outside and demand an explanation and get everyone in the building in an uproar, or I could hop in and ride a ways with them, then demand the explanation. It wouldn't take long, and I could walk back if I had to. Either Jesperson would explain, somehow, quickly, or I would bail out—and perhaps place a call, for Jesperson's own good, to a counselor at the university in the morning.

I trudged upstairs and, momentarily giving Jesperson the benefit of the doubt, put a few things in a valise, then returned to the ground floor. Soon headlights flashed into the dark room. "Mrs. Friend?" I called quietly. "Dr. Jesperson's picking me up. He has something urgent on his hands. I might be gone for—for a night." I didn't know if she heard me or even if she were nearby.

I stepped onto the porch. The air had grown chilly. Jesperson had drawn up to the curb but kept the engine running. I couldn't see his wife, in the passenger seat, as much more than an outline. I climbed into the back seat and plumped the valise down next to me. The Ford pulled away and we moved down the street. I looked at the backs of Jesperson's and his wife's heads. "Okay, sir. What's this all about?"

No response. We slipped past a stop sign without slowing down.

"Please. What's up!"

Still nothing. I looked more closely, and a chill pain shot through me. The sides of their faces were blank. There were no ears and, so far as I could see, no faces. Involuntarily I cried out.

I grabbed for the door handle, desperate to escape. The car had to slow down when, as we reached an intersection, a truck passed in front of us on the frontage road. I yanked the car door open and lunged out. I took off into the darkness at a stumbling run, crossing the frontage road and then the throughway, where, at that hour, there wasn't much traffic. I had forgotten the valise.

A long, low factory building sat behind a chain-link fence, bathed in the glare of tall lights. I ran for it and fell into a fetid ditch, pulled myself out and climbed. I dropped to the other side. Not looking back, I ran for a small building, a detached office or shed, from the windows of which light shone. I pounded on the door. "Hey! Hey! Is someone there!"

The door opened and a security guard-type studied me. His hand was on the butt of a pistol at his hip. "You're on private property, mac. It's posted. I'm in my rights if I give you a beating."

"Listen—some people tried to kidnap me. They might have seen me running here. I escaped from their car."

His shrewd eyes looked me over, taking in my disheveled appearance, my dirty, dripping trousers.

"Okay, sit down," he said and indicated a chair and shut the door behind me, locking it. He turned out the light and, standing well back, peered through the one window. "I don't see any—" He paused. "No, there's a car pulling up beyond the fence, down by the gate . . . your friends maybe? You just sit still and let's see what they do."

I became aware of my own breathing and the other man's, and the sound of a wind-up clock ticking. It seemed to take a long time for my pulse to slow down to normal.

After a while he said, "Name's Howie Sacker. I'm the other night guy. Bob Clary's in the building. Your name?"

I told him. I said I'd entered the car thinking that it was a friend behind the wheel. I was pretty sure it was, in fact, the friend's car.

"This is a funny place for a teacher to be at one in the morning—They're sitting out there with the lights shining through the fence at us. I don't think anybody's gotten out yet. So why'd they want to kidnap you? Do you have a relative with deep pockets—something like that?"

"I don't know why anyone would try this."

"Not some students of yours out on a prank?"

"No, it's nothing like that."

Sacker lit a cigarette, offered me one. The orange point of his cigarette in the darkness was somehow reassuring. Every twenty seconds or so he took another look out the window. "They're turning," he said after a while. "Driving away. They could come back, so let's sit tight for a bit." He offered me coffee from a Thermos bottle.

"Kellett, one of my buddies here at the plant, his kid was in your class last year. No names, but he said you were a good guy. His kid has straightened up, and enough so that people really notice. Maybe you know who I mean. Anyway, thought you should know there are folks who appreciate what you're doing over there."

"Thanks. I think . . . I guess it's safe for me to walk home now. We must be about fifteen blocks from Catalina Street?"

"That's right, but I don't want you out there if them guys could be keeping an eye on this place. You're welcome to stick around till sunup, if it suits you." He gestured to a sliding door behind him. "There's a toilet, so you don't need to leave even for that. I'd say let's play a game of cards, but I think we'll keep it dark here for now. Hmm, no sign of anybody out there, just trucks going by on the throughway like always. I used to drive truck when I lived in Minneapolis. You get to where you can't sit that long, back hurting, I have to be able to get up and move around. . . ."

The intervals between his glances outside became longer. Occasionally I got up and looked out as well, but I felt drained. All the while that Sacker talked, I was going over what had happened. Had the heads of my abductors really been featureless? Or had they been wearing some kind of a helmet? What had they wanted with me, and what were they doing in Jesperson's car? Was he safe?

"Can I use your phone?"

"Sure, go ahead."

This time I remembered Jesperson's number. There was no reply.

"I'm going to call the police," I said.

"Figured you would, if your story was on the up and up," Sacker said. He gave me the number from memory.

Not surprisingly, the cops thought my story justified a ride to the police station rather than just a conversation over the phone. They appeared before long at the gate, where the lights of Jesperson's Ford had shined earlier. Sacker and I walked slowly over and he unlocked the gate. We shook hands. He gave me a keen look. "My advice, Kellett, get a gun." Then he closed the gate behind me and strode back to his hut.

The cops offered to drop me off on their way to Jesperson's house, but I said I'd like to come along and would keep out of their way. One of the two officers, Hank Mander, said, "Good. Good, that's best."

We rolled through the silent streets. Sitting in the back, listening to the occasional remarks of the cops, I felt a surprising and childish sense of calm, being protected this way by armed law enforcement officers as I recovered from the tension of the past two hours. Soon, though, I felt somewhat guilty for my insulated attitude. Jesperson's place was likely going to be a crime scene, and I had been thinking mostly of myself. I wasn't sure that I indeed had been in *his* car, but I'd thought so at the time, and the car must, then, have been taken without his consent.

"All right, here we are. Stay in the car, Kellett. Stay—till we tell you to get out, you hear?"

One officer, Dan, walked directly to the front door. The other disappeared in the darkness at the side of the house. There was no response to the knocking. I thought the officer tried the door. But soon he turned and moved off from the stoop. I saw the door open behind him and Jesperson appeared. They conferred for a few moments and then the officer beckoned to me.

"Kellett. What's this all about?" Jesperson asked.

122

"I hoped you could tell us, sir."

"This officer says you claim to have been kidnapped by people driving my car."

"Yes—just after you called me to say you and Margaret were coming to pick me up."

"I made no such call, Kellett. Evidently someone has been impersonating me."

"Dr. Jesperson, you need to tell me what's going on. You drag me out to the lab at lunchtime, you call me up to look at the water tower—"

"That correct, sir?" the cop asked.

"Yes, it is— Won't you gentlemen come inside?"

"We sure will, let me find Hank. But everything's okay in here? Your wife all right?"

"Yes, Margaret went to bed quite early."

Jesperson turned on a couple of table lamps and I sat down on a sofa. Soon the two officers joined us.

"All I can do is tell what I know," Jesperson said. "Paul, I wanted to check my perceptions. I have seen and heard things recently that I wanted to verify, but I didn't want to ask my colleagues. If I were mistaken, that fact might compromise my ability to participate in research, let alone coordinate it. It might, in truth, mean the end of my career. But if I were hearing and seeing authentically unusual phenomena, I could determine whether they were significant. Well, yes: if they were real, then they were significant, there's really no doubt of that."

"Don't talk to yourself, Professor," Dan said. "Tell us what you heard and saw and what you thought might be going on."

Mrs. Jesperson silently entered the room. Jesperson glanced up at her and then away.

"Pardon the intrusion, Mrs. Jesperson," Hank said. Her eyes focused on him and she came nearer. "Go ahead, Professor," Hank said.

Suddenly she lunged for Hank's gun and tried to twist it loose. The two of them scuffled, Jesperson shouted hoarsely, and the other officer wrenched the woman away. For a moment she stood at bay, panting, a plain woman of advanced middle age in a faded pink wrapper, her face unreadable. Then, horribly, she began to wail and pluck at her clothes, her hair, and, reaching out, even my sleeve—I jerked back as if from something vile, repugnant. Dan seized her arms and put her in handcuffs.

"Surely, surely there's no need—" Jesperson began. "You can see she's terribly frightened already!"

"Look, Professor, she tried to take an officer's firearm—that's a serious offense," Hank said. "And there's the danger she might harm herself." Margaret Jesperson wasn't saying anything now, just shaking her head violently back and forth.

"She's seen things too," Jesperson said, with the air of someone making a confession. "You must allow for the strain we've been under, the two of us."

At that moment, Margaret's fit subsided into quiet sobs. As Dan held her, Hank took Jesperson by the arm and pulled him roughly away to a corner of the room where they spoke in undertones for some minutes. When the two men had finished talking, Jesperson, distractedly, muttered apologies to the officers and to me. Dan uncuffed Margaret, and Hank and Jesperson helped the distraught woman upstairs to the bedroom.

Dan and I sat on the sofa for a while, waiting, hearing an upstairs door open and, moments later, close. Then came the muffled sounds, again, of Hank and Jesperson talking. Twice Dan got up from the sofa to pace around the room, looking out the windows.

Once he asked, "Are you following the football this year?"

"Sorry, I'm not." I shook my head.

Dan shrugged. "You aren't missing much, believe me. It's gonna be one rough season for us."

In time, the other two men returned. Dan and I stood to meet them.

Hank looked from his partner to Jesperson and said, "If you're sure she'll be okay"—Jesperson nodded—"we'll take another look around outside, and drive through the neighborhood. Then we'll make a report and check back here in a couple hours, before our shift ends tonight." Hank turned to me. "Can we drop you someplace, Mr. Kellett?"

I looked at Jesperson's pained, weary face. "I'd like to keep you company awhile, Professor," I said. "If that's all right."

Jesperson nodded, and the officers left the house. We watched out the windows as, twice, they circled the house and then returned to their cruiser and drove away.

"I feel I have to apologize again for involving you in all this, Paul," Jesperson said finally. "I didn't know what to do. You've trusted me, taken a lot on faith and . . . and I know that can't have come easy."

"Professor," I said, "I want to help—I do. But I need some explanation. Tell me something. Tell me what you can."

"Ah, oh . . . well. Where to start?" Jesperson went to an armchair and sat, and I resumed my place on the sofa. "Really, it began in October, 1941. Two months before Pearl Harbor, a collection of extraordinary objects—glowing, purple objects—appeared beside a small stream in Allegheny County, Pennsylvania—fifteen miles outside Pittsburgh. There were ten of them and each hovered, stationary, about three feet above the ground. In size they ranged from that of a golf ball to that of a standard house door."

Jesperson paused and simply stared at me for a few moments. I said nothing, silently giving him permission to continue.

"In shape, a few of the objects were spherical. Others were very odd. Like pulled taffy. A look into the history of the location, this nondescript and undeveloped plot of ground beside a Pennsylvania stream, turned up exactly nothing. No previous unusual activity, no 'paranormal' incidents or dime-novel intrigue—no flying discs or Indian burial grounds. During those first weeks the federal government sealed off the area from the public, built a small compound on the site, and brought in scores of top scientists."

Jesperson stood up suddenly. "Do you want coffee?" he said, and I shook my head. He took a couple of steps toward the other end of the room, looking up at the ceiling, evidently thinking of his wife. Then he returned to his chair.

"This story, I'm sure it seems incredible to you," he said, eyes suddenly clouded with enigma and distance. "It was certainly that way with me, in the beginning."

"It's all right, Professor," I said. "I'm listening."

He looked for a moment at the front window, but his eyes turned back to me. "The objects came to be known as the Allegheny Group. What early analysis yielded is, essentially, what we

125

know about the Group now. The objects will melt, burn, or convert to steam anything that touches them, anything at all. Any beam or ray projected at them—be it light, sound, or what-have-you—passes through with mild disruption. To our techniques of measuring and testing, their existence appears vague, variable. Unstable. However, a quite simple method was found for transporting the objects: one only need move the small plot of soil beneath each object, and it will follow. An experiment was made with dispersing the soil from under one of the objects, with the result that about twenty-four hours later the object forever disappeared, just suddenly blinked out of existence. This was the only one of the objects ever to be lost. That is, until more recently."

Jesperson had begun absentmindedly to rub the center of his chest with the thumb of his right hand. Now he took note of this, regarding the hand, and then he looked outside again.

"Come into the kitchen," he said. "If you don't want coffee, I do."

"The windows bother you, don't they?" I said.

"So you've noticed. Yes. I think we can safely leave them for a few minutes."

In the kitchen, he started the coffee brewing and we sat on metal chairs at the narrow breakfast table. Jesperson had left open the door leading out of the kitchen.

"I hardly know how to continue," he said. "There is now so much research history with the Allegheny Group. But as for progress . . . almost nothing."

"So this is your quasi-military operation?" I said. "How did you get involved?"

"Yes, of course—you want my own story," he said. "One or two other matters, though, before we get to that. So. It wasn't long before the Allegheny Group was moved several hundred miles away to a government research facility. And almost a year later, Group II appeared in the same Pittsburgh location. Only this time it was just two spheres, both somewhat smaller than softballs. At four and then seven months following this, single objects—Satellites I and II—appeared. As the years passed, enthusiasm over the objects has dwindled, being that they so stubbornly resist our testing. Recently there has been talk of declassifying the phenomena. This will never happen, though. The specifics of the Allegheny Group are unique, but federal attention to the paranormal is not. And the government is not about to open even a single box in that collection of secrets."

The coffee ready now, Jesperson filled one mug and then, when I accepted it, a second one.

"Now, Kellett, I'm trusting you with a lot here. You trusted me, and it must run both ways. Just keep in mind the sensitivity of this information. Please." He looked almost sheepish, delivering this admonition. "What did change, a couple of years ago, was the classification of some of the objects. Group II and the satellites. They are now being loaned out around the country, short term, to research departments headed by individuals with the proper clearance. For the past five—almost six—months, the Allegheny Group II has been in the care of Rangell Lab under the guardianship of Dr. Sievers and myself."

Without warning my arms went strangely weak, and my hands shook a moment. Immediately suspicion took hold of me. For the first time since my abduction a few hours ago in the professor's car, I wondered how much of the situation might only be Jesperson's mad fantasy. But I *had been* abducted. I had seen those men, those things.

To cover how shaken I was, I cleared my throat and, after a false start, managed to say, "I don't mean to be rude, to doubt you. . . . But, Professor, I do not believe in the paranormal."

A loud knocking came from the direction of the front room, and I all but jumped in my seat. Coffee sloshed from my mug to the tabletop. Jesperson grabbed up something from the table, the salt or pepper shaker, I couldn't tell which. He stood and left the table, and I followed. As we passed through the kitchen, he hesitated, seemed to reconsider something, and set the shaker on a countertop before leading me from the room.

We reached the front door and, after peering through the window to one side, Jesperson opened it. Outside stood Officers Hank and Dan. They stepped just inside the door. Jesperson did not invite them further in and made it clear the door should remain open.

"We saw a couple of suspicious characters down the road a ways," Hank said. "We watched awhile but lost track of them and decided we'd better head back here."

"Yeah, we saw a couple of . . . ," Dan said and quickly trailed off into silence.

"Why don't the three of you wait just outside for a moment," Jesperson said. "I should do one thing, then we can continue this without waking Margaret."

So we stepped out, and moments later Jesperson joined us, locking the door behind him and carrying a broom in one hand and a smaller object in the other, a boxy red-and-white container smaller than his fist. A white cylinder as long as a toothbrush was tucked into the breast pocket of his shirt. He gave the broom to me and said simply, "Hold this a minute."

Jesperson began speaking quietly, and we all stood very near him.

"These people you saw," he said to the officers, "I assume they were men? Can you describe them?"

"Sorry," Hank said. "Umm, they were in the shadows—very dark. Very."

"Really sorry," Dan said. In the moonlight his features had gone slack, perhaps with exasperation.

Jesperson nodded and then addressed me, pointedly ignoring the other men, his eyes nearly hidden in the shadow of his brows.

"Kellett," he said, "there are at least two elements of all this that I haven't yet addressed. The more particular one, regarding my current situation, must wait a little longer. The other, though, is the general issue concerning my theoretical approach to Group II." He fiddled with the container in his hand, slowly turning it over and over between fingers and palm. "I had read everything—that is, everything available to my security level—regarding Allegheny. And I visited Group I on more than a dozen occasions. Then Dr. Sievers . . . she and I—"

"She?" I said.

"Ah, that's right. I forget how few people here have met her. An absolute recluse, you understand. Yes, Dr. Sievers is a woman. One of the brains—one of the geniuses—who came to prominence during the Second World War."

"She didn't . . . She didn't work on the bomb?"

Jesperson's mouth twisted upward at the ends, and he actually chuckled. It was the first expression of mirth I'd seen from him since all this began. He looked briefly at the officers, as if inviting them to share the joke. But they remained unmoved. In fact, they seemed only to be half-present, enduring Jesperson's talk with the non-expressive faces of bored students.

"I apologize," Jesperson said. "It's not a stupid question. It's only that, knowing Sievers—well, picturing her at Los Alamos is somewhat amusing. No, she was party to projects even more sensitive. More sensitive and, if they'd become generally known, more controversial.

"Anyhow, she and I submitted a report, a theoretical paper, really, arguing certain notions from the philosophy of science, with the Allegheny Group as our point of focus. In essence, the thrust of our argument was this: the scientific community must accept that the human creature has certain intrinsic limitations—hard boundaries both perceptual and conceptual, of the senses and the brain. Thus, it seems only reasonable that phenomena exist which we are unable to 'crack.' In other words, what proof have we that this sparse collection of five senses and a three-pound brain are enough to unlock every secret in the universe? And this rationale holds, even given the augmentation of our senses through technology and the networking of minds in a planetary population numbering in the billions. Indeed, when you consider our race's modest resources and the *sheer magnitude* of what lies beyond them, you must conclude that some mysteries will lie forever beyond us. Isn't it arbitrary and arrogant to insist that everything can be ground up by *our* senses and digested by *our* minds? Of course it is—ludicrous!"

The two officers remained silent, but shifted restlessly on their feet.

Jesperson opened the container he held, turned it over, and emptied a dark powder from it into the paper cylinder he'd carried in his shirt pocket. I could see now that the powder came from a kitchen spice tin. He leaned close to me and whispered, "Quick! Close your eyes, and cover your nose and mouth."

I did as he said, still holding the broom but raising my free hand to my face. There was a puffing sound, followed by the sounds of sneezing—some of it violent and hardly human. The broom was jerked from my hand, and now came thumping sounds.

I opened my eyes and dropped my hand from my face. With my first breath, I felt a burning in my nose. I began sneezing. Jesperson held the broom and was beating the officers with it, knocking both to the ground. He and the men below him, all, were sneezing. But Hank and Dan made great hacking sounds as they sneezed, and they rubbed vigorously at their faces with their hands. After watching for a few seconds I saw—and a shudder ran from my scalp down my spine—that as the two men rubbed their noses and eyes, their features blurred, were pushed about and distorted as if their faces were made of putty.

"Stop!" I shouted, then flailed out and grabbed hold of the broom handle. Lacking a clear course of action, I released the broom and stared into the professor's face, his eyes watering heavily. "Professor, what are you doing to them?"

He backed away from the two men, broom still in one hand, coughing. The two men on the ground twitched and continued rubbing at their faces, making no sound but the sneezing and no attempt to rise from their prone positions.

"These aren't people, Kellett," Jesperson said. "In fact, I'm almost certain they aren't alive."

"How can you say that?" I was beside myself, hugging my arms to my chest, all but ready to run off and leave the bizarre scene behind me.

"That was ordinary cayenne pepper I blew into the air," Jesperson said. He stepped to the side, using his foot to point out the paper tube now lying in the grass. "These creatures, whatever they are—I've learned that extreme physical sensations discombobulate them in a most dramatic manner, as you can see. Margaret was, er, confronted by one earlier. Her screaming had a similar effect. I'm coming to believe, actually, that they aren't any particular danger to us. A good kick or a blow, alone, would likely stop them cold. But they are undoubtedly disconcerting, if not to say an annoyance."

Hank and Dan continued to twitch on the lawn, their legs kicking out weakly and hands alternately rubbing at their warped faces and pushing at the grass below them. The horrible sneezing had begun to taper off. Still, they made no concerted effort to stand and seemed utterly confounded and unable to regain their bearings.

"They are human," I said. "How could they be anything else?"

"Hold this another minute," Jesperson said, and he handed the broom back.

He disappeared around the side of his house and shortly returned carrying both a running garden house and an unattached sprinkler head. He used the water on his hands, and then bent forward and ran it over his face.

"How are your eyes?" he said to me. "Are they burning?"

"No, they stung a moment. But I seem to have missed most of it."

From a pocket Jesperson pulled a handkerchief, which he dabbed at his eyes. Then he attached the sprinkler head and dropped it between the two men. Water bloomed upward from the sprinkler and fell on Hank and Dan. Suddenly the two went still, and somehow they began, ever so slightly, to alter.

"What is it?" I said. "What's happening now?" But I could see for myself. Their bodies were softening under the water, changing very slowly, like objects made of ice or sand. "It isn't possible."

"Of course it is, you're seeing it," Jesperson said. "And you noticed, didn't you, that they both are short one finger on each hand?"

I looked. It was true.

"I'm not killing them, Kellett. We don't know what they are, but they aren't like you or me. They intruded, we didn't want them, and now we're rid of them. Simple as that."

"But they spoke . . . They—"

"I know. Think of them as second-rate simulacra. As animated sculptures, psychokinetic modeling clay."

"You believe they're something like that?"

"I have very few data to go on. But it's a helpful notion, a placeholder in the chain of reason, if you will. A provisional idea."

Two minutes later we were sitting in the police cruiser, led there by Jesperson's curiosity. He started the car up and made a small, satisfied sound in his throat. "This, at least, couldn't be more *real*," he said.

We sat in the front seat of the cruiser, watching as the two bodies in the lawn lost their physical integrity all together, softened like cake turning to mush under the sprinkler water.

"If it helps," Jesperson said. "I'm almost sure you were brought here tonight by two real police officers. I could be wrong, but I think Hank and Dan do exist. Those two, out there, came later and were sent by . . . well, by heaven knows what." Then he groaned.

"Ugk, that coffee—my stomach. And the adrenaline. I should know better than to have coffee so late."

We stayed in the cruiser a long while, and there Jesperson told me the rest of his story, in great detail. He told me that Dr. Sievers had left for a conference four days before, due to return at the end of the week. Jesperson said that he was the only person with access to the lab while Sievers was away, and that, on the night after she left, he had spent a long evening alone with the two Allegheny objects in Rangell Lab. After several hours trying to muster some new approach to them, he did something quite strange, almost childlike, something that never would have occurred to him if a single other person had been present. He lay down on his back, between one of the objects and the eight-foot by eight-foot plot of contained Pennsylvania soil beneath. For a very long time he remained there, entranced by the object's purple glow as it floated above. He watched it with the calm reverence of a stargazer. And then, without meaning to, he fell fast asleep.

His sleep had been troubled, and he woke to an intense pain in, he thought, his heart. He opened his eyes and saw that the object above him had gone. In a panic, he lunged upward. But the pain doubled, and he vomited onto the soil beside him. His chest was warm, so he touched it and found that the very center of his shirt had burned away, and the hair on his chest as well.

"Had the sphere, somehow, entered me?" Still we sat there, Jesperson leaning forward with his hands crossed atop the cruiser's steering wheel. "That seemed the most likely conclusion, but I did not want to accept it."

Sitting up in the lab, still alone, he soon had realized there was a burbling, water-over-stones sound in the air. Finally he stood. But, try as he might, he could not determine the source of the sound. In the days to come, he would hear the sound again, often, and in different locations. He wondered, naturally, if the Allegheny objects hadn't in some way absorbed this sound from the stream bank where they first appeared. But why had no one at the lab heard it before?

"As I've said, we may have to accept that the Allegheny objects are unexplainable, are phenomena we cannot master," Jesperson said. "If anything, they may master us. It was at this point that I came truly to feel the validity of my ideas. As human beings, Kellett, we are in a sealed, impenetrable box, and that box is our physical and mental limitations. While we may be able, with much labor, to map out the interior of the box, we will never get beyond it. This was the challenge that Sievers and I took on. Instead of mounting another aggressive assault on the objects themselves, we hoped to use them to learn about humanity's limits. Could we discover, like a marathon runner who knows intimately both his abilities and his constraints, exactly how far we could 'run' at the objects before further inquiry became meaningless?"

"And has it worked?" I said.

"We have made . . . very modest progress," he said. "Very little progress, in fact. As I expected." He grinned ruefully. "It's a new approach, a new field of inquiry. It'll take time, and much work. At this stage it appears quite abstract, I admit. And not many people can see the value of it yet."

"It seems, I don't know—" I said and struggled to find words. "It seems almost heretical to the spirit of science to give up trying to find a definitive explanation."

Jesperson tilted his head slightly to one side and then to the other, seeming to weigh the validity of what I'd said.

"It's not that I propose giving up on an explanation, exactly," he said. "If something can be learned, and put to use, then I'm all for it. If only you could read the hundreds upon hundreds of theories that have been floated to account for Allegheny! Human beings have a distinct talent for theory. But I'm mainly interested in two goals: identification and adaptation. Often times, anything more is mere smoke. Do you know what Mark Twain said of science? 'One gets such wholesale returns of conjecture out of such a trifling investment of fact.' I used to have that posted on my office door."

Jesperson was silent awhile. It seemed like we spent half the night sitting there, in the cruiser, watching the weird pool of water forming in his yard and draining into the gutter, and listening to the night sounds, traffic out on the throughway, breezes in the trees, a house-door closing way off somewhere in the darkness.

When he spoke again, somehow he convinced me we should take a ride in the cruiser. There was an important errand he needed to run, and he didn't want to pull his car out of the garage and risk waking Margaret, though she had taken sleeping pills when he and

Hank had helped her to bed earlier. Jesperson got out of the car, turned off the sprinkler and checked that the front door was locked.

"You drive," he said when he'd returned to the car.

"I can't . . . no," I said. "I'm not driving a police car. Professor, you're going to get me into serious trouble."

But he talked me into it. He was exhausted, his face haggard and suddenly old. Yet he talked of tonight being a night of "exceptions," of free passes and of the universe "turning a blind eye," a Twelfth Night. I have no other explanation: he mesmerized me. And I took the driver's seat.

"What about Margaret?" I said.

"She won't wake till morning. I've encountered these . . . simulacra four times now, and I've never seen them appear at the same place twice in a day. Anyway, I have to take the chance, now, that she'll be safer with me away."

Jesperson wouldn't say where we were going, but gave me directions as we went.

Then he asked, "Speaking of theories, Kellett, what about you? Can you imagine a scenario to account for the phenomena I've described to you tonight?"

I was silent for a time but found that, indeed, I did have a theory, something that had taken shape in the back of my mind as I listened to him.

"It doesn't have to be sensible," Jesperson said. "Just the first thing that comes to mind."

"Well, yes," I said. "I've been thinking of the idea of Ultimate Reality, found in Plato's metaphor of the cave and his metaphor of the sun, and found also in many world religions. If there is such a thing as Ultimate Reality—a realm of archetype and permanence, of which ours is only a copy, an approximation—then the Allegheny objects may belong to that realm. Or, if there are more than one 'shadow world,' like ours, these worlds may surround the Real in layers. And perhaps the Allegheny objects have, for some reason, penetrated from a dimension *closer* to the Real. Assuming all of that, we might also speculate that there's a realm further distant, in its orbit, than ours is from the Real. It could be that this is where these creatures, these simulacra, come from. Leaking into our reality from a place where everything, to our eyes, is half-formed and shadowy."

A clap sounded in the car, startling me. Jesperson had actually clapped his hands in delight. He looked at me with great interest.

"Wonderful, Kellett," he said. "Wonderful. Your theory, in fact, has one or two points in common with my own. Though mine relies not on Plato but on Einstein on one hand and Polanyi on the other. I won't inflict the theory on you now, however. Still: I hope you see my point—we do have a talent for theory. Speculation is a creative act, not always strictly deductive or rational. We fill in the blanks with what comes to hand. Just be careful never to put your full weight on a plank of theory."

It was the dead of night, and ours was the only vehicle on the road. I knew the town well and recognized, as we went, each of the streets which Jesperson pointed out to me.

"We're headed for the water tower, aren't we, Professor?" I said. We were only a couple of blocks away now.

"Yes, we are. And considering what you may see here, I want you to know there are different, well, grades or classes of simulacra that have appeared over the past few days. Some are more convincing and more resilient than others. One, in particular, was—ah, deeply upsetting. So whatever you do see at the tower, don't let it get the upper hand. Keep safe. Do what you must, Paul, to make your way back, unharmed, to your regular life."

His voice became insistent, pleading. "Promise me you won't interfere," he said, "that you won't risk yourself."

I nodded. Me risk myself? Not likely. A moment later we rolled to a stop below the water tower. I parked the cruiser and turned it off.

"He's here," Jesperson said.

Without question, a figure now stood on the platform above the ladder leading up the side of the tower.

"On that first morning—was it just three days ago?—I came here," Jesperson said. "I'd left the lab, putting on a coat to cover my burned, ruined shirt, and I walked aimlessly for probably an hour. I ended up here and realized that for a long time I'd been half-consciously following that sound, the burbling sound. Can you hear it?"

I listened. Both of us had our side windows down, and I could hear it. A faint sound like a running stream.

135

"I walked to the foot of the ladder then and, not knowing why, started to climb," he said. "I went up only a few steps, then looked up and saw *him* above, at the very top. He started to descend, and I hurried back to the ground and left. Since then, I've caught glimpses of him up there. He's waiting for something."

The figure on the tower was far enough away and so well hidden in shadow that I could make out nothing, except that it appeared to be an adult man. And just at that moment, when Jesperson finished speaking, the figure began making his way down the ladder. He moved methodically, in no great hurry.

I heard Jesperson's door click open, and suddenly he was outside. I got out as well.

"Stay here, Kellett," Jesperson said. He came to me and clapped me on the shoulder, then backed away. "Or leave. Just don't follow me."

"Is . . . is this the one—the simulacrum you found more convincing than the others?"

"No. I've never been close enough to him." Now he turned away from me and began to walk fast. "That other," he said over his shoulder as he left, "was Margaret. Or not-Margaret. It's all become . . . so . . . strange now."

Immediately I was pulled back towards panic, that sense that none of this could be true, that it must all be of Jesperson's own making.

He reached the foot of the ladder just as the other figure came to the ground. I'd taken a few steps toward them but soon stopped. There were two Jespersons before me now, identical, at least at this distance. The hair, the faces, the clothes, the postures—every detail was there, in duplicate.

They stood apart a few moments, then moved closer. The second one, the simulacrum, reached out and embraced Jesperson, pining Jesperson's arms to his torso. They struggled a moment before going still. The babbling sound had grown louder and louder, and, as before, it was impossible to guess its source.

My breath was coming fast now, and in near-unbearable horror I saw Jesperson's back begin to glow, with something bulging out between the two arms enfolding it. A small, purple-blue sphere emerged slowly from the professor's back like a pebble being pressed through cellophane. When it was free of his body, the sphere dropped slightly, then rested, motionless, a few feet above the ground. The simulacrum released Jesperson. He slumped, as if dead, to the earth.

Then the simulacrum looked in my direction and slowly lifted a hand to shoulder height, as if in uncertain greeting. The sound, the rushing noise of water, seemed to be everywhere now, coming down from the stars, coming from the throughway, coming out of the ground.

I turned from the tower and gave in to the impulse that had been my companion for much of the night, the impulse to flee. I paused at the cruiser, leaned inside, and with a trembling hand flicked on the switch to activate the rooftop lights, the flashing red and blue. Then I ran, ran till I was home.

After I'd closed my door and locked it, I sat on the floor in the darkest corner of my bedroom, hugging my knees. I fell asleep there after a while and woke up terribly cramped before dawn. After sunrise, I used Mrs. Friend's telephone to call the school office and feign that I was ill. Like an animal fled to its burrow, I refused to leave my home all that day. Panic, imagination, and guilt, together, trapped me. Though Jesperson had told me not to interfere, the truth was that I'd abandoned him. I knew now that I, at bottom, was a coward. It was a revelation that would take getting used to.

However, by nightfall I'd faced down the panic. I crept down my exterior staircase and walked cautiously to the Rexall Drug, where I bought cough syrup I didn't need and an evening newspaper. The paper had nothing about Rangell Lab or Jesperson and only a two-paragraph item about a stolen police cruiser discovered, empty, at the water tower with its lights flashing.

The next day I returned to school. The routine of a day spent teaching kept me afloat, prevented me sinking into the sorry state of the day before. Still, I was far from my usual self that day. During a composition period, a potential disciplinary issue arose—one of our routine problems, young men at the back of the class talking dirty and making obscene gestures which only they think clever. Apathetically, I ignored it.

After leaving the school grounds that afternoon, I again stopped into Berglund's Hardware. Two days earlier I'd come to replace a bent cabinet hinge, but I had failed to notice that the companion hinge, too, was about to fail.

Approaching the cash register, I caught sight, out one of the store windows, of a familiar car.

I left my errand unfulfilled and hurried out, catching up to Jesperson's Ford at the corner. He was behind the wheel, alone.

"Professor!" I shouted, running to the car and rapping at the passenger-side window.

I backed away, and he pulled to the curb. Jesperson leaned into the seat beside him and rolled the window down.

"Good afternoon, Kellett," he said. "You gave me a start, son."

"But you're . . . you're all right?" I said. "Nothing came of it, then? The other night?"

I found myself counting the fingers on Jesperson's hands and feeling foolish.

"Kellett," he said, "do you know—you're white as a sheet! What's the trouble? What's worrying you?"

"Do you have some time, now, sir? To talk?"

So he got out and we went into a dim and smoky diner, quiet in the pre-supper hour. Talking with Jesperson there, it quickly became evident that he understood nothing of my references to our bizarre adventures, and soon he said as much. When I'd accepted that he knew none of it, I tried both to explain and to be tactful, even cryptic. But he wanted nothing except the full story, and after a difficult, circuitous hour he learned all I could tell him. When I'd finished—completing the story with the incident of my cowardice, my shame—Jesperson called to our waitress for more coffee. Finally, he began to talk.

"Kellett," he said, "there's only so much I can say, and I hope you'll understand. At one time there was an especially sensitive government project that visited Rangell Lab, but that came to an end almost two years ago. What you described, well, it resonates. There are similarities . . . more parallels, actually, to things that occurred then. To a sort of accident we had. But nothing so fantastic, of course. And, as I say, there's much I'm forbidden to speak about. Yes, despite all your questions, you have to leave it at that. I wish I could help you somehow. At most, I can say this: I feel as though we shared something like a linked dream, you and I."

"What"—I faltered a moment—"what do you remember of the past few days?"

"Me?" he said. "I had a very uneventful week. Margaret was out of town, returning yesterday from an enjoyable time with family. I had great plans for the week but came down with an awful flu the day after she left. I spent several days in bed, taking medicine and getting a quantity of sleep that I rarely enjoy in an entire month."

"And Dr. Sievers?"

"Ah, yes." He looked at me with a suspicious but amused narrowing of eyes. "I can't imagine that it ever came up—is it possible that sometime I mentioned to you that 'Sievers' was Margaret's maiden name?" I shook my head. "She has no scientific background, you know. And I haven't worked with, or even met, a Dr. Sievers. Ever."

"That other Professor Jesperson—both of them—they must *both* have been . . . simulacra? And his whole story . . . ? Was it nothing more than pixie dust?"

Jesperson spread his hands wide in a gesture of helplessness, of surrender.

I took a few sips from my coffee, then said, "I don't know what to do with all of this, Professor."

"What do you do . . . with a troubling dream?"

"Forget it, in time. I suppose. But I can never forget this."

"Go on with your life, regardless."

"It might not be so hard if I hadn't run like that, at the end. It's the act of cowardice that sticks with me."

"But, to some degree, we're all cowards in the face of the unknown," he said with a smiling look of unconcern. "Think of your students. All the cheating, the classroom hijinks. Isn't it all a reaction against the unknown, against the burden of their own potential—or of their limitations?"

"I'm worried that I'll be preoccupied, that it'll interfere with my teaching."

"Don't let it," he said. "Be brave in the classroom, Paul. Start there. Every solution gets its start in some simple, fundamental environment. Be brave with your students."

As I write this, it is December and school is out. These past months have been good months of teaching. Not easy, but good. Every day

I have thought about what Jesperson said then, in the diner. And every day I expect to see the silhouette of a figure on the water tower or to receive a telephone call from Jesperson, telling me that he and Margaret are again on their way to take me away in their car. "Identification and adaptation" is something Jesperson, or not-Jesperson, talked about on that strange night. I have had an experience I cannot explain; now I must adapt. Adapt and continue on. Perhaps this will be—or so it seems now—the great challenge of my life.

Pastor Arrhenius and the Maiden Brita

Chapter One: *Bergtagen*

Henning Arrhenius meant to be a more conscientious pastor than his predecessor at Stavnäs church apparently had been. Having settled in, he began to visit the people in the farther parts of Kåröd parish, and as the spring advanced and the roads and passes opened, his horse bore him to the dwellings of people who had not stirred from the neighborhood of their steads for months. This was how many of the folk of the parish met their new pastor, who had left Uppsala only months before.

The stead at Vinterasa was tenanted, Arrhenius had heard, by a farmer, woodcutter, and trapper named Lindow who had a large family and might not be able to care for all of the children.

A dirty little boy wearing only a tattered shirt opened the door. The reek from the dark interior made the pastor draw back for a moment. He stepped inside. As his eyes became used to the dim light, after the late-morning brightness of snow outside, he saw that the room was full of children, the oldest being young folk who would be doing the work of adults, the youngest a babe-in-arms. People were coughing, whispering.

He sat on a plain chair that was pointed out to him and explained who he was and what his errand was. There was a sour smell that might have indicated illness; he asked after the health of the family. Then: "I heard that there might be some need up here among a family," he said at last, trying to speak circumspectly.

"Oh aye, you see there's not enough room here for a flea to tup his wife," said a black-haired, stooped man who crouched by the fire.

Arrhenius didn't like to rebuke the man within a few moments of the first time he had crossed his threshold. He didn't think the man was mocking him or testing him; nevertheless the new pastor was being tested.

"My friend, should the little ones hear their father speak so," he said.

The man looked uncomfortable. "I'm sorry, sir, if I said what I shouldn't. It's what my father used to say."

"Maybe he had some better words," the pastor said, kindly.

"Well, he used to say too that there wasn't enough room here for a flea to cross himself."

That was profane and no better than the other, but the pastor looked down and let it pass. "The parish can help, Lindow, if you're too crowded. A child or even two children could be fostered. Would you and your good wife like to consider that?"

"They're not all ours," Lindow said, unexpectedly.

"You're caring for children of relatives?"

"There's that Brita there—she on that blanket there—she's been handed around among us up here." He indicated a girl who looked to Arrhenius to be of about fourteen years. It was warm in the stuffy room. Clad as she was in only a shift and a shawl, her undress was not modest.

"Handed around? Why, is she an orphan?" Orphans one always had in a parish, but he had not seen record or heard yet of any orphans up here, among the five families in the corner between two steep sides of the mountain.

"No, she's Sandklef's daughter."

"Why doesn't she live with him, then?"

The pastor expected the reason would be an illegitimacy scandal. Young as she was, the girl had borne a bastard and had been turned out of her home. He waited for Lindow's answer.

Lindow was looking at his wife. Then he looked back at the pastor.

"They found her hard to live with."

Arrhenius waited, but the woodcutter didn't say more.

He leaned forward and said, softly, "She steals?"

"No, she's honest," Lindow said. Pause. "She sees things. . . she sees things others don't see."

"She's mad then?"

"No. Look at her," Lindow said. "She's quiet. A good worker."

Arrhenius prompted the man: "She wants more than her share of things?"

"No, no."

They sat without speaking. The children were all looking at the pastor—except for Brita, who seemed to be looking at her knees. The shift barely covered them.

Arrhenius didn't like to turn from the head of the household to address the children without his consent, but the man was uncommunicative. "Brita?"

"They don't see what I see," she said.

"She was under the mountain," a woman whom Arrhenius took to be Lindow's wife said. "When she was a young girl, she went under the mountain. They found her in the woods. She was wandering around. But Sandklef took her back. She was his daughter. But he wouldn't keep her. She made his other children scream when she swept in front of her and when she stepped aside from them."

"Why?—was she irritable? Did she think they should get out of her way?" Arrhenius asked.

"No, it wasn't Sandklef's children. When she would step aside for those *others*. The invisible folk. That's what she said. . . . You still see them, girl, don't you?"

Brita continued to look at her knees.

"You *still see them—every day!*"

"No, but often."

"You. The queen of Fairy-land that would have been."

Arrhenius felt that all of them—Lindow, his wife, their children—were against him and the girl somehow.

"Pastor, we have all had her among us. Gudbrandson, Tiedeman, Sandklef, Bengtsson. You could take her away. Today. She has been in my house before, and now for three months. She acts strangely. I don't know that about the mountain or not. I don't think she is a mad girl. I would trust her with a newborn babe. But she's not wanted, not here or anywhere on the mountain."

"Brita, do you want to come with me? I can take you to the village. I suppose I could take you today."

"Will they pass me around down there?"

"I don't know."

"I'll come with you."

He stood up. "Well, let's go, then. Lindow, send that boy August to me for Catechism on Sunday afternoon. It's long past time a lad his size was confirmed. Put your things on, Brita. Lindow, I'll come back with the parish record book for you to sign, giving me the right to take the girl."

"She's not mine to give, pastor. You'll need to ask her father, Sandklef."

"Yes, of course. Can you tell me where he lives?"

Lindow gave Arrhenius directions. He wasn't going to offer a meal, Arrhenius knew. The pastor and the girl stepped out into the damp air. Mist had risen.

The girl's clothes were rags. She was a slight creature. The horse could have carried them both—he could have placed her on his lap—but he helped her onto the saddle. "Did you hurt your hand, Brita?" Her left hand was swollen and discolored.

"Lindow hit it."

"Why?"

"He saw me using it. He said the devil signs his name with his left hand. Christians should use their right hands."

"Can you read and write then, Brita?"

"Maybe so. Most of them don't know their letters. I learned some, but I don't know if I could read a book or not.—I was using my left hand to thread a needle. Lindow's wife told me not to. I answered her back. I told her it is hard for me to use my right hand. That's when Lindow hit it."

"For some people, it is easier to use the left hand—"

"When I was little, I was right-handed."

"—God made them both, Brita. The Bible never says anything about not using one or the other. People in my village scold children who wanted to use their left hands—I remember that. But poor girl, they never said in my town that it was a devilish thing to use your left hand." He led the horse, holding the reins, and they left the yard, where Lindow's door was shut against them. The path through the pines was only a track. Arrhenius realized that he had nibbled the inside of his lower lip ragged while sitting in the ill-smelling dark cottage.

After a long while they came to the end of the path and stepped onto a wider road, which was muddy and churned by wagon wheels and the hooves of horses. They didn't talk. Drops of moisture formed in his beard and at the ends of locks of her lank hair.

While the horse's hoofs pulled loose from the sucking mud with each step, he tried to stay on the firmer ground at the edge of the road, to keep from getting his boots burdened with the sticky mud. The moist, grey air was cold and smelled of soil.

"Before I went into the mountain, I used my right hand," Brita said, quietly. Her breath was visible.

"Brita. . . did you really go into the mountain? Did you really meet the Underground People? Don't be afraid to tell me what happened to you. You can tell me now or tell me sometime at home."

"I would tell you the truth, Pastor. Only I don't remember all of it."

"Brita, do you see things, truly?—that other people don't see?"

"Yes. . . . Sometimes. . . . Not so often now."

"Do you see anything now?"

"No."

"What do you see sometimes?"

"Other ones . . . I see them driving their cattle, or hunting . . ."

"Are they people like us?"

"Oh no, you can always tell."

Arrhenius remembered chimney-corner stories from his own village. "They have tails?"

"You would see them with tails, maybe, if you ever saw them when they didn't know you were looking, but when I see them, I see them the way they see themselves, without tails. When I was in the mountain they wore the most beautiful clothes, more beautiful than you can imagine. Only I can't think of how those clothes looked, now. But I know it was so!" To Arrhenius she didn't seem vain, proud of her knowledge, or what she thought she remembered and knew. She had corrected him without false humility. He thought of a question to follow what she had just said.

"Do the pretty girls have hollow backs?—are they rotten logs in back? That's what the coal-seller's boy told me when I was a boy in Ollvi."

"No.—Oh, I hope you never see any of those girls. They love to meet a Christian man in the woods and . . ." She stopped.

Arrhenius was sure that she was going to say something like, "lie with him," but she was modest. He approved of that, too.

"Behave improperly," he said for her.

"Yes."

Now they were walking by a small lake. The ice had broken up. They would pass through a wood and come to the village. Arrhenius was footsore and hungry. He didn't know how long it had been since the girl had eaten, either. She didn't look like she ate very much, he thought.

"I ate some of their food when I was in the mountain, and drank of their drink," she said. Arrhenius looked sharply at the girl. He had said nothing. She was looking past the horse's head at the road in front of them, and her face was expressionless.

Light rain began to fall.

It was dark by the time they arrived at the parsonage. Two people had looked at them curiously as they walked the short street of the village, but most were inside their dwellings.

Brita slept in the parsonage kitchen, wrapped in an old horse blanket. The brown bitch, pregnant, lay nearby in a bed of clean rags. The kitchen was the warmest room in the house, Arrhenius had told Brita, smiling. After breakfast the next morning, Arrhenius left the kitchen and entered his study. The woman Eva helped her wash herself. Eva had risen early, as always, and heated a basin of water. Cleaning the girl took a long time. Mrs. Arrhenius stopped Eva, who was carrying a basin of dirty water, outside the kitchen door. "Did she have lice?"

"Yes, madam."

"Burn her clothes and the blanket she slept in. She can wear those things your daughter grew out of last year, when she was working here for Pastor Boberg. Now, what else did you see?"

The woman understood the question. "She looks as old as she told me she was. I asked her and she told me she was sixteen. I asked her about women's curse and she said it's been for three years. I didn't ask her anything more, madam, there was no need—it's my belief she's an honest maiden. One not used to soap."

Eva went back into the kitchen and found the girl dressed and drying her hair.

"Go to the pastor's study when you're ready."

146

The pastor had a desk on which he wrote his sermons, a table, three chairs, one bookshelf. There were twenty-seven books on the shelf, all of them old and most of them massive. In his lifetime, Arrhenius could expect to add perhaps ten more. There were a Greek grammar, a Hebrew grammar, a geography of the Holy Land, a book of travels in the Holy Land, an edition of the *Aeneid* and a volume of Greek plays. There were three volumes of Luther's sermons, an edition of Melanchthon's *Loci Theologici*, a massive treatise on the old Israelite Temple, a Greek Testament and a Hebrew Old Testament, a single volume from a four-volume edition of Johann Gerhard's sermons, a hundred-year-old atlas of the world, an *Antiquities of Southern Sweden and Jutland,* an almanac, and a compendium of medical knowledge. The remaining volumes were sermons of Swedish divines and miscellanea. He had bought five of the books while a seminarian at Uppsala; the rest had been passed to him by his father or other relatives, looking to help the youngest son of five, or had been left by Boberg. Also, but not on the shelf, Arrhenius had a personal journal. Behind the chair in which he sat, a crucifix was mounted on the wall.

He called her into the room when she knocked at the study door. He indicated a chair for her. The rain had passed in the night and fresh sunlight came through the window behind her. He took in at a glance that, despite the scrubbing she'd had and the new clothes, she was not at all an attractive girl. That was good. Village housewives would be much more ready to take her in as she was, than if she had been pretty. He noted also that her hands, now clean, nails trimmed, were rough and red. She was used to work.

All through their conversation there was the sound of dripping from outside, as drops of melted ice fell from the eaves of the house into puddles.

"Good morning, Brita."

"Good morning, Pastor."

"Brita, today I will inquire in the town about a foster home for you. If we find a place for you, I will get your father's permission for you to live here in town permanently. I'll need to talk with you about the work you can do. But first: did Pastor Boberg confirm you?"

"No, Pastor."

147

"You knew who he was, of course; but you did not often come to church?"

"I didn't know him, Pastor. He never visited us on the mountain."

"Well, he must have spoken with you at the church door at least."

"No, Pastor, I can't remember that I have ever been to church."

Arrhenius could not feel surprise about this. "Well, say the Lord's Prayer for me."

She was looking at her knees.

He prompted her: "Our Father . . ."

Pause.

"Brita, is it possible that you have never been taught the Lord's Prayer?"

"I'm sorry, Pastor."

"So you don't know the Ten Commandments."

"No."

"Or the Creed?"

"No, Pastor."

"Dear Lord Christ, have mercy on us sinners. . . . Well, do you know this, Brita?" And he crossed himself.

She crossed herself readily, looking not at him but at the crucifix. "'Jesus save me,'" she said. Then, to the pastor: "Little Theodor taught me to do that. Gudbrandson's boy. He's my age, but he hasn't grown well. He's a hunchback and very small and thrawn. But he's as kind as anyone. And he taught me to do that a long time ago. His family goes to church sometimes."

"You lived with them for a while?"

"Yes, but when they went to church, they had me stay home and mind the house. But Theodor had already taught me how to cross myself and say 'Jesus save me,' when we were little, when I was always living at home with Father. We would play together, and he taught me that. He said that no harm would come to me if I would cross myself and say those words."

"Brita, this was before you went into the mountain?"

"Yes, before."

"That was when?"

"Five years ago."

He studied her.

148

"Brita, I'm wondering if you wandered off, as children will, and fell asleep in the woods one day, and dreamed that you were taken by the Underground People. Child, I will tell you something: I am not sure that there are any Underground People, any Invisible Folk. People used to talk about them in my village. I know the same stories that you know. But my father didn't like such talk. He said it was left over from heathen days. And he was a learned man. Because of what he said, some of the people stopped telling such stories."

"Really, did they?"

"Yes. Well, I suppose so. But about you."

"Everyone knows I went into the mountain, Pastor. They found me the next day. Father took me home."

"Couldn't you have fallen asleep, though? And dreamed?"

"No, Pastor," she said sadly. "Before I went into the mountain, I was like most folk, I used my right hand. And I saw what others see and nothing more."

"What did Lindow's wife mean, yesterday, when she said the other children didn't like it when you would sweep?"

"When I came back, I would see little people doing things, and I would try to sweep them away. They would laugh at me, stick out their tongues. I never could hit them no matter how I swung the broom. Now I just let them be. Only I can't help it, I step aside for them."

"Well, perhaps it's so. . . . What did Lindow's wife mean about you being the queen of Fairy-Land?"

"It only makes folks spiteful—I never should have said. But when I was in the mountain, they would have crowned me the bride of the King. They put the bridal crown on my head. He was taller than any man and his hands and face were so beautiful and white, and his eyes were black as coals. 'I will give you a new name,' he said. And I was frightened, and I crossed myself and said 'Jesus save me!'—and then I was in the woods, and they all were gone, and my fine clothes, and I was wearing just the plain things I had on before. And it was night and I couldn't find my way home. But my father, Sandklef, and the other men found me in the morning."

Then she said:

"Pastor, yesterday when we walked by the lake, my heart was troubled. Is there something bad about the lake?"

And Arrhenius lost his temper. "What, some nonsense about water serpents, is it? Or a big church bell that was being carried across the ice one winter day, and fell in, and still tolls down below when someone's going to die?"

"No, Pastor."

He sighed hard. "Well, what do you mean, then, Brita?"

"I'm sorry, Pastor. Only it seemed that someone had died there." She paused, remembering. "A baby."

"I don't know anything about such a thing, Brita. I have lived here in Stavnäs only for a little while, but I have never heard anything about the lake except that there are fish in it that people catch sometimes." Pause. "Whatever may be in the lake, we'd better get something into that head of yours." Pause. "And *this* is truth, Brita."

For the next hour, he began to instruct her, using Luther's Catechism. He also advised her about winning the confidence of householders who might consider bringing her into their homes. She should keep her memories and impressions (or imaginings) to herself.

And he told her that she would continue to sleep in the kitchen, but under a clean wool blanket.

Chapter Two: Confirmation

No one in Stavnäs with whom Arrhenius talked that first day wanted to take in the girl, but he was not much discouraged. The pastor thought that they had heard she had been "taken into the mountain" and that they mistrusted her for that. In time, surely he would meet a decent family that was not frightened of the rumor of the elves.

"We'll find someone, Maja," he said to his wife. "Now—how has it been for you today?"

"Just the sickness in the morning. You saw me at my worst of the day. While you've been out I have felt quite well. Poor Henning, with a sick woman in the house but hardly a wife."

"Well, Maja, I was twenty-three years old before before I married you, and a bachelor every one of those years. And in seven months I'm to be a father!" Pause. "If no one will have Brita, should we keep her?"

"You'll find someone who wants her," she said.

"But would you be willing to have her here?"

"We'll be having our own child without raising that one. As for help about the house, Eva sees to everything that I don't do myself. I never expected to be waited on like a fine lady when I married a pastor who had no patrons."

"Well for you that you didn't! But tell me, do you like the girl?"

"Isn't it soon to be saying?" Pause. "Henning, the child's not canny. This morning she suddenly turned her head and looked at me—here" (and she placed her hand lightly on her belly) "—and put her hand to her mouth, as if she were frightened."

"Her left hand?"

"I suppose it was. Then she went about her work. . . I had her polishing our bits of silver."

"Oh, so you trust her well so soon! I'm glad, Maja."

"She's an honest girl. At least, I think so. Perhaps she says things that she dreamed or imagined sometimes, but thinks were true. I never believed in elves, Invisible Folk, trolls, such things, growing up. They were country-folk's talk." Maja Arrhenius was the daughter of an Uppsala wagoner, a man who worked for a warehouse owner and delivered goods in the city. "And surely it's not likely, even if there were such beings, that they would marry a slip of an eleven-year-old girl who was . . . not yet a woman."

"My people would not be so sure," he replied.

"One other matter about that girl: such an appetite!"

There was a meeting of the parish council the next evening at the diminutive town hall. It seemed to the young pastor that the village elders wanted to size him up; to see if he were a preacher of Law, Gospel, the awakened conscience, the decisive repentance, the consolatory Sacrament, or if he were a good friend, a shrewd, lettered man, able, to be sure, to preach a lurid Lenten sermon or two, just to whet one's appetite for Easter beef and beer, but no meddler. Most of the business concerned the worldly affairs of the parish. On his walk home, Arrhenius saw Olsavius, a blacksmith, leaning against the wall of a building. The man was drunk. Arrhenius didn't stop to speak to him.

"Maja," said Arrhenius, standing in the doorway of the parsonage sleeping chamber. The meeting had been a long one, but his wife was still sitting up. "You should be in bed.—Why, what troubles you, dear one?"

"I wasn't able to sleep. I was sitting by the lamp after Brita went to the kitchen for the night, and I started thinking about how she looked at my belly this morning. You said that she said something about a baby being dead in the lake. Henning, perhaps she has the sight. Maybe our child will drown in that lake one day."

He hadn't supposed that his wife, a city girl who doubted the country-folk's belief in forest spirits, trolls, elves of the mountain, and the like, thought much of the second sight. Like any instructed Christian, she knew that God might warn someone in a dream. But the sacred Scriptures neither affirmed nor denied the Second Sight.

He began to talk about the Sight, but Maja cut him off.

"Henning, who really doubts that some people have that gift? But I don't like to ask her. I don't know her well enough yet to trust her completely, whatever she would say. And if she did say that— that our baby was going to grow up and drown. . . ."

"You're wise, as always. *Don't* ask her. Don't burden yourself with such things. If the Lord chooses to warn us, or . . . to prepare us, He will do that in other ways, too; and not by such uncertain means. And Maja, the girl is hardly a Christian. God be thanked, I sense no vices in her—"

"Nor have I heard bad speech from her, or light talk about sin."

"Yes. But she has been taught almost nothing. I must begin next week to visit those people on the mountain, assemble them in someone's home, and teach them. I'm ashamed of Boberg. Oh, they liked him well in the town, I see that. There are men on that board of elders who smile at sin, and Boberg asked of them no repentance. Let well alone—that, I'm thinking, was his way; and let the folk on the mountain, or at Varso"—an outlying farm district that was part of the Kåröd parish—"go to hell." He sighed.

"Jesus said, 'Take no thought for the morrow; sufficient unto the day is its own evil.' It's to bed for you and me, Maja."

Lent would end soon. Arrhenius knew that many who had not come to church for a long time would come for Communion at Easter. All of his Lenten sermons included exhortations to frequent

Communion. He sought to connect their sense of these forty days with the forty years of the Israelites in the desert, wherein they were fed upon the bread from heaven. The snuffling, coughing congregation contained some who already were faithful in coming to church and receiving the Sacrament. There were probably many who thought it seemly to come to church in Lent but who would fall away for the rest of the year, till Christmas, once they had received the Sacrament at Easter.

A dozen children of varying ages came to the church on Sunday afternoons to be catechized. Soon some of them complained that Pastor Boberg had not asked so much when he confirmed their elder brothers and sisters. "Maybe they were better learners," he said in a manner that he hoped was kindly, though he guessed that Boberg had asked little of his young scholars. Brita was noticeably older than the other pupils, but she did not seem resentful or awkward.

Maja told her husband something that Eva had said: "'It's my belief that girl will never take the Sacrament,' she said. 'Those who eat *their* food and drink *their* drink can never bear that it should touch their lips.' I asked her where she had heard such a thing. 'It's what everyone knows,' she said. 'And where did you hear that Brita had eaten the food of the Underground Folk?' I asked—"

"She spoke of that to me," Arrhenius said.

"Yes, Eva said that the girl just let that fall."

"You corrected her, I'm sure."

"Yes, but these country people stand fast by their superstitions, don't they? I could see she didn't believe I had the right of it, when I told her that even if there are Hidden People, and even if Brita had tasted their food, this was no reason she could not partake of Communion after she is confirmed. When my husband had catechized her well, she'll be ready to receive, perhaps as soon as next year, I told her. I hope that was all right for me to say."

"Yes, I think if she and I work together, she will not have to wait till Easter two years hence. And you may tell that Eva that St. Paul permitted Christians to eat meat that was sold in the marketplace and that had previously been consecrated to idols. By this we may take it that, if a Christian did eat of the food of the Underground People, it were no sin."

"She also said that she was surprised that Brita hadn't fallen over dead when she passed the threshold of the church the first time!"

"Is there no end to the woman's foolishness!"

"You may ask! She *also* said she thought it was a wonder, how Brita eats and stays so scrawny. She said perhaps the girl isn't flesh and blood at all, but a changeling—that the true Brita has never left the mountain, and this among us is an Undergrounder with no soul!"

"I'll send her away!"

"No, no, by that time she was smiling at me. Teasing the pastor's wife—"

"The pastor's pretty young wife," he said, laughing. Pause. "It's a pity that the girl went on talking to Eva. The woman thought well enough of her at first."

Easter passed, and then there were fewer people in church on Sunday. A few of his parishioners clearly approved of their new pastor, and a few of the women seemed pleased to be visited by his wife and to set out, as if of everyday use, their few things of city origin—a tablecloth, a few cups, spoons. There was a burial, and Henning got to know Oskar, the sexton, a grizzled, middle-aged man whose teeth were all gone, who smelled of sweat, and whose muscles bunched and relaxed visibly as he dug on a warm summer's morning. Like most of the adults in the town, he could read and write. His handwriting was unexpectedly fine. He abstained from all strong drink. His father had been a drunkard. Oskar had been a soldier and knew more of the wide world than most of the people in the village, Arrhenius guessed. His family had been in the area for many generations, and Oskar could tell those he deemed worthy of the knowledge where there were good places to fish, hunt, trap, and gather mushrooms and berries. He had never married and was shy around Maja.

He kept the graveyard, within the walls surrounding the small whitewashed church, in good order. In winter snow was swept or shoveled from the paths between the graves, and in summer the grass that grew up against the church walls was clipped.

On the morning after the burial, Arrhenius stopped to talk with the sexton, who was washing earthy hands in a rill from a small pump. "You're the third pastor I've known here, sir, and our pastors stay on a long time."

"Who was here before Boberg?"

"Gjerdman. He had fifteen children."

"Do any of them live in the parish now?"

Oskar dried his hands on the end of his shirt. "No. There was a visitation of sickness and that carried off those who remained here with their own families—three of them, years after Gjerdman moved on to Sorbygden."

"Yes, I heard of that."

"He was a one. One time he was preaching a course of sermons to drive away the people from bad living, and there was a youth, Erik from Millesvik, and his brother, who scoffed: 'There's no soul,' they said. 'You die and rot, and that's the end of you.' Gjerdman defied them. He said even such louts as they weren't such fools as that is. Well they knew that we are souls, he said. He thought they were just making game of him; but he didn't like light talk about such things, either. So he decided to play a trick on them. One evening, late, he comes to their door. 'Let me bring away your sons for an hour,' he says to their father, and he lets them go. And Gjerdman takes them to the graveyard wall, and it's a black night, and he says: 'Behold! There are the souls of those who scoffed, and now they have no peace.' There were several lights moving slowly around in the dark, there in the graveyard. 'They crawl about on their hands and knees, trying to find a way to the peace of the grave,' he said. He told me all about it. Well, the lads are just staring at it all. 'This could happen to you!' he says. But then he says, 'Now I have taught you a lesson. You see that for all your talk, you know and believe that we are souls.' And neither of them is saying anything against that. And then Gjerdman says, 'I have proven my point. In your hearts you know.' But then he doesn't want to deceive them. 'Now, young men,' he says, 'Remember how you felt this night. Know that those lights are not corpse-candles—but you knew they could have been.' And he takes them through the gate and explains that he bought some crabs at the market, and lit candles, and put the candles on the backs of the crabs with melted wax! Even as he's explaining, one of the candles falls off into the grass. But the other crabs keep crawling about with the candles on their backs." He paused.

"Well, we were never taught how to design such tricks at seminary," Arrhenius said. "That's an odd way to commend faith to an unbeliever. Did the two lads cease their mocking?"

"Perhaps they didn't, I don't know. . . . I could tell you other stories about Gjerdman, but that one's the one I like best."

"You should write a chronicle of this village."

"Well, it's true, there are some stories that shouldn't be forgotten. But when it comes to men's sins, what do you think?— Isn't it better that they be forgotten?"

"Yes, if they have been repented of, and if there is no necessity to keep alive the memory of them. 'Whatsoever things are lovely, whatsoever things are pure and of good repute, if there be any virtue, think on these things.'"

"And there are things that can't be mended. What's done is done."

"Yes, but a man doesn't have to be bound to his sin always. Christ through his minister will absolve the one who confesses."

The sexton reflected. "There are some who will never confess, I think."

Maja Arrhenius went into labor prematurely. A midwife, Märta, was sent for and came promptly. She came out of the sleeping chamber, where the pastor's wife was, with bloody towels. She didn't look at his face. Arrhenius was sick with terror. He sat on a chair outside the room trying to pray. The door was shut. For a while he heard Märta talking, and murmurs responding. Then for a long time he heard only sounds of the midwife moving around. Märta came to him and said the child was stillborn. He went into the room and was with his wife for a few minutes. Her face was distorted by suffering. The midwife sent him out. He sat for a long time.

It was dark in the hallway. A little breeze from an open window somewhere passed him. He smelled growing things.

Märta stepped into the hallway and said rapidly, "I'm sorry, sir, your wife is dead."

Women from the town brought things to eat. Arrhenius stayed in his study. He often fell asleep with his head on his desk, or even lying on the floor with his coat, rolled up, for a pillow. Stavnäs was the only town in the parish with a church; there were no other clergymen nearby. He conducted the funeral himself. The sermon was something he read as he found it in the forty-fourth of Gerhard's *Sacred Mediations*.

Bente Ståhle, one of the members of the church council, came to the parsonage the day after the funeral. "On behalf of the town, I tender to you our most profound sympathies, Pastor Arrhenius. I know that you have much comfort from God in this time of trial, but it is surely His will that we all help one another when necessary. The women will continue to bring supper to you each day. The council also thought it would be acceptable if you did not preach this coming Sunday, during your time of bereavement. If you would like to stay in another town for a few days, where, perhaps, you have friends or relatives, we will be most understanding. The council has authorized some money to pay your costs while you are gone if you elect to do so. Oskar will continue to tend your property as usual unless you would prefer that he stay away for a few days in respect to your feelings. If we direct him to exercise your horse, should you choose to leave it here, he will do that. If you have any friends or family on the road past Hacksäng, you might wish to ride alongside Elias Lundell, who is taking a wagon that way in two days to pick up some articles from his brother-in-law. He will be leaving at six in the morning and arriving there around three in the afternoon. If you wanted to go the opposite direction, I would mention that I have a cousin named Wigström at Angersdshestra who keeps a good wayfarers' tavern. Your horse would be well cared for. I would be glad to give you a note for Wigström; he would give you his best."

While Ståhle was talking, Brita appeared at the open doorway of the study for a few moments. She had removed her brown headscarf and was abstractedly scratching her scalp. She disappeared from Arrhenius's view.

After the councilman left, she knocked lightly on the open study door.

"Yes, Brita?"

Her left hand was pressed below her lips and one knuckle was raised to where she could bite it lightly.

"What is it?"

"That man is a bad man."

"Such childish talk."

157

"I know it's so, though."

"Come in, sit there. Brita, I haven't been sleeping very well and I have a headache. If there's something you need to tell me, please do."

"He has something to do with the lake. When we came here, I thought a baby died there." Arrhenius was motionless. The girl had her left hand slightly raised, as if to request silence while she thought.

"His baby. Yes. But he didn't want him. There's a girl and he's making her drown the baby. It's their baby."

"Brita, do you see this?"

"When he was here, I looked in. I saw him and I looked away into this dark hall out here. And it was as if I was standing in trees near the lakeshore, and I could see him with a woman and a little baby. It was night-time, but I could see everything. I remember it. I think he had sent her away someplace. He didn't want anyone to know. But they met at the lake. He told her to bring the child. When she and the baby got there, he commanded her to drown him. Then he sent her away. He gave her money."

"Child, I don't know what to say. I feel as if I should tell you that you're a bad, imaginative girl. Ståhle is a good man. Or I should say he's a respected member of this town that we have come to live in." Arrhenius thought of Ståhle as one of the worldly men on the church council, though his conscience often accused him of being too ready to think ill of this man and his cronies: only God knows the heart.

"Pastor, do you believe I see true things?"

He smiled and shook his head. "I've never been able *not* to believe it might be that you do. Maja and I used to talk about that." Pause. "You knew she was going to lose the baby."

"I didn't know. One time I looked at your dear wife *and I knew* that something wasn't right."

"No one had even told you that she was with child yet. She didn't show."

For a time, they said no more.

"I think that way of seeing things is going away from me. I hardly ever have it now. But this man, Ståhle. I thought I should tell you."

"It's a horrible thing you accuse him of, or, not accuse him, but say that you saw. I will have to go on as if you never had said that, Brita."

"Yes, Pastor."

"It seems useless knowledge, really. But God forbid that the pastor should start going among the people and trying to tease out other people's secrets. God forbid."

"I won't tell anyone else without your permission."

"That's a very good promise to make, Brita. And I won't be giving you that permission."

"No."

"The Lord bless you." He looked through the study window. "This is no time to hang about a house all day. Go for a good walk and bring us back some flowers for the table."

Arrhenius was coming home late. There was Olsavius again, this time lying in the churchyard. He hated to approach the man, but drunkards sleeping on church property were intolerable.

"Get up, Olsavius."

The drunkard stirred a little, then was still. He groaned.

Arrhenius smelled it.

"You've fouled yourself, man. Now get up. Here," and he took hold of the man and struggled to raise him to his feet.

"I'm brandy-shitten," the man said.

"Yes, you are. Now where do you live. We're taking you home."

"I want to sleep. Leave me alone."

"You can't sleep here." They were almost to the lych-gate. "Now come on. Where do you live? I'll help you get home."

They got past the gate. The man pushed against Arrhenius, slid against him, lay on the ground.

Arrhenius went back and closed the gate. He looked at the man.

"Come on," he said at last. "You're not sleeping in the street."

It took the better part of an hour to get him home. A few people watched them. The pastor heard laughter behind him as he continued on with the intoxicated man. At Olsavius's house, he pounded on the door with his fist. An adolescent boy came to the door, one of the sons of Olsavius's married brother. The brothers shared the smithy. Arrhenius's eye was caught for a moment by the boy's.

The youth helped Olsavius into the house.

The pastor was not able to find a home for the girl who had been taken into the mountain. Now that he was a widower, it was unseemly for her to remain at the parsonage. Eva slept at her own home, as before. Brita was a diligent Confirmation student and treasured a copy of the Catechism that Arrhenius had given her from his own library. She also loved poring over the atlas. Most of the other children ignored her. All of them, even August Lindow, were younger than Brita, so perhaps, Arrhenius thought, they were shy of someone so grown-up as compared to themselves. But without question the story of her having been taken into the mountain was the chief reason. The strange sweeping and stepping aside that he had heard of, he had never seen, and he didn't like to ask her about whether she saw the Other People; perhaps if no one brought them to her mind she would almost forget them. Another reason for their awkwardness around her was that she belonged to a household upon which great sorrow had been visited. She had to be aware that she was avoided, even shunned, by most of the town-children.

Arrhenius worked with the girl on her own, also, hoping that she could be confirmed after one year rather than two years of instruction, because of her age. One family in the village seemed willing to take the girl in if she were confirmed and had partaken of the Sacrament. Arrhenius understood: they were not sure that Brita was an unenchanted human being, or even that she was human at all. If she could receive the Sacrament without incident, they would be satisfied. Arrhenius could confirm her even now, before she thoroughly knew her Catechism, and before the customary time of Confirmation, just prior to Easter; the sacred Scriptures did not require that someone be confirmed before he could partake. He could finish her instruction later, able to count on her continuing to be a good pupil, and, in the meantime, he would have her off his hands. And he'd have scotched the mutterings about the girl being a changeling, or a human who belonged to Them. She would be out of his house.

But he would not do it. The Sacrament was given for the forgiveness of sins and the strengthening of a Christian's faith, and it was a good custom that only those rightly confirmed should receive it. All the same, the pastor had often to be aware that he was declining to take an action that would have cleared away some of his, and, he thought, most of the girl's, difficulties in a moment.

One night Eva was looking for one of the puppies. In the churchyard, she found Olsavius lying between two headstones. Arrhenius went out.

"Olsavius, you disgrace yourself. You lie here like a lump of earth. Look at these stones. Don't they tell you, 'Olsavius! Rise up and cast off your drunkenness! Your last hour approaches. You'll sleep here indeed, soon enough'?"

"Leave me alone."

"You're going home. Up, now."

"Boberg would have left me alone. Was a good man. Why can't you leave off bothering a man?" He turned over and lay his head on an outstretched arm.

"Surely you are mistaken. If Boberg found you lying drunk here—or anywhere—he'd have warned you to repent. No drunkard shall enter the kingdom of heaven."

Olsavius sat up, with effort, and rested his back against a stone. "You didn't know him."

"Did you?"

"I did know him. We used to drink together in the tavern! I remember. He said this. He said, 'The Lord Christ was born in a hot, bright land. Plenty of sun. Not like here. Us, He gave us drink. You drink it down, men.' That's what he told us."

"I don't believe that."

"I'd make you believe it if I could stand up."

Arrhenius went to a neighboring house where a young lad lived. He paid the youth to run to the tavern to hire a couple of men to carry Olsavius home.

Winter arrived with cold wind and wet snow. The sun stayed in the south during the short days. Lent came. He visited Ståhle at the merchant's office, intending to encourage the man to confess his sins, alluding to how men sometimes mistreated young women in their employ, but becoming tangled in his words as the man stared at him in seeming incomprehension and, then, real anger. The visitation ended with Arrhenius attempting to smooth things over

161

by resorting to generalities about Lent being a proper season for all Christians to examine themselves.

On Holy Saturday a few children who had received instruction from Pastor Boberg, and Brita, were confirmed after a service of public examination in the afternoon. None of Boberg's pupils had had more than a few weeks of instruction under Arrhenius, but they had come out of the woodwork as Easter approached, and he felt it was almost impossible that they not be confirmed, given their ages and his reluctance to reproach his predecessor's negligence, and the danger of making them bitter against the church if he did not accept them. They had consented to a few long sessions of instruction beforehand.

Arrhenius, standing in the church porch after the examination service, thought that he no longer felt melancholy. It was as if the springtime stirring was in his blood, irritating him. There was a young wife among the people of the congregation at whom he caught himself looking. Once, recently, in his study, he'd clapped the pages of his book together suddenly in self-reproach: his imagination had been at work.

People of the congregation were walking to their homes. He looked for the young wife, but didn't see her. She was too young to have a child of her own confirmed, he thought, and perhaps had no relative among the youths examined that day.

Brita, for once, was in the midst of a group of youths, the new confirmands, all of them talking at once and laughing. Her homely features were ones he'd seemed to know from long custom. The other young people were almost strangers. They set off together— Arrhenius hoped it was not to some unseemly revel. From somewhere, Ståhle joined the departing group. Arrhenius hadn't noticed him before. The merchant seemed to have his eye on Lottie, a pretty girl with a long yellow plait.

Brita stepped up to where Arrhenius stood on the church porch. She looked happy and didn't say anything about Ståhle.

Chapter Three: Wood

And so he was alone.

In most of the dwellings in the town, he was received with cold courtesy, though he knew a few folk tried to show him kindness. Of those who came to church, some conveyed by looks and words that they sympathized; some did not. The parsonage was quiet. He knew he must get rid of the girl or, inevitably, gossip would establish that she shared his bed. Stout Eva now stayed in the house at night, and her presence, he hoped, inhibited the invention of the scandal-talkers, but that effect would not last; and she did not like the girl.

Arrhenius roamed the forest, taking long, weary walks that did not always tire him enough for sound sleep at night. Sometimes he encountered wood-fellers, charcoal-burners, fowlers. They said little to one another. He carried a gun and thought he might try to kill a grouse if he got the chance, as he had done a few times in boyhood.

Often he sat with his back against a tall tree, his Bible across his knees, his mind wandering from the text; and much of the time, at home, he could not read it at all. He trusted that this state of mind would pass.

Desire had vanished during the terrible days and nights of immediate bereavement, but now was troublesome. Arrhenius might abruptly shake his head over an open book: he'd drifted from the text into a shameful reverie. It was as if, he thought, his mind were a chamber that had again and again to be swept because dust drifted and spiders spun webs. He knew that he was missing his wife, the only woman who had ever lain at his side. He had to repent often because his thoughts so frequently were not memories of their times together (so quickly past; he had looked forward to her recovery from pregnancy and the resumption of love, never dreaming that the few months of bed-fellowship they'd known would be all they would be granted). No—his reveries, reveries he could not seem to stop devising, were often coarse. At times he was Ståhle, forcing the servant girl against the wall; he'd never seen her, and in his imagination her features were hardly defined. At other times his imagination reared for him partial images of meticulous vividness, glimpses of a woman who appeared in his chamber by night or whom he encountered in the forest—but never did he see her whole; he was tormented by sudden, vivid glimpses of a fall of hair, or breasts or thigh momentarily emerged from darkness; and he'd suddenly realize what his heart was doing, curse, leap to his feet, and pace his chamber, or seize cloak and hat, and, saddling the horse, ride from the town as if on some errand. Or he might walk to the least-frequented part of the lake vicinity and step along the path, slashing with his walking stick at tall swamp grass growing near. "'It is not good for the man to be alone,'" he quoted; but his wife had bled to death in their bed, for all his begging prayers, and their child was stillborn. Joys of this world are fleeting: he'd known that, he'd preached it.

He found some relief in his rides and walks among the woods and rocks of the mountainside, when his work permitted him to take sufficient time for a long, long ramble—up there, where he rarely saw people other than distant shepherds or goatherds with their animals. He studied the forms of the land, making a map in his mind. On one occasion, after nearly an hour of looking about him from a height, he realized that if there should be heavy snows in a winter, followed too soon by a spring warmer than the common sort, or if there were exceptionally heavy rains, there would be dangerous flooding down below; the curve of the valley would direct the turbid streams towards Stavnäs and its lake. On another occasion, he sat on a lonely goat-path at the top of a ridge, throwing stones at a heap of scree a hundred feet below. One could fancy oneself a giant hurling boulders. Sometimes, in the untroubled peace of a feeding rabbit or the flick of a snake into the brush, the bustle of birds in the leaves, the unrolling of a scroll of white clouds and immeasurable blue depth, Arrhenius was solaced, not lastingly.

The Wild Hunt

He started later than was his custom one hazy July day. He wanted woods, shadows, and he wanted to tire himself, so he tethered the horse in a shady spot with good forage, and strode upwards, ever upwards, needless gun in hand. Heavy clouds occupied more and more of the sky, but he refused to acknowledge their threat. A hawk soared, far away across a depth of heavy air. Suddenly it dropped from his sight, for the kill.

He sat on a large, flat stone that protruded from the grass. Lichens mottled it. Part of the stone had broken away from the main mass. What had done that? He didn't know.

He lay back, an arm flung across his eyes to protect them from the sun, which was still high, but the sky had filmed over. The gun lay at his right side.

Angry thoughts of townspeople and dwellers at Vinterasa, and others in the parish, hard-hearted men and women who had few prayers for a widowed young pastor. Their drunkenness; their sharp practice; unforgiving brother against brother. Uncle and nephew quarrelling about a boundary. Rumors, with or without names, of fornication and adultery. Complaints about the church tithes. A few idle young men watching him from across the street as he unlocked the church door, not speaking when he began to walk towards them because of profane language he had heard and for which he must rebuke them; denials, resentful eyes. But also, the image of the young wife. Her husband's father had died a year ago and he had inherited some money, and was gambling it away, slowly but steadily, as petty stakes in weekly parties. Twice that Arrhenius knew of, the man had been in fights that arose over accusations of cheating. As a boy in Ollvi, Arrhenius had heard his father preach about gamblers and drunkards who committed murder, maddened by their vices. If the man died, the pastor could approach the young widow. The young wife would come to church, unsmiling, worn-looking; but, Arrhenius thought, if she could have a different husband, she'd bloom again. Then the light and heat were taken away. Arrhenius sat up. The dark clouds, out of the southwest, were moving swiftly. Thunder rumbled.

He watched the clouds for a little while. Then he began to walk back, around the side of the mountain. The wood where his horse waited for him was there, some distance below. Now the day was darkened, chill breezes rose and fell, branches moved, leaves turned up, then down. Arrhenius smelled the rain that was coming. Thunder drummed nearer. A horn sounded, a hunter's horn. Quite close there was a crack of thunder, and rain began to pour. Hounds were crying.

Arrhenius ran down the side of the mountain towards the indistinct black region that was the wood. Again he heard the horn bray. Above the dull clamor of the thunder he heard the sound of hooves from behind and above him.

He looked back the way he had come. Something appeared at the top of the ridge but was out of his sight before he could tell whether it was an animal or a human being. A moment later the shapes of eager hounds, then the shape of a horseman appeared there, then it too turned aside. White glare of lightning and racket of thunder followed.

Arrhenius looked away and continued to run toward the trees. He got under their shelter as the rain fell harder. He could hardly see, in the downpour that the wind hurled, The horse was somewhere in this darkness. He couldn't see it.

Again he heard the hunter's horn, and, turning to stare in that direction, saw beyond the dark shapes of the trees, in the open space through which he had just passed, a woman running, her clothing soaked by rain, her long braid stuck to her back. Black tree trunks and the grey curtain of rain hid her from his sight, but a moment later he saw the dogs again and the horseman gallop past. He heard the heavy hooves pounding the ground despite the roar of the wind and the thunder's shouting.

Arrhenius found his horse. It was dripping with rain and the whites of its eyes showed, and it was trembling. Arrhenius took the reins in his left hand and with his right patted the animal's neck, speaking to it in a low voice.

Then, over the horse's shoulder, Arrhenius saw the huntsman trotting through the woods, and at his side stumbled the woman. Her long braid was in the man's extended fist. She looked his way, unseeing, her face a white mask of anguish. In horror, Arrhenius raised the gun and fired over the man's head. Lightning flashed and for a moment Arrhenius could not see; sight returned; the rain lessened. He saw no one.

He looked among the crowding trees. The clouds passed over, the sun shone again. Birds called. He found no sign of anyone, nor of any horse but his own.

The Lover

Another summer's day: a slow waking from a hillside nap, to the sight of two white feet in the new grass, in front of him. Tiny twinflowers bowed before the motionless feet. A small bird stepped across the left foot and continued to hunt in the grass. The air was warm and scented. He saw slender ankles, and fine petticoats and a white apron over a red dress edged with embroidery. He raised his eyes to those eyes regarding him. Strands of pale-golden hair gleamed in the strong sunlight from behind, strands escaped from a bright green scarf. Then clouds passed in front of the sun and he could look into the face above his own. He began to rise, but had no strength even to speak, and fell back against the tree trunk, though he felt completely awake and clear-headed.

The woman, with captivating gracefulness, lowered herself to her knees, crouching. From somewhere she brought a woven basket. She was humming, or perhaps the sound was from something else, even from the land, the trees, the birds, the sky and all around him. She placed white bread in his hands.

Now the shadow had deepened to twilight and still was deepening. Perhaps he was the source of the humming tune himself. He looked away from the watching woman. A deer was standing close by, under motionless branches. It was a doe. It stepped across his gun and stood by the woman's side. The doe and the woman became dark forms against the dimness of a summer's night.

He sighed. Something tickled his hand in the grass; he looked down at a small black ant in the bright warm sunshine. His forehead was damp from the day's heat. The forest was silent; it was mid-afternoon, the quietest time in the wood, the birds hushed, deer in the brakes dreaming or keeping watch, flicking their ears to keep off midges.

Arrhenius thought he must have been slumped there only a few moments, although now his thirst was intense. Yet he felt invigorated and more at peace than he had for a long time. When he returned to his study, after dark, and lit the lamp, his books seemed fresh again, and he read with much enjoyment for hours.

He was able to carry out the duties of his calling. Sometimes, writing a sermon, he wrote rapidly, God's Word alive and endowing him with understanding of the heart and God's provision for it, and he looked forward to reading his sermon to the folk on the Sunday morning. He felt at times as if he had never understood that life was forgiveness. Some of the people greeted him after the service with a new warmth.

Ståhle and some of the other men of the parish, however, rarely attended divine service, or left before the concluding prayer.

Rarely, now, was anger interwoven with lust in his thoughts, but still his reveries were only sometimes, although then with gratitude, of his wife. For a time, he had thought over the vision of the woman with bread; but he fell away from that. Again he found his thoughts turning to the young wife in the church, she who was another man's wife. Often he simply thought about how she looked, sitting in the church, usually not looking at the preacher, or standing to sing with the congregation, her eyes on the hymnbook, but sometimes he caught himself imagining himself as her new husband.

Arrhenius returned at times to the secluded, sunlit hillside above a dark ravine where he had seen the woman who had stood, possessing peace, a deer at her side. He had no real expectation of meeting her there; if he ever did see her again, he had thought on one occasion, it would be somewhere else, in the busy world of men and women. Yet he came back to the hillside, making it a shrine.

One Monday, he settled himself with his back against what he was sure was the same tree-trunk that had supported him on that afternoon before; and waited. His fingers idly plaited ropes of long yellow grass.

It seemed that his watchfulness was ebbing out of him. Clouds slowly came up. A few very fine drops fell on his face, but he made no effort to brush them away, unwilling to make a movement, as if he were a hunter keeping still, so that his quarry would unsuspectingly wander close enough for a bullet. But he wanted to be, not hunter, but prey.

It was deep twilight now. Suddenly an owl voiced in the darkness: and someone settled down beside him. An arm went around his neck and lips were on his cheek. He reached out to embrace, and his hands touched cool cloth and warm skin. At the same time, he felt that he was sinking into the earth, that the warm mold was rising about him, and its sourness was in his nostrils. He heard the movement of insects in the grass and, too, the chewing of worms in the earth. Puffballs pushed through the moist earth. Now he was no longer held around the neck; she was lying in the grass beside him, her arms raised, hands reaching to draw him to her. In the dimness he could not see her face, only a pale shape with dark eyes and dark hair.

"Lie with me," the voice said, and as he heard it, he knew that this was what he had wanted to hear; and yet he checked against it. And he remained with his back against the tree.

He seemed then to see more clearly. "Who are you?" he whispered.

"What are names to trees, streams, breezes? What are names to fire, snow in the hollow places, clouds, a stone?"

"Who are you?"

"Nay, give me your name, man. I will take it away and put it in a dark place, under roots, behind a tree, down out of the stars' sight."

"I'm Arrhenius. I'm pastor of Stavnäs parish."

"Give me your name, man. There are no names for us, under the mountain."

"I'm Henning Arrhenius. I was christened with that name."

"Give it to me. What use is it? When Boberg lay in my arms, he needed not his name."

"Boberg!"

"I have missed him, man. But not so sorely as he missed me, I swear by stone and tree. Has he died, as your fashion is, man? Lie with me."

Arrhenius got to his feet. He didn't see the woman-shape rise; she stood before him.

"Come under the mountain with me. You will eat and drink and lie with me and my sisters. By stone and tree I swear, you will never be sent away. Give to me your name. Lay it aside as did Boberg."

"Boberg died!"

"In the mountain you will not fear death, man. And you will see forests grow from seeds, and rise, and be cut down or burnt, and forests rise again." She stepped close to him. "Give me your name."

Arrhenius said: "It was given to me at my Baptism."

"Give to me your name, and with it goes that water. And our water has no bitterness like that water. It is sweet, man."

He drew away. "I will not. Leave me."

In the dimness it seemed to him the woman watched him.

"You will leave this place now, and then I will leave. Never come here again," he said.

He could see almost nothing, now. But he heard her voice, harsh now: "Where is Boberg?" She laughed. "I miss him so!"

Then Arrhenius was running, stumbling against roots. He struggled across the side of the hill in thick growth of ferns. His foot went into a depression in the ground and he fell, wrenching it. He struck the ground heavily, but the pain seemed to clear his head. His hand closed on a thick dry stick from which most of the bark had fallen. He seized the piece of wood and held it in front of him to defend himself. Coming up the slope towards him he saw a deformed creature, its face raised to him: saucer eyes, gleaming like dull oil; a nose like a long wooden spoon; hair that was tangled grey moss. "Where is Boberg?" it croaked. "He misses me, where he is!" Arrhenius held tightly to the wood. It felt to him like he was holding a rough-cut beam, very heavy, but he did not let it drop. And then there was a change, and he was just a benighted traveler with a stick in his hand.

Arrhenius trudged into the village. He had to pass the churchyard on his way to the parsonage. From among the gravestones he heard a horrible sound—his heart leaped into his mouth. Then he knew it was the sound of the drunkard retching. His hand tightened on the walking stick. He could give the wretch a real beating and neither Olsavius nor anyone else would know who had dusted off the blacksmith's coat for him.

Instead he walked to the gasping man. "Come on, Olsavius. I'm too tired to go to your house and get someone to drag you home. Here, come on, get up. You're going to have to manage on your own. I'm not fouling my clothes with your vomit." The blacksmith reeled after the pastor. He led him to the stable. Olsavius sensed where there was hay tossed and fell into it. Arrhenius went into the house and came back with a basin of water and a cloth and wiped the man's face and the front of his shirt. The stench made him dizzy.

In the morning Arrhenius rose and walked to the stable. He expected the man would be gone. Instead, Olsavius was sitting on a barrel, his head in his hands. He looked up as the pastor approached. "I'd swear I'll never touch another drop, but I'm afraid of one more sin on my soul."

Arrhenius waited.

"It was the winters, the nights. The clouds. Now I want to drink whenever I'm not busy at the forge."

Arrhenius felt a fresh stirring of pity and disgust, and without premeditation said, "Get on a ship. Leave the smithy. Your brother can take the work. Get on a ship, Olsavius. Sail to sunny lands. You need the sunshine. Go to Italy, the Greek islands, the Ottoman lands. You'll drink yourself to death if you stay here."

"I've never been in a boat and I'm no boy to learn the craft."

"A blacksmith should be able to get work on a steamship. Go to sea, Olsavius."

"Today, if you wish it."

And it was done. Before Olsavius left, two days later, he came to Arrhenius's study and confessed his sins. The man was sober, but his confession rambled. Arrhenius thought that he managed to get some Gospel words through the man's ears—which, he realized for the first time, were dulled from the noise of the smithy. Maybe it had been easier for the man to turn to drink as the years passed and voices became blurred by deafness. At last, after two hours, the man had brought to light everything that troubled his conscience. Arrhenius pronounced the words of absolution. He shook Olsavius's hand afterwards, then pressed a little money into his hand. Through the window he watched Olsavius shuffling away. "I need a drink," Arrhenius muttered in the quiet room, looking absently at the Figure on the crucifix. Then he grinned and snorted through his nose. He went into the kitchen and summoned Eva and Brita to drink a glass of wine with him. He read to them the first verses of the second chapter of St. John. They all felt merry. Eva told about her wedding years ago, and how everyone danced in the warm rain.

A few days after Olsavius' departure, Arrhenius asked Eva to send the girl Brita to his study.

"They won't have you on the mountain, and they won't have you in the village," he said.

"No, that they won't," she said. They both smiled.

"Do you know, once I was tempted to have you take the Sacrament before you were confirmed, so that folk would see you took no harm from it, and maybe the talk about you would die down. And now you have been confirmed and you partake of the Body and Blood, and they still won't have you."

"I don't know why," she said.

171

"They're afraid that you might know things about them they want kept quiet. At least, I think that's the reason some of them aren't asking me if you can come and live with them—and work a long day everyday for them. For others—it's one thing, it's another."

"Some of them don't like the way I've stayed on here since Mrs. Arrhenius died," Brita said softly.

Pause.

"You know this?"

"Oh, one of the Confirmation pupils was telling me. I'd rather not say a name. I was helping this one once—you were visiting someone who was sick, and he came for the lesson, not knowing you would be gone. So I helped him. But he told me that his father said to him to stay away from that girl who lives with Arrhenius, and, you see, he could tell that his father was thinking bad things about you, and me."

"Brita, I have relatives in Nybo. They'll take you in till you can find a home to work in there. Could you do that?"

"Anything would be better than this."

Pause.

"You're not even left-handed any more, are you?" he asked.

"No," she said, smiling sadly.

So Arrhenius hired a trap. He told Eva frankly why he was taking Brita away. She said nothing to dissuade him. After deliberation, he also told Bergstrand, the parish council member who lived nearest to the parsonage. He was an old man whose head shook always. Arrhenius didn't know whether the man was fairminded or not; he was as tired of reproaching himself for wondering whom he could trust as he was of weighing the soul of now this, now that one. Judging others not only violated the Lord's counsel; it made him miserable. If he must challenge a man because of his conduct, he must; but he meant to cease from efforts to measure the good and the evil in another man's soul.

And when he told Bergstrand, the man proved true; for he said, without dissembling, "People will say you've got her with child, and that's why you're taking her away."

Arrhenius said, "I suppose they will."

172

"We won't all believe that," Bergstrand said, looking into his eyes steadily.

They were standing behind Bergstrand's son's store, where two men were unloading barrels of flour from a wagon.

"I'll return in three days," Arrhenius said.

"See that you do! I'm counting on you to bury me one of these days."

Arrhenius's Nybo relatives, cousins of his mother, received Brita in kindly fashion. On the morning of his departure for Stavnäs, Håkan Blom, the head of the household, asked Arrhenius if he would be able to come to the town again someday to see how Brita was doing; he already had a family in mind that likely would take her in and give her good work.

"You should come, and make sure you come when that Hanna marries our Helmer. He's been away at sea for two years, all the way to America. We expect him back sometime in the next few weeks; and they are to be married."

Blom indicated a woman who passed into a dark stable on some errand. Before she disappeared, her green scarf and white blouse were bright against the shadow.

"We had a letter from him in the winter. He said he was in Philadelphia. He said there are lots of Swedes in Pennsylvania. Good opportunities there for a man. I don't know if he is looking forward to settling down back here, now, though the understanding the two of them had when he left was that he would work for me. I think she's wondering if he will come back."

"I should ask Bergstrand if there's much work for young men in Stavnäs. Maybe Helmer would like to live closer to the woods and the mountain."

Blom stared at the pastor. "Meaning no disrespect, sir; but Nybo's three times the size of your little town. There's precious little work here. That's why so many young men are leaving for Stockholm—for America. You send your promising lads to America. And send the best girls there, because those Swedes need wives. If you have any young fellow who would like to know about America, you bring him along with you the next time you come here. I'll show him Helmer's letter. He tells all about it."

"Well, Blom, I hope I can come here again before too many weeks pass. You'll remember me in family prayers?"

Arrhenius had told Blom about the talk that he expected would be going on in Stavnäs.

"We will pray."

And Arrhenius returned to the town, to grief, to the people to whom he had been called, the Book, the crucifix, the Mysteries of which he was steward, and the lesser mysteries of the human soul. There was a letter awaiting him, signed by Ståhle and several other elders and influential men, requesting a meeting to discuss certain tensions that had arisen of recent months between the reverend pastor and his flock.

Chapter Four: Summer 1937

A student enrolled in the Department of Swedish Language and Culture at the University of Wisconsin, Allan Ridderstad, spent a summer in Sweden, part of the time consulting the archive at the University of Lund, and the rest of the summer taking down stories told by elderly countryfolk. This fieldwork was the heart of his eventual master's thesis. Ridderstad found that the storytellers were usually pleased by his interest, especially when he told them that his grandparents on his father's side were from Sweden, although Ridderstad's forefathers were from the southern coast rather than inland regions.

"I'll tell you a story we like up here," said a woman named Louise Hammarstedt. "It's about a place called Winter Ridge. That's about thirty miles from here, northaways, below the dam. My grandmother used to say that the elves lived there in the old days. People used to disappear sometimes. They were taken into the mountain (*bergtagen*)." She paused.

"I'd like to hear that story, mother," Ridderstad said. They were sitting in a small, tidy parlor in a farmhouse that was three hundred years old. It didn't have electricity. She smiled at him, put out her cigarette, smoothed her skirt across her knees, and began.

"A long time ago, when wishing still helped one, there was a young girl who was an orphan. She lived with the pastor and his wife. One day, she went for a walk in the woods. It was getting dark. Suddenly she heard her name called from the dark trees. But nobody could she see. She started walking faster. Again she heard her name called.

"She thought it would be a good idea to turn around and go home; but it was getting dark, and she became confused. The voice kept on—now from one side of the path, now from the other. She kept on walking along, faster and faster.

"Then all of a sudden sitting across the path she saw a big bear. The poor girl turned around and went back the way she came. And then in front of her on the path was another bear. She didn't know what to do. So she left the path and ran into the woods. The voice kept calling her. Soon she came to a place where there was a door in the hillside. She was afraid to go in, but behind her the two bears were coming, *huff-huff*, she could hear them breathing and panting. Of course we don't have bears here nowadays, not for a long time.

"And a voice said to her,

"'Come inside, come inside, come inside,

"'You'll be the king's own dear bride.'

"So she went through the doorway. And it was all more beautiful than anything. There were people in fine clothes, and in the midst of them was none other than the Elf-King himself. And she was to marry him. But she was afraid, and cried out the name of Jesus; and everything disappeared, and there she was, in the woods.

"In the morning the pastor found her. 'What did you mean, wandering in the wood?' he said. And he said if she ever did it again, he wouldn't come looking for her, naughty thing that she was.

"But the people in the town talked against her. They accused her of one thing and another, I don't know what, though none of it was true. And she remembered how fine the people under the mountain were, and all the lovely things. So at last, when she couldn't bear it any more, why, she went up onto the mountain, and into the wood, and looked for the door. And after a long time, she found it. And she cried at the door for them to let her in. And the door opens, and she goes in.

"'Come inside, come inside, come inside,

"'You'll be the king's own dear bride.'

"Well, back in the town, the pastor noticed the girl was gone. So he says to his wife, 'She's gone to the wood again, and I told her not to. The wolves can have her.' But his wife said, 'God forbid. You go and bring her back. The Good Shepherd went and found his one lost sheep.' So he *had* to do it after she said that, for he was a pastor and all.

"So he came to the place.

"'Let me in, let me in,

"'For I am a man without any sin,' he said.

"So they had to let him in. Then he demanded that they let the girl go. But the King of the Elves brought to him a beautiful woman instead.

"'Seek no other within the hill,

"'For here is one who is fairer still.'

"But the pastor wouldn't have her. And she was really just a stump of a tree that had been struck by lightning. But the King brought him a woman who was still more beautiful.

"'Seek no other within the hill,

"'For here is one who is fairer still.'

"But the pastor wouldn't have *that* one, either. And she was really just a rotten log. So the King went to bring him another beautiful woman. And while he was fetching her, a little dog, that the pastor had given a bowl of milk to once, came out of a corner, and said, 'Tell him to give you the broom behind the door.'

"The King came back. And this woman was so beautiful, it would make your heart ache to see her.

"'Seek no other within my hall,

"'For here is the loveliest one of all.'

"And the pastor was tempted, for she *was* more beautiful than any earthly woman. But he reached down and pinched the little dog hard, on purpose, and made it yelp and bite his ankle, and the pain of it broke the spell the King was weaving all the while. No, he said, he wouldn't have that one either, but the broom behind the door. And the fair-seeming woman was a pile of dirty old blankets. And the King had to let the girl come home with the pastor, for the King had made her look like a broom. So they left the place and came home, because now she wanted to come home again. That's the story people here tell about Winter Ridge." She smiled and recited: "And I was at her wedding feast. They gave me beer, but it all ran down my chin."

Ridderstad laughed with her and said he would have been glad to give her a good glass of beer if he had had any. The other people there in the bright room were pleased to see that the American understood. Ridderstad had the storyteller repeat some things, and got the story written down, nearly word-for-word, in his notebook. He stayed all the evening in the farmhouse parlor, while the people there told stories.

It got towards midnight and he had to leave. He was staying at the parsonage, and the pastor would be driving over to pick him up soon. Before he left, the people were telling stories of their families, memories of the influenza epidemic of almost twenty years before, and the story of the great flood of 1847 that destroyed several hamlets in the region and numerous farmhouses. Also they related legends of ghosts. Ridderstad perceived that this type of narrative (*sägn*) was understood to be factual, or based upon fact, unlike a fairy-tale (*saga*). One legend was about a parish councilman who had violated his servant girl and, when she became pregnant, had forced her to drown the baby. The man's name was Bente Ståhle. After his death, he was seen haunting the lake where the baby had been drowned. It was said that he would be glimpsed running, all in hell-flames, trying to arrive in time to prevent the servant girl from drowning their child so that he could be delivered from his torments. Ridderstad thought this was an interesting legend because parish records did indeed list a man of that name, a merchant of the town of Stavnäs, who had been a church councilman, born 1782, died 1846, and because usually in such tales it is the girl who murdered the child, or the infant itself, that haunts the scene of the crime.

Afterword

Since the present book is—loosely speaking—a collection of ghost stories, the reader might be curious about my personal notions regarding the supernatural, supposing there is such a thing. That topic is, in a sense, irrelevant with regard to the enjoyment of the stories, which must stand on their own as works of the imagination. From my own point of view, most of them were attempts to work within an existing genre of fiction. This is especially true of the first several stories, which are antiquarian ghost stories in the mode associated with the master of this kind of fiction, M. R. James.

James was asked for his opinions on the topic of ghosts and responded, "I am prepared to consider evidence and accept it if it satisfies me." The thoughts that follow may scandalize some of my readers, not because I allow for the possible existence of ghosts, but because I consider the topic on the basis of authority. I affirm the historic creeds of the Church, and to do so implies recognition of the prophetic and apostolic writings—the Old Testament and the New Testament—of which the creeds are epitomes. In the Old Testament, I find an account of the visible manifestation of the dead prophet Samuel. Nothing is said there to suggest that the apparition is an hallucination in Saul produced by mental illness, or is an artifact of hypnosis effected by the witch of Endor, or is a nonhuman spirit masquerading as Samuel, although that theory is ancient, seeming to have been the opinion of Tertullian, Eustathius, and St. Gregory of Nyssa; but Origen and Diodore contended that Samuel himself appeared. St. Augustine wasn't sure. (See Rowan A. Geer and Margaret M. Mitchell's *The "Belly-Myther" of Endor: Interpretations of 1 Kingdoms 28 in the Early Church* [2007].) In the New Testament, Christ, walking on water, startles a group of disciples and assures them that He is not a ghost. After His resurrection, He eats fish with them, thereby demonstrating to them that He is not a ghost. It would seem that each of these incidents provided the Savior with a "teachable moment" in which prevalent beliefs could be corrected (compare St. Matthew 5: 21, 27, 31, 33, 38, 43): if

179

ghosts never do, in fact, appear, it would be opportune to say so. But this is not said.

On one occasion, I was studying St. Luke, Chapter 16. I read verse 26, which appeared to me to say that there is a great gulf between the living and those who have departed this life, and the latter cannot appear to the former. On that account I was prepared to abandon the ghost story as a fictional genre; it wouldn't be appropriate to write stories that were predicated on something of such importance that was ruled out by sacred Scripture. However, I eventually realized that I had misread the passage. It states that those who have departed this life for perdition cannot cross to heaven, nor can the souls in Paradise go to the damned; a blessed soul cannot succor a damned soul (even with a drop of water such as the rich man has begged for himself). The gulf of which the text speaks lies between heaven and hell (and obviously it is not so absolute as to preclude some kind of communication, since Abraham and the rich man are able to speak to one another; of course, a parable is a story and one must be careful about using details of a story to establish doctrine). Once this fact is established, the damned rich man then asks that someone from heaven go to his brothers, still alive on earth, and warn them about hell. Abraham doesn't say that no glorified spirit can go to earth with such a message; rather, he says that even if such a one did so, the message would not be believed if the warnings in the sacred Scriptures were not sufficient.

So far, then, I find that the 66 books[1] of the canonical Scriptures do not seem to preclude the appearance, to those living this earthly life, of the spirits of the departed. However, persons of some authority—an authority contingent and derived—in my own circles do tend to reject the possibility of "ghosts" appearing

---

[1] The more extensive canonical lists of Roman Catholicism and Eastern Orthodoxy do not, so far as I know, contain any material that relates specifically to the topic of ghostly apparitions, as opposed (arguably) to prayer for the departed.The Lutheran Confessions expressly permit prayer *for* the departed, but not prayer *to* the departed as in Roman Catholicism or Orthodoxy.

(though not of angels). For example, Dr. Robert H. Bennett, in *Afraid: Demon Possession and Spiritual Warfare in America* (2016), affirms that there are no such things as ghosts; therefore reports of "ghosts" are due to dishonest reporters, or "overactive imagination," or mental illness, or demonic imposture (pp. 106-107). My sense is that most pastors and teachers in the Lutheran Church-Missouri Synod, of which I'm a lay member, would agree, if they've ever had occasion to consider the matter. However, Dr. John Warwick Montgomery, also a member of the LC-MS, set out half a dozen possibilities relating to apparitions in *Principalities and Powers* (1973; pp. 140ff.), which I summarize below.

Montgomery considers as possible these six or seven ways of interpreting "spectral evidence."

First, it is possible that impressions, even dreams, from one living person to another may be received telepathically as hallucinations. Of course, the mere existence of telepathy is controversial at best.

Second, apparitions might register in the brains of living persons with their source being "brain radiations" that had been generated by persons now dead. I take it, by the way, that something like this is imagined in Arthur Machen's late and enigmatic story "The Exalted Omega." Montgomery is summarizing another writer here and doesn't seem inclined to give the notion a lot of regard.

Third, a ghost may be a "residual human aura." *If* a "subtle body" exists, it might be possible for someone to perceive that of someone else. The apparition need not be understood to be a manifestation of an immortal soul. Residual auras of dead animals might occur.

Fourth, ghosts might be "the dead themselves, on their way to the reward determined once for all by their relationship or lack of relationship to Christ" while they lived in the body, "but not yet entered fully into that reward. . . . Only the time-lag between death and heaven, or death and hell, is extended to account for ghostly phenomena that show more self-direction than the 'human aura' would allow for, and yet do not engage either in angelic or in demonic missions to the living."

For his fifth category, Montgomery introduces two possibilities, namely "Ghosts as the damned sent back to haunt the living or as Satanic counterfeits of the dead."

Sixth, some ghosts could be "the saved sent back to earth by God for a special mission." Montgomery cites the account related by the Bible translator J. B. Phillips, who said (in a book called *Ring of Truth*) that the ghost of C.S. Lewis had appeared to him to encourage him about a difficulty in his life.

Montgomery adds that his openness to the possibility of ghosts is another matter entirely from being open to attempts by the living to conjure the departed, an activity that is expressly prohibited by the Bible and Christian tradition. By the way, he has a few interesting sentences on the once-famous Episcopalian Bishop James A. Pike, with whom Montgomery was a featured speaker at McMaster University in Hamilton, Ontario, in 1967. By then Pike had given himself to attempts to communicate through séances with his son, dead by suicide. Pike himself seems to have come to an unhappy end too, in the Sinai desert.

My taking the trouble to set out Montgomery's scheme may give the impression that I am more occupied with such matters than I am. In fact I have read little about the theory of and evidence for ghosts, etc. As of the time that I am drafting this afterword, in mid-May 2016, I haven't yet read Montgomery (whose book I just received) or Bennett all the way through, nor any other book devoted to ghosts except for the Victorian clergyman John Mason Neale's *The Unseen World*. I was interested to read, in Bengt Hoffmann's *Theology of the Heart*, the account of Luther's dead daughter appearing to the Reformer in a dream. A Lutheran pastor told me a story, from the 1930s, about his great-grandmother's cousin, whose grandson appeared in her bedroom to tell her that he was going to be with Jesus. Telephones were not yet common, and so it was not until a state trooper drove to the house that the family learned that the young man had been killed in a motorcycle accident. The family calculated that the young man had appeared to his grandmother at the time of the accident. I would like to emphasize that life after death and related topics are matters that, in my circles, we seek to understand above all on the basis of the Bible, not on the basis of anecdotes, nor on the basis of psychic research or occultism, and that our hope is not in psychic "survival," or a Platonic hope of return to the realm of the Forms, or in the planes-of-being schemata of the East, but is the Paschal hope, of resurrection to glory in Christ (1 Corinthians 15).

As for almost any given account of a haunting, etc., skepticism is likely to be in order.

But I wrote my ghostly stories largely because for years I'd enjoyed reading literary entertainments of the antiquarian type. In 1982, when I began to date the woman whom I married, we found that we both liked such stories, and we would read them to one another from time to time. We didn't like everything in Academy Chicago's paperback of H. Russell Wakefield stories, but "The Red Lodge" was a favorite. When we moved to Urbana, Illinois, for grad school, I discovered that I had access to abundant books in the M. R. James tradition, in the stacks of the huge research library and, especially, through interlibrary loan. It was like being a kid in a candy shop: Munby's *Alabaster Hand*, Rolt's *Sleep No More*, Malden's *Nine Ghosts*, Gray's *Tedious Brief Tales of Granta and Gramarye*, in original editions. Getting hold of James's eerie children's book *The Five Jars* was easy. Also, Penguin republished James's ghost stories in an omnibus volume and I reviewed it for a nonconformist campus paper. My wife and I tried more recent authors too; I read Susan Hill's *Woman in Black* aloud to her in two long sessions—as I recall, in the space of 12 hours or so with a night's sleep in between; and immediately after finishing that, we started H. F. Heard's Trollopean-Jamesian *Black Fox*. Robert Aickman was a big discovery, though perhaps he shouldn't be mentioned in the context of the specifically antiquarian ghost story. Furthermore, I met a distinguished practitioner of the traditional ghostly tale, Russell Kirk, and interviewed him on the topic for the paper. He had the excellent manners and the appearance of an incorruptible country judge. Naturally, I took to writing ghost stories. I composed a few stories of traditional type that survive as handwritten drafts, and which were meant to be read aloud to my wife. In the early 1990s, I began to write ghost stories for publication. (My thanks are due to Andrew, Lucy, Richeldis, and Linnea for their patience when their father was monopolizing the computer to type one or other of these.)

My discovery of the Jamesian story probably occurred in 1968, with "Casting the Runes" by James and several antiquarian tales by others, in the impressive Whitman collection for young readers, *More Tales to Tremble By*.

As for the Faërian stories, notably "Pastor Arrhenius," there I'm connecting with imaginative experiences that predate the Jamesian discovery. I had the fortune to grow up with woods and paths and sea, and Northern folktales and myths and Tolkien.

Story Notes

These notes are intended to be read some hours or more after the stories are read.

Lady Stanhope's Manuscript

This story was first drafted as "The Tutor" 30 years ago, in 1987. It's one of several stories that I wrote with the example of M. R. James's antiquarian ghost stories in mind. The present in "Lady Stanhope's Manuscript" is the late Victorian period, from which point in time the characters look back to Lady Hester Stanhope's time (say around 1820) and then, much farther back, to the time of the Seventh Ecumenical Church Council (AD 787),[1] and to the even earlier time chronicled by Procopius, whose *Secret History* (mid-6th century AD) is authentic—including the reference to the weird transformation of the emperor's head.[2] The creatures that kill Mr.

---

[1] Tessaracontapechys ("a magician, a soothsayer, and a servant of demons"): see *A History of the Councils of the Church* by Hefele, 1894 (which has recently been reprinted by Wipf and Stock, 2007), p. 268. Constantine Copronymus: see *A Select Library of Nicene and Post-Nicene Fathers of the Christian Church, Second Series, Translated into English with Prolegomena and Explanatory Notes*, Vol. 14: The Seven Ecumenical Councils, tr. Schaff and Wace, n.d., rpt. Eerdmans 1988, page 550.

[2] From the Penguin Classics translation by G. A. Williamson (1966, rpt. 1988, p. 103): "Some of those who were in the Emperor's company late at night, conversing with him (evidently in the Palace)—men of the highest possible character—thought that they saw a strange demonic form in his place. One of them declared that he more than once rose suddenly from the imperial throne and walked round and round the room; for he was not

Trefillan may derive from a reference, in C. S. Lewis's *Out of the Silent Planet,* to Chaucer's "airish beasts." In my reading, I'd come across good things to put into a weird story; this was an enjoyable story to write.

The occult is often a mode of what Blake warned against as "mind-forg'd manacles." "Lady Stanhope's Manuscript" is based on this conviction. The writing known to Geoffrey Cleeve as Lady Stanhope's manuscript was a composite, preserving an ancient fragment but eked out by an apostate clergyman's forgeries, intended by him to fascinate Cleeve and thus make him vulnerable to Trefillan's psychic vampirism. The unwholesome ritual that Geoffrey remembers from childhood, which occurred when the "old man" visited him in his room, was a sorcerous parody of 1 Kings 17:21

Trefillan might with profit have reflected on the Hebraic warnings to schemers who are liable to fall into the traps they intend for others, or the animadversions of St. Paul with regard to the makers of "cunningly devised fables." Qoheleth (the Preacher) wrote, "Lo, this only have I found, that God hath made man upright; but they have sought out many inventions." (That exceptionally intelligent storyteller Kipling borrowed the last two words for a collection of his tales.)

Along with the things mentioned above and documented below, I have borrowed a couple of anecdotes from Rider Haggard's *The Days of My Life* to help bring my characters to life: the trial story and the donkey story.

---

in the habit of remaining seated for long. And Justinian's head would momentarily disappear, while the rest of his body seemed to continue making these long circuits. The watcher himself, thinking that something had gone seriously wrong with his eyesight, stood for a long time distressed and quite at a loss. But later the head returned to the body, and he thought that what a moment before had been lacking was, contrary to expectation, filling out again. A second man said that he stood by the Emperor's side as he sat, and saw his face suddenly transformed to a shapeless mass of flesh: neither eyebrows nor eyes were in their normal position, and it showed no other distinguishing feature at all; gradually, however, he saw the face return to its usual shape. I did not myself witness the events I am describing, but I heard about them from men who insist that they saw them at the time."

Powers of the Air

In his letter accepting "Powers of the Air" for what was, I believe, Tartarus Press's first hardcover anthology, publisher Ray Russell told me that my story was a refreshing change from the gory submissions he'd been receiving. In a November 1992 letter to me, Russell Kirk mentioned that he found the setting memorable.

Originally, the story—called "The Persecutions" when first drafted in January 1988—was set on "the heaths of Exmoor." This handwritten version was never typed and I don't suppose anyone else has ever seen the original draft, although I may have read it to my wife. I don't remember just how, a few years after writing the Exmoor draft, I came to recast "Powers" as a story of the Dirty Thirties in the American Midwest. That decision had been made already, I believe, when I came across *Dust Bowl Diary* and the excerpts that appear at the story's beginning with the permission of the University of Nebraska Press.

The antiquarian bit—the material from St. Athanasius's *Life of Antony*—is genuine. I'd read the work as translated for the Paulist Press Classics of Western Spirituality series, having bought the book on 13 Dec. 1982 at Powell's magnificent bookstore in Portland, Oregon. In western Oregon I'd never endured a dust storm, but experiencing one was part of my family's initiation into the weather of North Dakota (where we'd moved in late August 1989). On the afternoon of 10 January 1990 a brownish "fog" developed, which I observed from my third-floor office on the university campus. I walked to the house where my infant daughter Lucy was being babysat, bundled her into the stroller, and pushed the stroller home, a matter of a few blocks, struggling a bit with the wind even in town. Later, we heard that, due to the high winds, a semi truck had blown over and its driver had been killed, and a man who'd been walking by, or on, a road in the dust and darkness had been struck by a vehicle. He might have been disoriented by the storm. Fields had been churned up during harvest in previous weeks, and so loose dirt, not yet covered by a snow blanket, was ready to be raised by winds of 60 mph or so.

It seemed to me that the harsh Midwestern weather and remoteness could be related to the desert wilderness of early monasticism, though perhaps struggles somewhat like Astrid's have happened also in nondescript urban neighborhoods.

I meant for the story to generate suspense, but to come pretty close to being a comedy of misunderstanding. When the soot tumbles down the chimney onto the interesting young man, Sigrid is reminded of some half-fabulous account, perhaps from a more widely-traveled neighbor or from some stray bit of reading matter, about Africans. She can hardly believe such folk really exist. When bizarre phenomena happen under his nose, Pete Vinje must assure himself that they are explicable in terms of some stray bits of psychology that he's caught wind of. Sigrid possesses natural gifts of resilience and good nature and perhaps a special vocation to the cloistered life as well—of which she has no notion. Her parents are out of their depth as well. The story's narrator is a pastor in a mainline Lutheran church, who looked forward to a career of comforting the afflicted and afflicting the comfortable with calls to inclusive social justice. His education was in a tradition going back to Schleiermacher. His interlocutor is a traditional Roman Catholic priest and would be regarded as behind the times by many of his peers today.

The Ergushevo Icon and Aqualung in Svalyava

Here are two more antiquarian tales. These are my two "Orthodox" stories, dating from a time in the 1990s when I was exploring the ancient Church Fathers such as Sts. Irenaeus and Athanasius through correspondence courses and self-directed ventures, listening to the music of John Tavener during his Orthodox, penultimate period, reading *Again, Epiphany Journal,* and the writings of Fr. Alexander Schmemann and Fr. Seraphim Rose, and thinking about the distinctive features of the Eastern Orthodox family of churches.

Icons are important in both stories. Both deal, in differing ways, with "false icons" as well as with legitimate icons. Of the latter, Anthony Ugolnik wrote, "The placid icon is but a prototype for the transfiguring power of the illumined image over the mind. The icon's form is static and unchanging, faithful to a body of convention that preserves the mind of the church but that discourages too much interpretive 'individuality' on the part of the artist" (*The Illuminating Icon,* 1989, page 62).

"The Ergushevo Icon" was influenced by my friendship with a reporter for the Grand Forks *Herald* who often wrote on religion, and, no doubt, by my journalism courses and student newspaper days. I also had in mind a remark attributed to Martin Luther, to the effect that when God builds a church, the devil builds a chapel next door. This story provided the opportunity for a small nod to M.R. James. I hope that, if someone eventually attempts to synthesize a "Jamesian Mythos," this story will included in the canon of stories if only on account of its expansion of an allusion in "Count Magnus." "The Ergushevo Icon" uses a bit of material relating to church politics drawn from *Not of This World*, the original version of a long and inspiring biography of Seraphim Rose, which I read in 1993.

The story might have been influenced by Charles Williams's *Descent into Hell*, in which the historian Wentworth knowingly countenances an inconspicuous error relating to a costume that a group of amateur thespians wants to be completely authentic. In "Ergushevo," perhaps the narrator's situation at the story's end owes something to an outburst in T. S. Eliot's essay on Baudelaire: "the recognition of the reality of Sin is a New Life; and the possibility of damnation is so immense a relief in a world of electoral reform, plebiscites, sex reform and dress reform, that damnation itself is an immediate form of salvation—of salvation from the ennui of modern life, because it at least gives some significance to living."

"Aqualung in Svalyava" aspires to be a horror story that turns out to be a wonder tale. Tessa saw what seemed to her a frightening apparition, reminding her of jacket art on a record with a title song about a depraved vagrant. Modern culture stocked Tessa's mind with such ugly imagery, disposing her to think along lines that, in this case, were *malapropos*. She and Mark will learn better, I think; perhaps the icon of St. Prokopy will become the nucleus of a "beautiful corner" (Красный угол) in their home. It may become a locus of beneficent influence. If the reader likes this tale, perhaps he or she will look up Robert Aickman's fine story "The Houses of the Russians," which didn't inspire my story, so far as I am conscious, but may have some degree of affinity with it. (Aickman's story appears in the collections *Sub Rosa* and *Painted Devils*.) My story draws on the concept of the *yurodivy* or holy fool,

189

about which I read in *Epiphany Journal* and elsewhere. Long after this story was written, Eugene Vodolazkin's *Laurus* was published, a marvelous novel that will provide many readers with their first encounter with holy fools. "Aqualung" is one of two stories I've written with a Russian setting, the other being "Rusalka."

Dr. Wrangham's Garden

This little piece was meant almost as a parody of the M. R. James type of antiquarian ghost tale. As I recall, I wrote it while home sick from classes one day. In some book or other, I'd run across a paper by the novelist, Trollope commentator, and bibliophile Michael Sadleir on Archdeacon Francis Wrangham (1769-1842), which included the mocking rhyme upon which my powers of invention went to work.

Around that time I became interested in Victorian clergymen such as the industrious John Mason Neale and the very learned Edward Bouverie Pusey, also the lyrical diarist Francis Kilvert. It was the Victorian clergyman C.A. Johns who wrote the book that J.R.R. Tolkien identified as his favorite volume in adolescence, *Flowers of the Field*. I suppose there are few identifiable groups about which popular notions are more inadequate than that of the Victorian clergymen; one could devote decades to exploring their biographies and literary remains, and, of course, novels about them.

"Dr. Wrangham's Garden" was published by M.J. Logsdon in his *Salinas Valley Lewisian*, an obscure magazine that was largely given over to the debate between Kathryn Lindskoog and the defenders of Walter Hooper, whom she had accused of tampering with, and falsely adding to, the legacy of C.S. Lewis. Why I showed the story to Logsdon I don't remember, but he liked it enough to want to print it where it would hardly have been expected to have found a home.

Trolls

This might be this book's story that goes back the farthest in my imagination. It seems to me that in the mid-1980s *troll* appeared in the press as a word that some people used to refer to a homeless person who slept under a highway overpass. It doesn't seem that that usage lasted very long, but it got me thinking. This was, of course, long before the "Internet troll" usage.

I was a fill-in instructor at the University of Wisconsin-Parkside during the 1987-1988 academic year. We lived in Racine, which, if my memory is correct, had suffered some economic decline in recent years, such as I have attempted to suggest in "Trolls." We moved twice in a matter of months, but both neighborhoods were decent; however, I seem to have been aware of abandoned buildings and manufacturing areas close in to downtown. They were not common sights in other places where I had lived.

Along with whatever impressions I absorbed from this locale, an influence on "Trolls" was probably *Castaway*, a novel by James Gould Cozzens, which I had read to my wife in November 1985. It concerns a man in a sort of Crusoe-like situation, in which he forages from the contents of a vast department store.

Finally, though "Trolls" is not much like a Robert Aickman story, the British author's freedom to use folkloric or mythological creatures in banal settings may have encouraged me to feel similarly licensed.

Gone with the Wind, or Whatever It Was

This story is indebted to a March 2004 news article by Associated Press writer Jeff Barnard, reporting the offer, for $2 million, of the Oregon Vortex House of Mystery near Gold Hill, a small town about half an hour's drive from Ashland, the city where I lived in the 1970s.

The story is also indebted to H. P. Lovecraft, whose "Shadow Over Innsmouth" I have briefly quoted verbatim.

It won a blue ribbon for First Place and a purple ribbon for Class Champion in creative writing at the Greater Grand Forks Fair—alas, I didn't record the year.

Rusalka

When I drafted this story in 1997, one of my students, Jason Carlson, saved me from a howler. Kuritsin's fiancée was originally named Sadovaya—*sah-do-vie-yah*—which I thought sounded alluring and supposed would be a nice change from the usual practice of Western authors who name their Russian heroines Katya, Olga, or Irina. Jason politely informed me that the name means "of the garden"—it's a place-name, not a personal name. I think he also told me that my title, "Russalka," was questionable, as Russian

191

doesn't double the consonant S. At the time, I retained it because that was how the word (for a dangerous fairy-creature) was spelled in the translation of Turgenev's "Bezhin Meadows" wherein I found it. That seems to have been one of the first Russian stories I ever read, and it remains a favorite. The translator who prepared the atmospheric version printed in Norris Houghton's Dell paperback *Great Russian Short Stories* was the gifted and industrious Constance Garnett. Readers of the Turgenev story will see why I didn't conceive of the rusalka as being a mermaid in the familiar sense. Second thoughts did eventually prompt me to use the more correct transliteration of the Russian (Русалка), with just one S.

I'd seen Akira Kurosawa's superb film *Dersu Uzala* at the Varsity Theater in downtown Ashland, Oregon, years ago and never forgotten it. Years later, the Kino videocassette release came my way, and the film proved even more wonderful than I'd remembered. McPherson & Company reprinted Malcolm Burr's 1941 translation of Arseniev's *Dersu the Trapper*, and my young son and I loved that. (This was perhaps my first encounter with Russian nature writing—not counting passages in novels, such as Levin hunting with his dog Laska in *Anna Karenina*—which I've subsequently found in translated works by Aksakov, Paustovsky, and Skrebitski.) It was the first story I've written whose inspiration was largely cinematic rather than literary. I was gratified by the compliment I received from a Russian lady regarding the authenticity of the story, though perhaps she was just being nice.

The story that Kuritsin was attempting to write, mentioned at the beginning of "Rusalka," derives from an anecdote I heard on 2 February 1997, on a ride to Moorhead, Minnesota. The driver and other passengers were older than I and knew our area better than I, including "where all the bodies were buried." I don't mean that they were gossips but rather that they were interested in our region, in the drama and humor of the people's lives, and could impart their interest. A few years later, my wife and I started a campus-community reading group dedicated to classic literature (mostly novels by Scott, Dickens, Austen, Tolstoy, Dostoevsky, and other nineteenth-century authors). Some of the people with whom I'd gone to Moorhead on that Sunday became members of the reading group, and others participated as well. On occasion someone's memory was triggered by our current book, and a true, warm narrative would be related, brought forth from a well-stocked imagination. The reading group lasted for eleven years and these "digressions" were as good as the discussions proper.

Dobronravov's account of the Black Death as a hag is, so far as I remember, my variation on an entry in *Folktales of Norway* (1964), Reidar Christiansen's contribution to the University of Chicago's attractive folktale series from a generation ago. Shchelkalov's story of Matvei and the goblin is my invention.

It's almost twenty years since I wrote "Rusalka," but from my files it appears to me that I drew upon "Siberian Exile in Tsarist Russia" by Alan Wood, from the September 1980 issue of *History Today*, and articles in *Sky and Telescope* (June 1994), *Astronomy* (December 1993), and *Discover* (September 1996) on the Tunguska event. The *Sky and Telescope* article, "Journey to Tunguska," is by Roy A. Gallant. The 1958 edition of Gallant's book for youngsters called *Exploring the Planets* was one of the great library discoveries of my childhood, largely due to John Polgreen's pictures, which fascinated me—particularly the picture of Saturn from Titan on pages 100-101 (which must have been derived from one of Chesley Bonestell's paintings). I suspect that the art in Gallant's book, and the illustrations in one or two Golden Books taken from Rudolph F. Zallinger's mural of the dinosaur age for the Peabody Museum of Natural History, did much to set my imagination towards science fiction and fantasy when I was a boy.

In my Afterword, I've characterized "Rusalka" as a "dark Faërian story" rather than as a ghost story. The wraith that appears at the story's climax is not the spirit of the drowned Raisa—notwithstanding the idea that a rusalka is the ghost of a drowned girl. Raisa's earthly remains are buried and her spirit reposes in blessedness. The wraith is a spirit of another sort.

"Rusalka" is, a little, an attempt to work within the mode of Algernon Blackwood's best stories, "The Wendigo" and "The Willows," in which the realm of wild nature gives way to, or even is equated with, what is sometimes called Faërie—notably, by Tolkien. Only writers with a poetic responsiveness to nature can evoke the desired atmosphere. (The reader will have to judge whether "Rusalka" succeeds.) Tolkien possessed this ability, as seen throughout his imaginative writing, with the Withywindle Valley sequence in *The Fellowship of the Ring* and *Smith of Wootton Major* as examples. Chekhov's novella *The Steppe* has something of this

193

quality even though it remains located in the fields we know. Turgenev's short story mentioned above ventures closer to the borders of the Perilous Realm. In "Rusalka," Arseniev passes those borders.

Shelter Belt

With this story, I was feeling my way towards the "dark Faërian" tale (see "Rusalka" and "Pastor Arrhenius and the Maiden Brita") that succeeded my efforts in the antiquarian ghost story mode.

"Shelter Belt" is one of several stories I've written from a child's point of view. Others don't appear in this book, since they are not stories of the supernatural, and were written in the context of my freshman composition instruction, to illustrate the use of sensory detail or the manipulation of point of view. "Unsuspecting" has a little boy witness some older boys who shoplift in a convenience store; "What He Found" has a youngster discovering a stash of nude photographs in the woods; "In Their Yard" is about a boy who knocks a baseball into a neighbor's dog turd-strewn property. "Claws" is about a boy and his mother, like "Shelter Belt," and takes the boy's point of view, but the situation it describes is different from that of "Shelter Belt." A grade school boy gets in trouble because he brought a gun to school. The gun is about an inch long and was part of the equipment of a G.I. Joe action figure, but the school officials enforce their "anti-weapon" policy and suspend the inoffensive lad, and incur the wrath of the boy's mother, who has till then been too preoccupied with her job to pay much attention to him. The story was inspired by a 1997 incident that occurred in the Seattle School District. "The district has a zero-tolerance policy on weapons, and it is mute on size," said Dorothy Dubia, a spokeswoman for the school. Principal Elaine Woo was unavailable for comment to the press. The boy was expelled. I recall being surprised and disappointed when I used "Claws" in a class discussion and students who commented on the story sided with the school district.

Use of a child's point of view invites attention to sensory details of which adults may commonly be unaware and to issues relating to the soul that many adults overlook or dismiss. So, I suppose, does entering Faërie.

The Allegheny Exception (with Adam Walter)
I love many stories that feature a leisurely development of atmosphere. The present story began as a different kind of effort— to write an exciting story that would start immediately and move rapidly. I'd liked the idea of telling a weird story in the vein of the first season of the original *Outer Limits* TV series, complete with a laboratory in which eerie sounds could be heard. If readers care to imagine the story realized as a black-and-white *Outer Limits* teleplay, directed by Gerd Oswald, with Conrad Hall as director of photography, they'll be very much on the right track. Readers may do their own casting from the ranks of television actors who were busy circa 1964, as regards who will play the roles of Paul Kellett and Mrs. Friend, who the roles of Dr. and Mrs. Jesperson, etc. I started writing without knowing where the story would go, curious to see if I would manage to write a complete story that resolved all the details that I strewed around in the first pages.

In the event, I wrote as if I knew where I was going till I reached the point where I was stumped. My friend Adam Walter continued and completed the story, and invented the title. About 60% of "The Allegheny Exception" is Adam's work. The draft was complete in 2010. We've been over the story several times, making changes in parts drafted by the other writer. "The Allegheny Exception" was submitted for publication in *Fungi*, where it appeared with editorial changes that we had not had the chance to consider, and saw print there under a new title, "Kaleidoscope of Shadows." It's easy for me to imagine "The Allegheny Exception" as the title of a script submitted to *The Outer Limits*, with producer Joseph Stefano devising "Kaleidoscope of Shadows" as the title for the show as televised.

Adam's stories have appeared in *Dappled Things*, the *Journal of the British Fantasy Society*, *Big Pulp*, *Supernatural Tales*, *Flashquake*, and *Fungi*, as well as the anthologies *100 Lightnings* and *Day Terrors*.

Pastor Arrhenius and the Maiden Brita
Some earlier stories in the present book, and a few not printed here, were conceived as exercises in an existing genre, namely the antiquarian ghost story founded by M. R. James. This story and

195

"Rusalka" especially are "dark Faërian" stories, like the narrative in Tolkien's "Sea-Bell" poem in *The Adventures of Tom Bombadil*. With "Pastor Arrhenius," the starting point was folklore, particularly "Anne Rykhus" in *Scandinavian Folktales* (1988), a Penguin collection edited by Jacqueline Simpson. Ever since I was a youngster I had loved the Viking Press edition of Asbjørnsen and Møe's *Norwegian Folk Tales* (1960), so hauntingly illustrated by Theodor Kittelsen and Erik Werenskiold. I own 4,000 books, and if I had to winnow my collection down to, say, 200, that book would be retained. I wrote a piece for *Fungi* introducing Kittelsen to American fans of the weird. I think cinema was important too: for example, "Pastor Arrhenius" might owe a little to Tarkovsky's *Andrei Rublev*. I revisited Sibelius's symphonic poem *Tapiola* while working on the story, and maybe also his *Wood-Nymph*, which had been released on a Bis CD that I snapped up not too long before I started work on the tale.

However, without doubt an important inspiration was a book that, outside Lutheran circles, is hardly known in America—Bo Giertz's *The Hammer of God* (published to considerable success in Sweden, 1941, as *Stengrunden*, and published in an English version in 1960). The first hundred pages are about Savonius, a young Swedish pastor who is precipitated, around the year 1808, into an unforeseen crisis and conflict when he has to leave a wedding party to attend at a rural deathbed, and finds that his education has not prepared him for what happens there. Arrhenius has things to learn and to unlearn as well, but happily he is not as handicapped as Savonius was. My story is mostly quite different, but I don't think it would ever have been written if not for Giertz's novella. I have no doubt that readers who would never try anything that could be considered as fiction for the "religious market" might, even so, find Giertz's tale absorbing.

The anecdote about the crawling crabs with candles on their backs derives from an old book by H. D. Inglis writing as Derwent Conway, *A Personal Narrative of a Journey Through Norway, Part of Sweden, and the Islands and States of Denmark* (Constable, 1829). I began reading widely in travel literature during the same mid-1980s period in which I explored the Jamesian ghost story tradition. One turns up interesting bits in forgotten travel books, such as the use of the Central Asian concoction known as tarantula schnapps to immobilize unsuspecting journeyers so that they can be robbed. Gustav Krist, in *Alone Through the Forbidden Land* (1939): "If you want to brew it you catch a number of poisonous spiders, put them in a glass, and throw in some scraps of dried apples or apricots. The furious brutes fling themselves on the food and bite into it. They thus inject their poison into the dry fruit, which you then mix with fermented grapes. Thirty or forty tarantulas make about a quart of the deadly brew. A tiny glass of this liqueur is enough to drive a man insane. Half an hour after he has drunk it the victim is so paralysed that he cannot move; an hour later he is raving mad." Curiously, in *Somewhere East of Life*, if one can judge by a Google excerpt, Brian Aldiss seems to have incorporated this passage from Krist. I read much of Inglis and Krist in 1992.

With regard to a couple of names in the story: *Lindow* is a nod to the author of *Swedish Legends and Folktales*, which I was reading at the time of writing this story; and *Arrhenius* is a name in my ancestry. Our Arrhenius was not the one who received the Nobel Prize for Chemistry—in fact, if I'm not mistaken, our Arrhenius was born with a different name but appropriated that of the chemist upon emigrating to the United States.

List of Original Appearances

"The Allegheny Exception" [with Adam Walter]
Originally appeared as "Kaleidoscope of Shadows" by
August Jacobs in *Fungi* no. 20 (Spring 2011)
"Aqualung in Svalyava"
Originally appeared in *Fungi* no. 18 (dated Summer 1998,
but published in 2000)
"Dr. Wrangham's Garden"
Originally appeared in *The Salinas Valley Lewisian*, 3 no. 1
(Issue 9, Winter 1994)
"The Ergushevo Icon"
Originally appeared in *Fungi* no. 15 (Spring 1997)
"Gone with the Wind or Whatever It Was"
Originally appeared in *The Doppelganger Broadsheet*, circa 2010
"Lady Stanhope's Manuscript"
Originally appeared in *Lady Stanhope's Manuscript and Other
Supernatural Tales* (1994), ed. by Barbara Roden
"Pastor Arrhenius and the Maiden Brita"
Originally appeared in *Strange Tales Volume II* (2007) [edited
by Rosalie Parker]
"Powers of the Air"
Originally appeared in *Tales from Tartarus* (1995), edited by
R.B. Russell and Rosalie Parker
"Rusalka"
Originally appeared in *Enigmatic Tales* no. 6 (Autumn 1999);
revised in *Fungi* no. 22 (July 2015)
"Shelter Belt"
Originally appeared in *Strange Tales* (2003) [edited by Rosalie
Parker]
"Trolls"
Believed to have appeared in *The Doppelganger Broadsheet*,
circa 1996

Made in the USA
Middletown, DE
24 September 2017